Madison Avenue Shoot

A *Murder, She Wrote* MYSTERY

Madison Avenue Shoot

A *Murder, She Wrote* Mystery

A NOVEL BY
JESSICA FLETCHER & DONALD BAIN

Based on the Universal television series created by
Peter S. Fischer, Richard Levinson & William Link

AN OBSIDIAN MYSTERY

Obsidian
Published by New American Library, a division of
Penguin Group (USA) Inc., 375 Hudson Street,
New York, New York 10014, USA
Penguin Group (Canada), 90 Eglinton Avenue East, Suite 700, Toronto,
Ontario M4P 2Y3, Canada (a division of Pearson Penguin Canada Inc.)
Penguin Books Ltd., 80 Strand, London WC2R 0RL, England
Penguin Ireland, 25 St. Stephen's Green, Dublin 2,
Ireland (a division of Penguin Books Ltd.)
Penguin Group (Australia), 250 Camberwell Road, Camberwell, Victoria 3124,
Australia (a division of Pearson Australia Group Pty. Ltd.)
Penguin Books India Pvt. Ltd., 11 Community Centre, Panchsheel Park,
New Delhi - 110 017, India
Penguin Group (NZ), 67 Apollo Drive, Rosedale, North Shore 0632,
New Zealand (a division of Pearson New Zealand Ltd.)
Penguin Books (South Africa) (Pty.) Ltd., 24 Sturdee Avenue,
Rosebank, Johannesburg 2196, South Africa

Penguin Books Ltd., Registered Offices:
80 Strand, London WC2R 0RL, England

First published by Obsidian, an imprint of New American Library,
a division of Penguin Group (USA) Inc.

First Printing, April 2009
1   3   5   7   9   10   8   6   4   2

LIBRARY OF CONGRESS CATALOGING-IN-PUBLICATION DATA:
Bain, Donald, 1935–
Madison Avenue shoot : a Murder, She Wrote Mystery   by Jessica Fletcher and Donald Bain.
p. cm.
"Based on the Universal television series created by Peter S. Fischer, Richard Levinson & William Link"
ISBN: 978-0-451-22603-7
1. Fletcher, Jessica (Fictitious character)—Fiction. 2. Television commercials (Advertisements)—Pro-
duction direction—Fiction. 3. Celebrities against—Fiction. 4. New York (N.Y.)—Fiction. I. Murder, She
Wrote (Television program) II. Title.
PS3552.A376M23 2009
813'.54—dc22   2008047027

Set in Minion
Designed by Ginger Legato

Printed in the United States of America

*To all our friends at the Association of
Independent Producers (AICP):
Matt, Anima, Farah, Denise, Ileana, Jane, David, Paul,
Laurie, Maryann, Lena, David, and Kristin.*

*And to the Southeast Consortium for Special Services, Inc.,
helping Down Syndrome children—whose abilities
and personalities are as varied as yours and ours—
achieve the best they can be.*

Acknowledgments

Many people helped us along the way to this book. The commercial production world is filled with wonderful, friendly, talented professionals, too nice to kill anyone. Here are a few of them.

Many thanks to Jon Kamen and the crew from @radical.media in New York City for letting us hang around their commercial shoot, in particular to director Steve Miller, DP Eric Schmidt, and Producers Matt O'Shea and Nancy Kagan. Thanks, too, to Derek Pletch and Bebe Baldwin of GSD&M in Austin, Texas.

We're grateful to crew members Michael Sibley, Anne Shratter, Kate Wilson, Peter Jackson, Geb Byers, Jennifer Koestler, Rick Nagle, Greg Addison, Kevin Smyth, Rick Liss, David Moshiak, Liz Maas, Julie Vogel, and Tina Murgas, who shared their knowledge and nomenclature with the authors. And a salute to all we didn't name, the other

ACKNOWLEDGMENTS

crew members too numerous to mention here, but who do a fantastic job making make-believe believable. You know who you are.

Special thanks to Jane Nunez of AICP, Sally Antonacchio of The Artists Company, and to Detectives Bruce K. Bertram and Roger Brooks of the Danbury Police Department, and North Salem Judge Ralph Mackin.

All those named above are the experts; any errors you find are ours.

Chapter One

"Aunt Jess!"

"Grady! How good to see you."

I gave my nephew a hug, stepped back from his embrace, and looked down. "And who is this young man? It can't be Frank. Frank was a little boy the last time I saw him, and that was only six months ago."

"I'm still a boy, Aunt Jessica, just not so little anymore."

"Indeed, you're not," I said, smiling. "You're going to be taller than your father before we know it."

"I already come up to my mother's shoulder."

"Well, I can see you're very grown-up, but not too grown-up to give your aunt a hug, I hope."

Frank shrugged, but he allowed me to give him a quick cuddle, and even managed a slight squeeze back. "What year are you in school now?" I asked, holding him at arm's length and examining his sweet face, a miniature version of Grady's, but with his mother's eyes.

"Fourth grade."

"As much as that? My goodness, where does the time go?"

"Excuse me, Aunt Jess. What does your bag look like?" Grady asked.

I turned to peruse the baggage moving toward us on the conveyor belt. "Brown tweed with a red ribbon on the handle. I think I see it now. Yes, there it is."

We were at a crowded luggage carousel in La Guardia Airport in New York. My flight had originated in Dallas. I'd joined it in Chicago, where I'd been attending a conference. Before I returned to Cabot Cove, I was stopping off in the city for some business meetings and, more important, to visit with my nephew; his wife, Donna; and my pride and joy, my nine-year-old grandnephew, Frank, named for my husband, who had died many years before this child was born.

"I can get it, Dad," Frank said, pushing his way in front of others waiting for their bags.

"Wait, Frank, it's heavy," I said.

"Hold on, sport," Grady said, following his son.

"I got it. I got it." Frank grabbed on to the handle of the suitcase, but the weight of it threatened to pull him into a crowd of my fellow passengers. Grady reached over his son and wrestled my bag off the carousel, nearly knocking over a large gentleman in a ten-gallon hat and intricately inlaid turquoise and black cowboy boots.

"What the heck do you think you're doing, man?" the

cowboy said. "You nearly ran over my foot. Do you have any idea what these boots cost?" He pulled a red kerchief from his pocket and bent to wipe off his pointed leather toe.

Apologizing profusely, Grady lugged my bag to where I stood.

"Aw, I could have got it, Dad," Frank said, shuffling along behind his father.

"Not without mowing down half the people over there," Grady replied. He turned to me. "What kind of rocks do you have in here, Aunt Jess?"

"Oh, the usual kind," I said. "I brought you and Donna some books." I eyed Frank. "And I might have a little something in there for a boy in the fourth grade."

Frank's eyes shone. "You brought a present for me?"

"We'll see if you like it when we get to my hotel."

"You know you could have stayed with us, Aunt Jess. Frank was happy to give you his room."

"You said I could sleep on the couch. Right, Dad?"

"Now, we'll have no more talk of that," I said. "I put you out enough picking me up from the airport. My agent tells me this is officially a business trip, since I no longer live in New York City. Besides, we'll all be more comfortable this way, and the hotel is only a few blocks from your building." What I didn't say was that from what they'd told me, Grady and Donna's new apartment in Manhattan was small enough without an out-of-town relative crowding in and taking up precious space. And selfishly, I'd reached a time in my life when I treasured my privacy and found a hotel room more relaxing than someone's guest room, especially when it meant rousting the room's rightful owner. The magazine ads for the hotel that my literary agent, Matt Miller, had booked for me bragged about their luxurious feather beds and European linens. I looked forward to testing their claims for a great night's rest, even though it could never be the same as sleeping in my own bed.

We exited the terminal and walked across to the garage where Grady had parked. Frank had insisted on wheeling my suitcase himself, and I was happy to let him, but Grady and I kept a sharp eye on his progress in case the bag became too unwieldy to handle. He managed it well—only one tip over—and the look of pride on his face when Grady opened the trunk was worth any bumps and scrapes the suitcase might have endured.

"I'm learning Italian, Aunt Jessica," Frank informed me from the backseat as Grady negotiated airport traffic, looking for the entrance to the highway.

"You are?" I said. "That's wonderful. I'm all for teaching languages in the elementary grades."

"I'm learning Spanish in school," he said, "but my friend Michele is teaching me Italian. His name is spelled like a girl's name, but if you say it, it's like three names in one, Mick-*Kay*-Lee. That's how they say it in Italy. He lived in Italy for a lot of years. I can count up to twenty already. Want to hear?"

"Of course," I said, winking at Grady while Frank recited the numbers in Italian.

"Michele lives upstairs in our building," Frank said after reaching *venti*. "He's cool. You'll have to meet him."

"I'll be happy to," I said.

Grady glanced at his watch. "Donna has dinner planned for six thirty. Would you like to stop at the hotel first?"

"Is there time? I don't want to keep her waiting."

"It's rush hour, so it may be tight. But if nothing else, we can drop off your suitcase and have them hold it for you."

"Let's do that," I said.

A little voice from the rear piped up. "But what about my ... um ... present? If you leave your bag at the hotel ... ," he trailed off.

"Frank Fletcher," Grady said sternly. "I don't want to hear selfish thoughts like that. I think you should apologize to Aunt Jessica."

"Sorry, Aunt Jessica."

"I did promise him a present," I said. "How about this? You let me off at the hotel while you park the car, and I'll meet you at the apartment."

"You don't have to indulge him, Aunt Jess. Frank's a big boy. He can wait."

"I know he can, but I can't. I want to see if he likes what I brought him."

There was a whoop from the backseat. I turned to see Frank cover his mouth with both hands, but his eyes were gleeful.

The hotel overlooked Union Square, a large plaza and park downtown in an area that was both commercial and residential. It was Wednesday; a colorful farmers' market was winding down in the square across from the hotel. Shoppers were snapping up end-of-the-day bargains from vendors who were reluctant to haul their unsold products back home. Gaily striped awnings announced booths selling apples, vegetables, breads, cheeses, and other goodies. Grady turned off Broadway and pulled up in front of the hotel entrance, maneuvering around the trucks double-parked on the busy street.

"Checking in?" asked a handsome young man dressed head to toe in black as he opened the passenger door. "You go right in. I'll bring your luggage."

"We made good time, so there's no need to rush," Grady said, climbing out of the car to open the trunk. "You have the address and our phone number?"

"Of course."

"You really can't get lost."

I laughed. "You'd think I've never been here before," I said. "I used to live here. Remember?" I gave him a peck on the cheek, waved to Frank, and walked into the hotel's granite reception area, passing a concrete trough of grass trimmed to five inches high, the only touch of color in the steel-gray lobby. The bellman followed with my suitcase, which he parked next to a massive column.

"Thank you," I said, handing him a tip.

"My pleasure, ma'am."

The front desk was busy, so I took my place on line and looked around. The decor was decidedly modern, all hard edges and walls soaring up to tiny pinpoint lights like stars in the ceiling thirty feet above. The people working behind the desk were young and fashionable in their black garb, the women perfectly made-up, the men with spiky, shiny hair, thanks to a generous application of gel. The atmosphere was more my agent's style than mine. Matt knew all the "hip" places in the city. But I was always up for something new, and staying in a trendy New York hotel might be fun.

Ten minutes later, I was standing in the smallest hotel room I'd ever seen.

A queen-sized bed covered in pristine white sheets and comforter dominated the space. On one side was a square table, which appeared barely large enough to hold my laptop computer and perhaps a piece of paper. On the opposite side, stuffed between the bed and the window, was an upholstered chair. The lamps flanking the headboard were hung on the wall, as was the telephone. At the foot of the bed, also mounted on a wall, was a small flat-screen TV. If I wanted to sit in the chair to watch television, I'd have to climb over the bed or risk knocking my shoulder into the TV as I squeezed by. There was no bureau, not even a nightstand with drawers. Instead, hanging in the closet was a canvas organizer with four shelves.

The bellman had spread a cloth on the bed to protect the linens, and heaved my suitcase onto it. Where I was to put its contents, and even the bag itself, was going to take some arranging. After he left with tip in hand, I scouted the rest of the room—what there was of it. The tiny bathroom had a glass shelf under the mirror on which I could put at least some of my toiletries. The rest I'd have to leave in their black nylon travel pouch hanging from a hook on the back of the bathroom door.

The narrow closet held only five hangers, all it could accommodate since it already contained the canvas shelves as well as an ironing board and iron—an exercise in optimism if ever there was one. Where an ironing board could be set up in this miniature room was anyone's guess.

I unpacked what I thought I would need in the next day or two, slid my suitcase under the bed—the only place available where I wouldn't trip on it—tucked the books I'd brought for my nephew and his wife in my shoulder bag along with the gift for Frank, and exited the room.

Grady and Donna's apartment building was only a block and a half away, and I had plenty of time to get there. I crossed Broadway and wandered among the remaining booths of the farmers' market, stopping to sample a tiny cup of cider offered by a vendor. Before he finished packing up, I purchased a half-dozen Honeycrisp apples to bring to my hosts. At an adjacent stall, I bought a jar of wildflower honey made in Maine from a beekeeper who, I discovered, lived only ten miles from Cabot Cove.

"I can't believe I had to travel all the way to New York to find your honey," I told him.

"We come down here every fall and hit all the farmers' markets in the city," he said. "We stay for two weeks or until we're sold out. The wife and me, we have a trailer we park on the West Side."

"Do you save any honey for us in Maine?"

"Oh sure," he replied, chuckling. "We sent a few cases to Charles Department Store before we left." Charles Department Store was a treasured landmark in Cabot Cove.

"Well," I said, "I'm giving this jar away to relatives here in the city," I said, admiring the hand-drawn label and the little piece of gingham tied over the lid with a strand of raffia. "I'll make sure to get another one from the store when I get back home."

"Say hello to David and Jim for me when you see them," he said, referring to the brothers who owned Charles. "Tell 'em Hollister sends his regards."

"I'll do that, Mr. Hollister."

Frank was waiting on the front stoop when I arrived at Donna and Grady's building. "Can I help you carry anything, Aunt Jessica?" he said, eyeing my packages.

"You can take the apples," I said.

"Okay."

He reached up and pressed a call button on the panel next to the building's front entrance. At the answering buzz, he pushed through the door and held it for me. Their apartment was on the first floor, down the hall from the mailboxes and the elevators. Frank skipped ahead of me, swinging the bag of apples. I followed with a wince, crossing my fingers in hope the plastic wouldn't rupture before we reached the kitchen.

"Oh, Aunt Jessica, it's wonderful to see you again," Donna said, embracing me and relieving me of my packages. "Frank, please put those on the counter and go wash your hands."

"You found us," Grady said, taking my coat from my shoulders.

"Of course I did, although I dropped bread crumbs along the sidewalk so I can find my way back to the hotel," I said, laughing.

"Goodness, Grady, she used to live here," Donna said. "You don't forget how to get around the city that fast."

"I know, I know, but she's been back in Maine for a while," he said, sighing. "Anyway, I was just kidding."

"Aunt Jessica, if you left bread crumbs, the pigeons will eat them up," Frank said from the kitchen, where he'd placed the apples in a bowl.

We laughed. "I have no doubt that you're right," I said.

"Are your hands clean, young man?" Grady asked.

Frank held his palms up for inspection. "Kind of," he said.

Donna pointed to the bathroom. "Wash. Now."

He ran down the hall.

She looked at Grady. "Why is he being so good?"

"He knows Aunt Jess has a present for him."

I held up the little box I'd wrapped in silver paper and tied with a red ribbon.

"Ah," she said. "Do you mind if he doesn't open it until after dinner? I'd like him to be on best behavior during the meal."

"Whatever you say is fine with me," I said.

We put the box with Frank's gift by his place at the round table, a visible incentive for him to mind his manners, and I looked around at the apartment. The table was next to a galley kitchen, closed at the far end, which Grady and Donna had painted a buttery yellow. It was a typical city layout with scant counter space, but including a good-sized refrigerator and stove. Adjacent to the dining area was the living room with two windows flanking a flowered sofa and leather-top coffee table. A cozy armchair was set against one wall opposite a floor-to-ceiling bookcase. In addition to books—some of them mine—the shelves were filled with keepsakes from their travels and framed family pictures, mostly of Frank as a baby, but also of their wedding, including one with the three of us together. There wasn't space in the living room for much more, but they had hung pretty prints on the walls, and the room was cheerful and warm.

"This is charming," I said.

"It's small, but we love it," Donna said. "The neighborhood is close to Grady's office and Frank's school, and there are always a million things to explore in New York City on weekends."

"New York's an exciting place to live, isn't it?" I said. "I enjoyed my time here, and I miss the city every now and then. But I found I'm happiest back home in Cabot Cove."

"And you can always visit New York," Donna said, setting a salad on the table.

Frank showed off his best table manners throughout the meal, although he couldn't resist reaching out once or twice to play with the ribbon on the gift box. But he pulled his hand back quickly whenever Grady aimed a frown in his direction.

"How's the new job?" I asked over dessert, a delicious pear upside-down cake Donna had made.

"Going well so far," Grady said. He'd just started working for a payroll company in the advertising industry. "It seems pretty straightforward. Carl, the boss, is training me on all the union requirements, pension and welfare deductions, that sort of thing. I'm fine with the regular accounting. It's the industry-specific stuff I needed to catch up with, and I have. I've got about ten production companies I'm working with directly. One of them is Eye Screen. They're one of the biggest shops in the business. Do you know them?"

"No," I replied, "but I can't say that I'm familiar with the names of any commercial-production companies—or many film-production companies, for that matter."

"They're shooting a commercial next week and he's going to bring Frank to visit the set," Donna put in.

Grady grimaced. "I only said I was *thinking* about it."

"Awesome!" Frank said. "Can I be in the commercial?"

"No!" his parents chorused.

"You'll have to promise to be quiet as a mouse," Donna told him.

"If you're not, they'll kick us off the set and my name will be mud," Grady added. He looked up at Donna. "I'm not sure I should take him. It's the first time I'm going to be on a shoot. Maybe I should just see how it goes before I bring him along."

"You already said you would, Grady."

"Yeah, Dad. I'll be good. I know how to be a mouse." Frank wiggled his fingers in front of his nose and made little squeaking noises.

Grady smiled fondly at his son. "Very funny, sport."

"What is the commercial for?" I asked.

Grady looked uncomfortable for a moment. "It's for Permezzo, the international credit card."

"I have one of those," I said. "I use it when I travel abroad. Their concierge service is very helpful."

"They're making a big advertising push in America.

The agency awarded Eye Screen the job to make a series of spots. They're using celebrity testimonials. You know, TV personalities, famous people."

"Who's going to be in the commercials, Dad? Anyone I know?"

Grady shrugged. "Anne Tripper and Stella Bedford, for two."

"I never heard of them," Frank said, clearly disappointed.

"I've seen Tripper on TV," I said. "She writes those industry exposés. I'm not sure about Bedford, although the name sounds familiar."

"You must know her, Aunt Jessica," Donna said. "She's the lady with the barbecue cooking show on the food channel. The one who always dresses in overalls."

"Oh, yes, I know who you mean. I don't believe I've seen her show, but she's written a cookbook."

"Several cookbooks, actually," Grady added.

"Her picture is on the cover," I said. "Overalls and a straw hat."

"That's the one," Donna said. "She—"

"That's not a real celebrity," Frank said. "They should use a rock band. I could give them the names of my favorites. How about Five for Fighting, or—?"

"Don't interrupt, dear," Donna said.

"They're also using Lance Sevenson," Grady said. "He hosts the program *It's in Your Stars.*"

"The mystic?"

"Yes. You know him?"

"We were on a panel together once. He's, well, he's an interesting man."

"He's nuts is what you mean."

"Grady!" Donna frowned at her husband and cocked her head toward Frank.

"But some people *are* nuts, Mom, aren't they?"

"We don't talk that way about people, Frank," Donna said, placing her hand on his and drawing it away from the loose ribbon. "We just say he has an unusual point of view."

Grady muffled a laugh.

"Your celebrities should get Permezzo a lot of attention," I said.

"They could really use someone like you, Aunt Jess."

"Me?"

"You're a famous writer. They'd be happy to have you in a commercial. I think I could arrange it."

"I don't think so, Grady, but thanks for the vote of confidence."

"No, really, Aunt Jess. They would be thrilled to have you in their commercial. I mentioned it to Dan Howerstein, the producer. The lady from the agency was there and they got all excited."

"Grady," Donna said, her brow knit, "you didn't promise that Aunt Jessica would be in the commercial, did you?"

"I didn't promise," he replied, holding up his hands in defense. "Not at all. I just, uh, I just said I would ask. Aunt Jess is a bigger celebrity than any of those people."

"Yay! Can I watch you be in the commercial, Aunt Jessica?"

"I'm not going to be in any commercial," I said, smiling

at Frank. I looked up at Grady. Misery was written all over his face.

"This is something we can talk about later," I said. "Now, I think this might be the perfect time to open the present."

Frank grabbed the silver box and tore at the paper.

"Take it easy, son," Grady said, putting a hand on Frank's shoulder. "Your aunt Jessica got you a very special gift that might be, well, fragile, or breakable. Be careful with it."

Donna smiled and hugged herself while she watched Frank, who now worked at the knot in the ribbon very slowly, his excited eyes flashing from his parents to me and back to the box. I had checked with Donna and Grady before buying Frank's gift. I wanted to be sure they approved, and also that Frank was old enough to take on the responsibility of something that wasn't designed to withstand rough handling.

"An iPod! You got me an iPod!" Frank bounced up and down in his seat, laughing. "I always wanted one. Michele has one and he listens to his all the time. It's his special treasure."

Grady cleared his throat. "What do you say to your aunt Jessica, Frank?"

Frank got up from his seat and came to where I sat. Clutching the iPod to his chest, he said solemnly, "Thank you, Aunt Jessica. It's what I wanted most in the whole world."

"Looks like I made a good choice, then," I said. "You enjoy it."

"I'm going to put music on it right now. Can I, Dad?"

"We have to read the instructions first."

"I know how to do it. Michele showed me."

"Nevertheless, we're going to read the instructions."

"You two go ahead," Donna said, rising from her chair.

"Yes, go on," I said. "We'll clean up."

"You'll do no such thing," Donna told me. "You're a guest. Besides, there's hardly enough room in this kitchen for one, much less two."

"I can be a guest another time," I said, picking up my dessert plate and carrying it to the sink. "How about if you wash and I dry?"

We had the kitchen clean and dishes put away in short order. I was folding the dish towel when Frank came back to the living room with a huge grin on his face.

"I'm going upstairs to show Michele my iPod. We called. His mom says it's okay."

"Just for a few minutes, sport. Your aunt Jessica came a long distance to see you. You don't want to be rude."

"We'll be right back, Aunt Jessica. I just want to show Michele the great present that you got me. We can dance together now. He's got 'Superman' on his, and now I put it on mine."

"Isn't that a movie?" I asked.

"It's a song."

"He really does know how to load that thing," Grady said, shaking his head. "Kids and computers. He's a lot faster than I am."

"Say hello to Mary for me," Donna said as Grady and Frank walked out the door, and we took seats on the sofa.

"He's so excited about his friend Michele," I remarked.

"He's a good friend," she agreed.

"Is he in school with Frank?"

"No. Michele is sixteen."

"Sixteen? That's quite an age gap between them."

"Michele is a Down syndrome child. He has a little difficulty with speech—Italian is his first language—but he's making great strides. He and Frank met in the laundry room when his mother, Mary, and I were doing the wash. They hit it off right away. At first, I thought that Frank was flattered by the attention of an older boy. And Michele was happy to befriend someone who accepted him for who he is. Then they discovered that they both like the same kind of music. And they laugh at the same jokes. Michele is quite the jokester."

"A good foundation for friendship," I said. "I'm proud that Frank is his friend. It says a lot about his character."

"Frank's a very generous, open boy, and so is Michele."

"You and Grady have done a fine job with Frank."

She laughed. "Tell me that on the days when getting him to dress for school is like pulling teeth. There's no one who can procrastinate better than Frank."

"Maybe it's in the nature of little boys. I seem to remember Grady putting off his homework until the very last second." I smiled at the memory. "He was a handful," I said, "always excited about something new. He's still a bit like that, I think."

Donna's eyes met mine. "I'm sorry, Aunt Jessica."

"About what?"

"I didn't know that Grady was hoping you'd be in one of the commercials."

"No harm done," I said. "I've always been curious about how commercials are made, but even so, I'm not sure I want this face on camera."

"Why not? It's a wonderful face."

"You're such a dear. We'll talk about it more later, maybe after Frank goes to bed and Grady can tell me exactly what he said to this producer."

I had a feeling that Grady had promised the producer that he could convince me to be in the commercial. He'd been impetuous from the time he was a boy, and it was his boyish enthusiasm that sometimes got him into trouble. While it was one of his most endearing traits, it could also be a trying one. How many times had I had to rescue him from the consequences of his eagerness to please? More times than I could count. I'd have to think about this. Did Grady need to be rescued again? I hoped not, but a little voice was telling me that that might be the case.

Chapter Two

"I think it's a great idea."

"You do?"

"Absolutely! Your next book is coming out in April and it could use some exposure. I talked to Vaughan Buckley just the other day." Vaughan had been my publisher for many years. "He says they're cutting back on marketing budgets, like most publishers. That especially impacts well-known writers like you. You know how it is—your books get published and they sell well because of your large and enthusiastic fan base, which means the publisher can spend less on advertising and PR. But being on national television could raise your sales to an even greater level. Your fans will see you up close and personal on millions of TV screens across America. I think doing a commercial makes a lot of sense, Jess. It's not something to walk away from."

"But it's a commercial for a credit card, not for my books."

"It's exposure, Jessica. Name recognition. Could save you the wear and tear of a book tour."

"I don't mind book tours, Matt. I enjoy meeting my readers."

"You can do that, too."

Matt Miller sat across from me at the City Bakery, a popular coffee shop, gourmet bakery, and salad bar close to my hotel and downstairs from his office. He took a sip of cappuccino and peered at me over the rim of the cup.

"I suppose," I said.

Frankly, I was surprised that Matt was so keen for me to participate in a commercial for Permezzo. I was a little suspicious, too. He'd never suggested I do anything of this sort before, and there had been other opportunities for endorsements that I had routinely declined.

He'd also acted strangely when I'd arrived at his office. He was standing by the elevator when the door opened, and immediately ushered me back inside it, not even giving me a chance to say hello to Paulette, his receptionist. He'd called over his shoulder to her, "Tell her I'll call her back" as he joined me in the cab and pressed the button for the first floor. "I can use a little caffeine to keep me going this afternoon," he'd said by way of explanation.

"Don't you need a coat? It's chilly out."

"Nah! It's right next door," he'd replied.

Now, at a small table in the City Bakery, I took a sip of

its famous hot chocolate and eyed my agent. Always well dressed, this day he wore a crisply tailored pink and blue striped shirt with his initials on the cuff, a navy silk tie, and suspenders in a miniature pink and red check. He'd left his suit jacket upstairs.

"Okay," I said, "what else should I know?"

"I don't know what you mean," he said, his eyes widening in an effort to appear innocent.

"Come on, Matt. We know each better than that. You're not telling me everything. I'll just keep drumming at you until you do."

"Am I as transparent as that?"

"Yes."

"All right, Detective Fletcher, here it is." He leaned forward and said in a low voice, "I have a new client. In fact, she'd called just as you arrived."

"Why didn't you take her call?"

"Because we had a date for coffee. Besides, I don't want to seem too easy to reach." He laughed. "I think you're my only client, Jessica, who doesn't call every day just to chat."

"Writers get lonely," I offered. "Writing is a lonely profession."

"Yeah, I know all that, but I can't spend my day holding their hands over the phone."

I raised my eyebrows and asked, "Is this client a big secret?"

"Not anymore, at least not from you. But you have to promise you won't talk to anyone about this. I haven't announced it publicly yet."

"What haven't you announced?"

"That I'm about to represent Anne Tripper's latest book."

"Anne Tripper? She's one of the other celebrities in the commercials for Permezzo. Did you arrange that?"

He shook his head. "No, but I encouraged her to accept the offer. I'd be a happy man if I could make a deal with Permezzo for all my clients. It's a great way to get them attention without making it look like they're pushing their books. Product placement, Jessica. Branded entertainment. Talk to the consumer about one thing while guiding them in another direction."

"Sounds a little sneaky to me."

"Just smart marketing. It's the way things are done these days."

"But it's just a television commercial for a credit card," I said.

"That's not all it is," he said. "It's a national cross-media campaign. Magazines. Billboards. Radio. Internet. Permezzo will put the spots on their Web site with profiles of the celebrities in their ads and links to learn more about them." He leaned forward to make the point. "Like about the books they've written." He sat back. "They're developing a travel-related video game. There's even talk of a reality TV show. Wouldn't surprise me if they posted the commercials on YouTube for your fans to download. We'll put a link to them from your Web site."

"*My* Web site?"

"Of course."

"My Web site is for communicating with my readers and for publicizing my books, not for advertising Permezzo."

"It's not advertising for Permezzo, unless you want it to be. It's just a link to something you're involved with. That's the beauty of it. It's all about you."

"And the commercial," I added.

"Yes, but it's the commercial you star in. This kind of stuff is done every day."

I sighed and sat back. "This is a lot more complicated than I bargained for. I thought I'd be helping out Grady, but I never realized I'd be making a commitment of this nature."

"It's the new world of advertising, Jessica, and I, for one, think it would be a good move on your part."

"And on Anne Tripper's part?"

"She's already committed. It'll do great things for her. Her books sell well, but by no means is she up to your level yet in terms of fame, but I think that might change. I have a feeling her new book is going to be a blockbuster. If there's anyone in America who doesn't recognize her name today, they'll know it once the book comes out."

"That's quite a statement. What's it about?"

"Can't tell you. Not that I don't trust you, but, well, actually, I'm not entirely certain myself. I assume it's another industry exposé—she's already written about nuclear energy, processed foods, and the toy market—but she's holding her cards pretty close to her vest. I can tell you that there *will* be a few people who won't be happy when it hits the bestseller list. She says she has the inside dirt on some heavy hitters."

"I'll look forward to reading it," I said, wondering why Matt would be willing to represent a book whose contents were still under wraps.

"Tell Paulette when we go back upstairs to put a note on her calendar to send you an advance copy."

I sat in Matt's office browsing the latest copy of *Publishers Weekly* while he returned Anne Tripper's call.

"Now," I said after his conversation had ended, "how about getting to my reason for being in New York."

"Right. Your next book. The way I see it . . ."

I left Matt's office forty-five minutes later and went to my hotel, where I called Grady at his new company.

"You're serious, Aunt Jess?" he said, his voice bubbling with enthusiasm. "You're willing to see the creative director of Permezzo's advertising agency?"

"We're only going to talk," I said. "I'm not committing to anything, you understand."

"Aunt Jess, you're going to love this lady. She's smart and sharp, really knows her stuff."

"I'm sure she's all that and more," I said. "I don't know if I'll feel comfortable making a credit card commercial, but I'm willing to learn more about it."

"Thank you, Aunt Jess. You won't regret it, I promise you. Frank is going to be so excited when I tell him."

"Grady, you're getting ahead of yourself."

"I know, I know. Sometimes I do that."

I smiled. "Sometimes" was an understatement.

"I'll call you as soon as I set up the meeting," he said.

"Just wait till I tell Carl. This is going to put me in good with the boss. You're terrific, Aunt Jess."

Oh dear, I thought as I hung up the phone and sank down on the soft edge of the bed in my tiny hotel room. *What have I gotten myself into?*

Chapter Three

"Mrs. Fletcher? We spoke on the phone. I'm Betsy Archibald of Mindbenders. We're the agency for Permezzo. I'm so glad you could come today. We're all excited about your participation." Instead of shaking my hand, the petite redhead handed me her business card.

"Nice to meet you," I said, glancing at the card and putting it in my pocket.

"And you are?" She directed her gaze to Grady.

He hopped forward with his hand outstretched. "Grady Fletcher, Betsy. Dan Howerstein introduced me to you last week. I happened to be in the Eye Screen production office when you were having the, uh, the pre-pro conference call. Remember?"

Betsy looked at Grady's hand and said, "I don't shake hands. If we'd met before, you should know that."

She turned away. "Please follow me. Your costars are here already."

Grady glanced at his hand and wiped it awkwardly on the side of his jacket. Then he extended it toward me. "After you, Aunt Jess," he said, forcing a smile.

Betsy rang for the elevator. Before it arrived, a musical chime sounded, followed by a simple tune. I looked around for its source. "That's mine," Betsy said, drawing her cell phone from a pocket, and squinting at the screen. "I hope you're on your way," she told her caller. "The meeting is about to start." There was a pause. "You know I can't pay you until the client pays me. Look, I can't talk to you now. We can discuss it tonight. You can take me to dinner." There was another pause and a shrug. "Break it!"

The elevator door opened and the three of us stepped in. We stood in silence as the illuminated numbers went from one to two to three, but it gave me the opportunity to observe the agency's chief creative officer. I estimated she was in her late thirties, although with her small stature I imagine there may have been times she was easily mistaken for someone much younger, especially when she wasn't wearing the open-toe black patent leather four-inch heels she had on. Even with the added height her shoes provided, she was more than a head shorter than I. She was dressed elegantly but in clothing far from the corporate attire I would have expected. She had paired charcoal harem pants, an Indian scarf tied at the waist, with an aqua off-the-shoulder knit top, which revealed the heavy sprinkling of freckles on her shoulder, evidence that her hair was naturally red, if perhaps not the bright coppery shade she wore in loose ringlets framing her face. When the elevator stopped at the third floor, Betsy led the way, her stride long and hips swaying like a diminutive version of a runway model. My eyes were drawn to the scarlet soles of her shoes. *How does she walk in those things?* I thought. I've made some sacrifices for beauty and fashion in my day, but chancing a twisted ankle from an impossibly high-heeled shoe was not one of them.

The office Betsy led us through was a huge loft space with tall windows at either end. All the utility pipes and ductwork exposed overhead were painted in brilliant colors—shocking pink, yellow, orange, acid green, deep turquoise. Everything else in the space was black and white. A series of eight or ten of what Betsy called "pods"—white tables lined up to form loose rectangles around the room's supporting columns—were occupied by small groups of people sitting in black chairs, working on black laptops, most of them wearing black as well. At every junction between the pods there was a lounge area with deep armchairs, upholstered in white canvas, and modern sofas in black felt. Several of them were used by employees enjoying a nap.

"We don't have regular hours," Betsy explained, pausing to straighten a chair. "Creativity can't always be summoned from nine to five. The office is open twenty-four hours a day. Some people prefer to work at night or very early in the morning, and we encourage our staff to take advantage of whenever they feel productive."

"Must be tough on family life," Grady muttered.

Betsy heard him. "Families have to make sacrifices for art," she said. "Our agency has won every coveted creative-advertising award there is—the One Club, the AICP Show, Cannes Lions, New York Festivals, London International, the Clios. We've won them all. We credit not only our staff but also their families in our success."

"Ex-excuse me, Betsy?" A young man had come up to her holding a board with a piece of white paper covering some artwork. Clearly nervous, he handed her the board, his hands shaking, the loose paper quivering. "Sorry to interrupt, but I thought you'd want to see this right away. I . . . I worked on it all night."

Betsy lifted the cover sheet and concentrated on the page beneath. I peered over her shoulder to see what she was studying so intently. It was a design for a logo with two *A*s intertwined.

Betsy glanced up at me and quickly covered the design. She aimed a brilliant smile at the young man, whose face immediately flooded with pleasure. "Perfect, Kip," she said.

"You really like it? I mean, thanks. Just thanks," Kip said, bouncing on his toes, obviously pleased.

"Don't forget what I said, though." She looked at him sternly.

He grinned at her, then moved his fingers over his lips as if zipping them shut. He backed away from us awkwardly, raised his hand in a wave, and walked quickly to his computer at the nearest pod.

Betsy flashed a brief smile at Grady and me, and continued on, stopping at a curved wall on the loft's periphery.

"Ah, here we are." She tapped on a door that had no knob. It was opened by a rotund gentleman in a three-piece gray silk suit.

"Jessica Fletcher! I have been waiting on—how you say?—needles and pins for you," he said, grabbing my fingers and bringing them to his lips.

The expression on Betsy's face was priceless. For a woman who didn't like to shake hands, the prospect of a kiss on the fingers must be terrifying, but she schooled her features quickly and made the introduction. "Mrs. Fletcher, this is our most important client, Antonio Tedeschi, Permezzo's president and chief marketing officer."

"How do you do," I said.

"*Ecco, bella*, you are exactly as I pictured you," he said, pulling my hand under his arm and escorting me into the room. He looked back at Betsy and winked.

A dozen people stood around an artfully arranged buffet table with platters of food, enough to feed a crowd three times our number. Antonio leaned close to my ear. "Such an important lady. Such talent. We shall make a big success together, yes?"

"I hope so," I said, trying not to appear rude by drawing away.

"I tell my Betsy I am so excited to meet you. I read all your books, and then look what she does. She brings you to me."

"Ain't he too much?" A lady with short blond hair and a big smile approached us. "Antonio, Ah'm goin' to take you home to Dallas so you can teach my honey Homer the right way to treat a woman."

"It would be my pleasure to visit your amiable home," he replied.

She didn't wait for an introduction. "Howdy, Mrs. Fletcher. I'm Stella Bedford," she said, pumping my hand after Antonio had released it. "I could say I'm a writer, too—I have a bunch of cookbooks out—but that would be a lie. All my books are written by a ghostwriter. I can cook up a storm, but Ah can hardly put two words together on paper. I do so admire someone who can."

"It's a pleasure to meet you," I said. "But please call me Jessica."

"Jessica it is." She was dressed in an elegant green and white shirtwaist dress, which showed off her generous curves, and had a pink cashmere cardigan resting on her shoulders. She wore shocking pink lipstick and her blue eyes were accented by jet-black mascara and a long set of false eyelashes.

Antonio turned to me. "May I bring you some coffee?"

"Tea, please," I replied.

"You can get me a coffee, hon. I take two sugars," Stella told Antonio. She turned to Grady. "And who's this handsome fellow?"

Grady blushed at the compliment.

"This is my nephew, Grady Fletcher. Grady, this is Stella Bedford."

He smiled at her, but after his experience with Betsy Archibald, he wasn't sure if he should offer his hand. He settled on "Nice to meet you."

"Actually, at home they call me Cookie," she said, taking Grady's arm. " 'Stella' is such a formal name, doncha think?"

She gazed up at him, batting her eyelashes. Still holding his arm, she addressed me. "I tried to get the TV folks to name my show *Cookin' with Cookie*, but they wouldn't. Said it sounds like I'm a baker, not a barbecue chef." She squeezed Grady's arm. "Bet you were expecting to see me with a piece of straw in my teeth, weren't you, hon?"

Grady's blush became deeper. "No, ma'am."

"Ooh, you were, too. Just admit it. They make me wear these silly overalls on the show. Said it makes me memorable. They may be right. My last cookbook's been flying off the shelves, not quite as fast as your books of course," she said, reaching out and tapping me on the arm, "but we're doin' good."

Antonio returned with a waiter holding a tray on which were two mugs, one with coffee and one tea, as well as a bowl of sugar, a pitcher of cream, and a small dish of lemon slices. He also brought with him a lanky man I recognized, and in their wake a young woman with dark hair clutching a clipboard to her chest and appearing ill at ease. The tall man batted his hand behind his back, stopping the young woman in her tracks.

"Jessica, my dear, it's been a long time," he said. "How is the world treating you?" He raised the half-glasses that were dangling from a cord around his neck, and peered at me through the lenses as if they were a monocle. He spoke with a British accent.

"Hello, Lance, nice to see you again," I said, taking my mug from the tray.

"Ah, you already have the acquaintance made of this gentleman," Antonio said.

"Mr. Sevenson and I were on a panel together in Wisconsin a number of years ago."

"It was before the success of my show when I was flogging one of my early books." He tapped a long finger on his thin lips. "*Crystals in Your Life*, I think that was the one. Book tours are the pits. All those housewives in hair rollers." He raised his eyebrows, leered at Stella, and slid his glasses on his nose. " 'Course, I'd love to see you in hair rollers."

"It'll never happen, darlin,' " she said, but her answering smile was brittle. "Excuse me, y'all. I have to find Jimbo, my manager." She took her coffee from the tray and walked away.

I introduced Grady to Antonio and Lance.

"Keeping your aunt out of trouble?" Lance asked.

"Actually, I work for the production company's, uh, payroll company," Grady said.

"Oh goody. Are you the one writing us the big checks?"

"Not really. No. The agency pays the talent, not the production company."

"And we are the 'talent,' " Lance said, guffawing. "Oh, I like that word. As if anyone could think that woman is talented." He cocked his head toward Stella Bedford's back. "Or that one, for that matter." He tipped his head down so he could peer over his half-glasses.

I followed his gaze to a woman with long straight blond hair who was arguing with Betsy Archibald. She wore a sleeveless black scoop-neck dress with knee-high black boots. A quilted red bag hung from her shoulder by a gold chain, leaving her hands free to wave in the air as she spoke animatedly, light reflecting off the many rings on her fingers. She was frowning, and I got the impression Betsy was not about to placate her.

"*La bocca,*" Antonio said, seeing the direction of our eyes. "*Mah!* She is a difficult woman. Yes. But *bella!* So beautiful. And many people listen to her."

"She's got a mouth all right," Lance said, "but no one pays attention to what she says. She's a total bimbo." He looked at me. "You and I are the only true stars in the firmament here, my dear. The others are strictly wannabes. Poor Betsy. No wonder she pushed me into this. I'll see you later. Gotta feed my genius." He patted his stomach and ambled off toward the buffet.

Antonio looked distressed. "Bimbo? I don't know this word."

"Just as well," I said.

"Is this a bad thing?"

"It's not a compliment. Apparently, Mr. Sevenson does not count himself among Anne Tripper's fans."

"But many do," Antonio said, reassuring himself that he had the right people to represent his credit card. "She is big on the television. Even in Italy, we know who she is. You have her acquaintance, yes?"

"We haven't had the pleasure," I said.

"But no, this is not right. Come! I will present you. All my wonderful people must know each other." Antonio steered me in the direction of Betsy Archibald and Anne Tripper, whose conversation stopped at our approach, although their facial expressions indicated they hadn't resolved their differences. Betsy appeared pleased to see us. Miss Tripper was obviously annoyed at the interruption.

"How do you do," Anne said, giving me icy fingers to shake when Antonio introduced us. She gave Grady a cool nod, and scowled when Betsy excused herself to find the producer, who was late in arriving.

"I understand we have an agent in common," she said to me.

"Matt Miller?"

"Yes. He's going to represent my next book."

Matt had told me not to say anything about his representing her, but here Anne Tripper was talking about it freely. "Matt's been my agent for many years," I said. "I'm sure he'll do a good job for you, too."

"He'd better. I plan to be at the top of the bestseller list by next fall. If the publisher he comes up with doesn't meet my timetable, it'll be the last time Miller gets a book of mine." She fiddled with a large black opal ring on her index finger, one of three rings she wore on that hand.

"He told me he expects it to be a bestseller," I said, "but it isn't the agent who markets the book. It's the publisher."

She waved her hands in the air as if dismissing my statement. "Any publisher will fall all over itself to sell my book. They have to if they want to make their money back."

"Signora Fletcher, she is a bestseller," Antonio said, smiling from one to the other of us. "Her books are very popular in Italy." Then he hastened to add, "As are yours, of course, Signorina Tripper."

"Nice of you to remember," she said.

Antonio seemed to start. I thought his response was to

Anne's chilly remark, but he pulled a case from his pocket and consulted his cell phone, which must have vibrated to alert him to a message.

"I'm published in a dozen countries, although God knows why," Anne said. "I write about the impact of American industries. Americans understand what I'm saying. No one else in the world does. They just put our books on their shelves to prove that they're well-read. They probably do the same with yours. Are you published in any *important* countries, other than our own, of course?"

"A few," I said, cringing inside for the insult she'd just paid Antonio's homeland, implying that it was unimportant. Fortunately, he wasn't paying attention to our conversation.

Grady, however, was. Not about to let Anne Tripper outdo me, he jumped in. "Aunt Jess! Your books are translated into at least sixty languages," he said.

"I see you have your own promoter with you," Anne said. Her lips formed a small smile, but it never reached her eyes. She looked around the room. "Everyone seems to have brought along an assistant. Perhaps I should have as well." Her eyes swung back to mine. "But then, I never have a problem speaking for myself."

"I don't imagine you do," I replied.

"I'm sure we'll be seeing more of each other," she said, "but right now I have to catch Betsy Archibald. We weren't finished with our conversation when your arrival cut it short. You don't mind, I'm sure." She walked away.

Grady's eyes met mine and he directed a long stream

of air toward his forehead, raising strands of hair that had tumbled down.

I gave him a little shake of my head, and he understood not to comment in front of Antonio, who looked up from his cell phone to realize Anne had departed. "She is gone?" He glanced at his watch. "*Ecco!* I must find the producer. The meeting, she should begin." He gave a short bow in my direction, grabbed my hand, and clasped it to his breast. "Signora Fletcher, so wonderful to acquaint with you. I am so happy you are to be in our patch."

He must have seen my confusion.

Antonio looked at Grady. "This is right? Patch?"

"Spot," Grady answered.

"Ah, yes. Spot. Thank you, my friend." He turned back to me. "I am so happy you are to be in our spot."

Grady waited for Antonio to leave, then leaned toward me. "Before anyone comes back, Aunt Jess, would you mind if we took something from the buffet? I never got any breakfast this morning. I was running late and had to take Frank to school. I'm starving."

"I don't mind at all," I said. "Let's take a peek at what they have. I could use a little fortification, especially if I have to spend a lot more time with some of my 'costars.'"

"Gosh, I'm sorry, Aunt Jess. I didn't know what they'd be like. At least Stella Bedford is nice."

"Very nice, Grady. And don't you fret about this. I've worked with difficult people before."

We picked up plates and napkins and walked to the end of the buffet, passing Lance Sevenson, who was berating the young woman with the clipboard. "You are to be ready whenever I need you, not wandering about the room," he said, forgetting for a moment to use his British accent. *What's his real accent?* I mused.

Lance breathed in noisily and straightened up. "I want you at my side recording everything I say. I must have accuracy. The next book will be on my wit and wisdom, and it is your responsibility to capture it."

"But you waved me off. I thought you didn't want me there."

"When I don't want you there, I will tell you. Until then, you are to be my shadow. If I snap my fingers, I want your undivided attention. Understand?"

She hung her head.

"Understand?" he persisted.

"Yes, sir."

Grady raised his eyebrows at me and grimaced. "Hoo boy. Wouldn't want to work for him," he whispered.

"Nor would I," I agreed.

We filled our plates with an assortment from the buffet and found seats at the large conference table, which was soon occupied by the others in the room. Stella Bedford perused our selections as she passed behind our chairs, and returned a moment later, taking a seat next to Grady. "I got one of those pastries you have, hon," she said, giving him a flirtatious smile. "They look yummy, just like you."

Grady, who'd been taking a sip of coffee, began to cough and Stella pounded him on the back. "I always seem to have this effect on young men," she said, grinning at me.

"Cookie, leave the boy alone," said a large gentleman in an aqua Western shirt and string tie as he pulled out a chair next to the cookbook author. He slid a paper plate on the table—it was piled high with three different pastries, two mini muffins, a croissant, and a bagel with cream cheese—and sat heavily, the chair bouncing a bit from his weight.

"This is Jimbo Barnes, my manager," Stella said. She turned to him. "You musta heard of Jessica Fletcher, the famous mystery writer. Well, here she is in the flesh. And this handsome guy is her nephew, Grady."

Jimbo nodded at me and reached across Stella to give Grady's hand a shake. "Nice to meet ya," he said. "Hey, don't I know you from somewhere?"

"You look familiar to me, too," Grady said, "but I can't quite place you."

"The airport," I put in.

Jimbo and Grady looked at me perplexed.

"I recognized the cowboy boots."

"My boots?" Jimbo looked down at his feet and smiled. "These were custom-made special for me in El Paso, boot capital of the world."

"Oh, right," Grady said, hunching his shoulders. "I nearly knocked you down with my aunt's suitcase."

"You and the boy. I remember now. That's all right; no harm done." He pulled a red kerchief from his pocket and wiped it over the pointed toes of his boots.

"You makin' friends behind my back, Jimbo?" Stella said, leaning into Grady.

"Don't pay no mind to this flirt. She loves to discomfort all the men. I think it's her hobby."

"Now, that ain't nice, Jimbo," Stella said. "I just like

to have gentlemen around me. Makes me feel young and pretty." She nibbled at a cherry Danish that she'd speared with a fork, and her eyes rose to the ceiling while she contemplated its taste. Startled, she swallowed and grabbed Jimbo's hand just as he was about to bite into a croissant. "Darlin', do you see the color of that air vent up there? That's exactly the shade that I want painted on the wall in my office, you know, the one I built with the pictures of me with all the celebrities." She leaned forward and shook her fork at me. "Jessica, we must take a picture together before this commercial nonsense is over. I got me this great wall at home—I call it my 'Wall of Fame'—and it's covered with photographs of me with every famous person I've ever met since the TV show started up. They're signed, too. Ah'm gonna put our picture together right at the very top." She patted her manager's arm. "Where's your briefcase, Jimbo? Get your camera."

"Not now, Cookie," he said, stuffing the entire croissant into his mouth. In a voice muffled by bread, he added, "The meetin's about to start."

Chapter Four

"Ladies and gentlemen. If I may have your attention." A man I hadn't noticed before had taken a seat at the head of the table next to Betsy Archibald, who carefully lined up the pencils next to her pad. He was dressed casually in a gray V-neck sweater over a white T-shirt, which half covered a gold chain around his neck. His hair was neatly cropped close to his head, but he appeared not to have shaved for several days.

"That's Howerstein," Grady whispered to me, "the producer."

"Daniel would like to go over the schedule," Betsy announced, nodding to two young people holding stacks of folders. The pair efficiently distributed them to those assembled around the table. The logo for Eye Screen Productions was prominent on the cover.

"I won't keep you long," Howerstein said without preamble. "We have a lot to do and only a few days in which to do it. I know how important your time is." He emphasized the "your," but from the way he kept glancing at his watch, I had a feeling it was his time he was concerned with. He riffled through several papers in his folder and drew one out. "We have planned the shoot for the middle of next week. We should be able to complete all four spots in that time frame. A car service will pick up the talent at their hotels each morning. Please let Jason or Lucy, our PAs— that's our shorthand for production assistants—know where you are staying." He pointed to the young man and young woman who had helped pass around the folders. Jason raised his hand and smiled.

"We'll start in the morning, going one at a time, continuing on the next day for whatever we haven't finished. We're holding the location for a third day, but I don't think we'll need it," Howerstein continued. "Please come prepared with your lines memorized. There aren't a lot of them." His gaze took in those of us around the table.

"Yes, please do," Betsy put in. "Every second costs money in production. And—"

Howerstein cut her off. "I hope you've had an opportunity to meet each other this morning. And to—"

"And to meet Mr. Tedeschi from Permezzo," Betsy interrupted again, cocking her head at Antonio, who took her introduction as a cue to speak.

"Yes, yes," he said, pushing back his chair and getting to his feet. "Permezzo are so pleased to have such distinguished celebrities as yourself endorse our service." His eyes roamed around the table till they made contact with each of us who was to appear in the commercials: Stella Bedford, Lance Sevenson, Anne Tripper, and me. "We have a little surprise for our distinguished guests, a *gratificazione*." He reached into an attaché and withdrew four packets, which he passed to us. On the front of my thick envelope, in an elegant script that must have been hand-lettered by a calligrapher, were the words "Jessica Fletcher Knows Permezzo." "Open, open, please," Antonio said, smiling benevolently at his recipients, his palms pressed together in front of his ample girth.

I lifted the flap of the envelope carefully, reluctant to damage the paper with its beautiful writing. Across the table, Lance Sevenson's assistant watched as he ripped the packet down one side and extracted the slim red leather case it contained. He lifted the lid, pulled out a platinum Permezzo card, and, holding it between his index and middle fingers, waved it at Antonio. I opened my package to find the same thing, as did Stella.

Anne Tripper, who'd waited to see what our envelopes contained, left hers unopened on the table.

"It is a little gift from Permezzo," Antonio said, his eyes twinkling. "We have put twenty-five thousand dollars on it for each of you to buy whatever you like." He raised his eyebrows waiting for the response.

"I hope you don't think that's all the money you're paying me to be in your commercial," Lance said, "because if you are, you've got another think coming."

Betsy had been leaning forward to see our reactions to Antonio's present. She frowned. "Really, Lance, this is not the time," she said coldly.

Antonio's face fell. "You misunderstand," he said sharply. "This is from the heart, a gift for you. This is not business."

Anne smirked. "It's all business, Antonio, or we wouldn't be here," she said, sliding her unopened package into her red purse.

Lance, who was sitting next to her, snatched up her hand and studied her large ring. "Buy yourself that black opal?"

"What business is it of yours?"

"Gems and stones are my business," Lance said, grinning at her. "It's bad luck if you buy an opal for yourself. Bet you didn't know that."

Anne pulled her hand away with disgust and hid it under the table. She started to say something in return, but I raised my voice to be heard above other conversation.

"Thank you, Signore Tedeschi," I said. "This is very generous of you. I'm sure we all can put it to good use."

He smiled at me, but it was a sad smile.

"Ah'm gonna skip on over to Tiffany's when we leave here," Stella said, winking at Antonio. "Would you like to come along? I always like having a handsome man on my arm when I'm buyin' jewelry."

"No. No," Antonio said, recovering his cheerful demeanor, "but you buy for yourself something very beautiful for a beautiful lady."

"Don't you worry your head about that. I surely will. And I'll show it off to you, too."

Anne gave out a loud sigh. "Can we get this meeting going, please? You may have time to go shopping," she said, giving Stella a baleful look, "but I have important appointments today."

"Hon, there ain't nothing more important than buying diamonds," Stella said, putting on a show of tucking her card in her cleavage.

Howerstein jotted down something on a piece of paper, folded it in quarters, and wrote a name on the top. From where I sat, I couldn't see whose name it was. He gestured to Lucy, the production assistant, and handed her the note.

Antonio cleared his throat. "Yes. We will begin now. I begin by saying that Permezzo has a celebrated history in Europe," he said, launching into what I expected might become a long speech. "We were first to include concierge service for our marvelous customers." He flicked his fingers as if shooing something away. "The other cards," he said, making a face, "they have only a few things."

"If I may?" Betsy broke in.

Antonio frowned at her, but she quickly added, "We are providing everyone with a history of this wonderful company so they can see how important it is. Inside your folders, ladies and gentlemen, you'll find this elegant brochure." She held up a colorful booklet with a picture on the cover of a smiling couple clearly delighted with Permezzo's services.

Antonio nodded at Betsy. "Yes, yes, this is a very good piece," he said, turning back to his audience. "You will see how we took all the experience of our competitors who develop their service in the twentieth century, and we—how you say?—do them better. Permezzo is on the toe to take over the twenty-first-century market to create the premier business service for successful executives, like yourself."

He prattled on for a few more minutes, praising his company's foresight in anticipating and delivering what the sophisticated traveler would need in the new millennium, but when he paused to take a breath, Howerstein jumped in.

"Thank you, Mr. Tedeschi," he boomed. "We are all big Permezzo fans here. And it is our goal to make Permezzo a household name in America. How are we going to do that? Well, we'll start with the commercials we're going to shoot next week." He lowered his voice as if giving confidential information. "If any of our distinguished guests have questions for Mr. Tedeschi, we'll arrange to keep the conference room open as long as you need it following the meeting." Howerstein shot a smile at Antonio. "Right! Now, let's go over the scripts and the storyboards. I'm certain Mr. Tedeschi will tell you that what's key for Permezzo's success is that the spots we're about to film go off smoothly."

Antonio bobbed his head in agreement and flopped back into his seat.

The production assistants, carrying trays, circled the table offering everyone bottled water and clearing away our plates from the buffet. For the next twenty minutes, we reviewed the material in the folders, going over sheets of paper that laid out the assignments for each day of shooting, who the crew would be, where the talent—us—was supposed to be at each point in the production, and what our lines were for the commercial. He also explained the storyboard, an illustrated version of the spot, something like a comic book page, giving not just the characters and dialogue but also a rough idea of camera angle, props, and wardrobe.

Lance raised a hand to get Howerstein's attention. "I have an important question," he called out. He poked his assistant, Lena, with his elbow, and pointed his chin toward her pad.

She quickly picked up her pen and sat with it poised over the paper, ready to take down the conversation verbatim.

"Yes, Mr. Sevenson?" the producer said, tapping on the face of his watch.

"Who is going to be directing this illustrious group, and why has he not deigned to attend this meeting?"

The scratching of Lena's pen was the only sound in the momentary silence that followed Lance's query.

Betsy jumped in before Howerstein could answer. "I can answer that. Our agency, Mindbenders, has selected a prominent Hollywood director, Adam Akmanian. He directed the hit *On the Planet Pluto.*"

Grady leaned close to my ear. "These days they'd have to rename it *On the Dwarf Planet Pluto*," he whispered. "It doesn't qualify as a full planet anymore."

The title of the film didn't strike a bell with me, but then I don't often get out to a movie theater. The last time must have been several years ago. I do like to read the movie reviews in the newspaper every week. And with cable service I can catch up with the latest films on television, even though it's a couple of months after they come out.

Lucy, the production assistant, leaned between Grady and me and asked in a low voice, "Would you like more water?"

I declined, but Grady took another bottle from her tray.

When she'd withdrawn, I noticed a folded note in front of Grady. I nudged his arm and pointed to the paper. Grady opened it. "Call me," it said. He looked over at the producer, who'd been watching him, nodded, and slid the message in his pocket.

Meanwhile, Betsy rattled off the names of three more movies from the Adam Akmanian canon, but those titles were also unfamiliar to me.

Grady leaned over again. "I've never heard of any of those films. Who is this guy?"

"And, of course, last year he directed *Battle of the Alien Space Cadets*." Betsy sat back and smiled.

"Okay. That one I've heard of," Grady said under his breath. "A real shoot-'em-up. Frank loved it."

"So is the Permezzo commercial going to be science fiction?" Anne asked no one in particular.

"Adam is tied up in meetings in L.A. today," Howerstein said, ignoring the aside. "He's flying in the beginning of next week, but he told me to tell you he sends you his very best, and that he's eager to meet and work with each of you next week."

"I doubt he sent any messages at all," Lance said, giving his assistant another poke. "Directors are prima donnas, or I should say prima donalds, since they're all male."

Lena began writing furiously on her pad.

"And I know all about Akmanian. He's a wack job!" he proclaimed.

"No. No. Only the best for Permezzo," Antonio said.

Anne waved a hand in the air. I noticed that she had removed her opal ring. "He's probably more like a has-been," she said, "but then I suppose doing commercials is not at the top of the wish list for Hollywood's A-list directors."

"On the contrary," Betsy said, working to control her temper. "Commercial work is prized by Hollywood directors."

"So you say. Name one," Lance said.

"I can name you dozens of Hollywood directors who have done spots," she replied, "including just about all the famous names." She started counting on her fingers. "Spike Lee, Ridley Scott, Michael Bay, Martin Scorsese, Michael Mann, Oliver Stone, Wes Anderson, David Lynch."

"All right. Let's stop this now," Howerstein said. "Betsy's right. The top guys in Hollywood are happy to direct commercials."

"I wouldn't have hired Akmanian," Lance said, leaning over to see what Lena had taken down.

"Well, fortunately it isn't up to you," Betsy said acidly. "We're very pleased with his reel. He's going to do a marvelous job for Permezzo. He's excited about the project, and I'm certain you'll find him very professional when you work with him next week."

Antonio seemed happy that his director was in the company of Scorsese and Stone; he clasped his hands together and smiled his approval at Betsy. She sat up a little straighter in her seat. "Daniel has to leave for another appointment. If you have any questions, now is the time to ask them. Or you can wait till you're on the set next week."

No one around me raised a hand, and neither did I, although, if pressed, I could think of a few, beginning with, *Is it too late to back out?*

Chapter Five

"Say cheese!"

"Brie!"

Stella Bedford had linked arms with me while Jimbo Barnes aimed his digital camera in our direction and clicked the shutter. "That looks good," he said, squinting at the tiny screen on the back of the camera.

"Are we both smiling?" she asked. "Take another one, just to be sure." Stella hugged my arm. "This is gonna be great. I'll send you the print and you can sign it to me. Make sure you use permanent ink, right?"

"I'll remember."

"Now, don't forget to give me your address."

"I won't forget," I said.

"Cookie, shut up so I can take the picture."

Stella tilted her head toward mine and gave the camera a perky smile.

"That's it," Jimbo said, turning a dial so he could view what he'd captured.

"Let me see," Stella said. She leaned against his arm, then pulled the camera out of his hands. "Look, Jessica. Don't we look nice?"

I put on my reading glasses to peer at the screen. "That looks like a good one," I said.

"Can I see?" Grady asked, peeking over my shoulder.

After the meeting emptied out, the four of us had lingered in the agency's conference room. Stella had prevailed upon me not to leave until Jimbo could take our picture together.

"That's a great shot of you guys, Aunt Jess."

Jimbo smiled. "I'll have extra copies made so you can have one, Grady."

"Thanks! By the way, what kind of camera is that?"

"I just got it," Jimbo said, taking the camera back from Stella. "It's a new Japanese model. Does video, too. Lots of bells and whistles. Comes with three different lenses."

"Men and their paraphernalia!" Stella said, rolling her eyes. "I swear, if it has a wheel or a speaker or a dial or a cartridge, they just love it. My Homer's no different. The surround sound in our media room back home could blow you out of your seat. Me, I'm a down-home girl. I like things simple. If it has too many buttons, I'm not interested—unless it's a dress."

"Does that preference extend to kitchen appliances as well?" I asked, thinking a professional chef must have a pretty fancy supply of tools, too.

"Now, there I might make an exception," she said with

a grin. "But only for a high-end fridge or stove. I'm just not good with technology. Computers! You can keep 'em. Lucky for me, my specialty is barbecue, and for that, a spicy marinade and a hot fire can take you pretty far. Look where it took me!" She struck a pose and laughed.

"That's some camera he's got," Grady said, coming over to us.

"Just so's it don't catch my extra chin," Stella said, patting the back of her hand under her jaw.

"You looked lovely to me," I said.

"You're gonna be my new best friend."

Grady glanced at his watch. "Ready to go, Aunt Jess? I have to get back to the office."

"Wait, Jessica," Stella said, settling a large tote bag on the conference table. "Tell me where you're staying and I'll get Jimbo to send the pictures over soon as they're ready."

I gave her the name of my hotel, but suggested that she send the prints to Cabot Cove instead, or wait until I returned. "I hadn't planned on staying in New York through next week," I said as I printed my address on a card. "I have to go home this weekend to tie up some loose ends, but I'll be back in time for the shoot. I'm not sure at the moment where I'll be staying when I return."

"Our door's always open," Grady said.

"I know, dear, and I appreciate that."

I'd decided it was too hard on the pocketbook, never mind the psyche, simply to stay in my dollhouse-sized hotel room for another week. While the bed was everything that had been promised—and I'd slept very well—it was impossible to relax in the room during the time I wasn't under the covers. I'd tried taking my book downstairs to the hotel lounge, but the lighting was dim, and the noise level much too high to concentrate on reading.

In addition, all the business meetings I'd arranged during my visit would be concluded by the end of the next day, and as I'd been originally scheduled to fly home Friday night, I made up my mind to keep to the plan. I'd decided that when I came back from Cabot Cove, it would be to another hotel, or Frank's room at Grady and Donna's apartment. They were urging me to bunk with them, and I was leaning in that direction.

"Jimbo and I are over at the Waldorf-Astoria," Stella said, tucking my card in her wallet and fishing out one of her own. "Not together, of course. His wife would kill me if she even heard me talking about it—she's one of my oldest friends—to say nothing of what my Homer would do. He's jealous of every man I talk with. We could have stayed at the Plaza; I hear it's opened again after the renovations. But it was easier to stay at the Waldorf, what with Permezzo paying for the nights when we're doing the shoot."

"They are?"

"They do that for all the talent, Aunt Jess."

"Well, for goodness' sakes, Grady. Why didn't you say something?"

"Gee, Aunt Jess, I guess I forgot."

"Tripper lives here in New York, but Sevenson is also staying at the Waldorf," Stella said, making a face. "Not that I want anything to do with either of them. Did you ever see such a pair of egos? Him with his assistant writing down everything he says, as if pearls of wisdom could ever drip from those lips. You should have heard Betsy take that little girl over the coals before you arrived."

"Why would she do that?"

"Does she need a reason? She's not the sweetest cube in the sugar bowl, let me tell you. Told little Lena she should be ashamed to degrade herself working with that charlatan. That's the word she used, 'charlatan.' Told her that if she had any brains, she would get a 'real' job instead of following around that phony like a sick puppy. I thought Lena was going to cry, but she didn't. Raised her chin and walked away. Didn't defend herself or nothin', just walked away."

"Good for her," I said. "You can't argue with someone when they're being rude or calling names like that. The best thing to do is not to give them the satisfaction of a response."

"That's what I tell Frank, too, Aunt Jess," Grady said. "Sometimes some kid will tease him at school. I tell him, 'Don't get into a fight. Just walk away.'"

"Well, Lena did just that, didn't give Betsy the satisfaction of a response. 'Course, that wouldn't have been the reaction of Miss Nasty Mouth, you can bet on that. She would have made it a knock-down, drag-out fight. I kinda cotton to that idea. Wouldn't you just love to see them two go at it?"

"Who do you mean?" Grady asked.

"Now, don't look at me like that, Jessica," Stella said, ignoring Grady. "You can't tell me you ever heard a nice word from Anne Tripper."

"Hoo boy, she's a tough one, all right," Grady said.

"I didn't have much of a conversation with her," I said.

"Well, consider yourself lucky," she said. "Doesn't even open her gift. Can you imagine? I worked too hard in my life to turn up my nose at twenty-five thousand dollars. Right, Jimbo?"

Jimbo nodded as he snapped closed the latches on his briefcase.

Stella turned to me. "Get Betsy Archibald to put you up at the Waldorf, Jessica. That way we can go to the set together in the morning."

"I'll certainly ask about it," I said.

"Station one to station two, do you hear me? Come in."

There was a crackle of static and then a reply. "Station one, I hear you."

"Where are you now, station two? Come in."

"I'm in the bedroom."

"It works!" Frank said into the two-way radio as he ran down the hall of the apartment into his parents' bedroom. "Now we have to go up to your house," I heard him say.

"What's he up to?" I asked Grady as I slipped off my jacket. We were going out to dinner together—my treat—and I'd come over to the apartment while we waited for Donna to arrive home.

"They're trying out a set of walkie-talkies that Michele got for his birthday," Grady said, hanging my jacket on a hook in the hall closet.

"Sounds like they're working just fine."

"They should. They're supposed to be long-range. I thought all the metal in the building would have an effect, but it doesn't seem to be interfering."

Frank bounced down the hall and jumped in front of me. "Aunt Jessica, look what Michele got." He held up the two-way radio receiver. "We're testing how far away it can work."

"I see," I said.

Frank waved the receiver in front of me. "Want to talk to Michele?"

"Where is Michele?" I asked.

"He's right here," Frank said, skipping back down the hall yelling his friend's name.

"Take it easy, sport. He's not deaf." Grady shook his head. "Lucky we live on the first floor. I'd pity anyone who had an apartment beneath ours."

"Come on," Frank said, gesturing to a boy behind him. "She's nice. I told you about her."

Michele, who was half a foot taller than Frank, shyly followed him to meet me. Dressed in jeans and an Aerosmith T-shirt, with his iPod wire dangling from a pocket, he moved slowly, brown eyes watching me warily.

"Hello, Michele," I said, smiling. "Frank has told me so much about you. It's a pleasure to meet you."

As if I'd made a joke, Michele threw back his head and laughed.

"See? I told you," Frank said to him, holding up his hand for a high five.

The boys slapped their palms together. Then Michele stepped forward and gave me a hug.

"My goodness!" I said, hugging him back. "What did I do to deserve this?"

"Michele always knows when people are good," Frank said. "He can tell just by looking at them. He's got a fifth sense."

"Sixth sense," Grady corrected. He clapped his hands. "Okay, boys, on your way. Aunt Jess needs some quiet time." He turned to me and waggled his eyebrows. "I'm going to fix you my special concoction."

"What concoction is that?" I asked as the boys whooped and thundered back to the bedroom.

"I call it the Fletcherita," he said dramatically, going into the kitchen, opening a cabinet door, and taking down three glasses.

"Is that related to the margarita?"

"Fourth cousin, once removed."

"Well, this should be interesting," I said, shaking my head.

By the time Donna returned home, the boys were upstairs in Michele's apartment, and Grady and I were deep in conversation about the afternoon's proceedings, our Fletcheritas half-consumed.

"You would not believe the lines at Whole Foods," she said, handing off two shopping bags to Grady. "You'd think they were giving away the food instead of charging top price for it."

While Grady emptied the contents of the bags into the refrigerator and the cupboards, Donna hung up her coat and greeted me. "How did the meeting go?" she asked, sinking down on the sofa.

"Good, I think. They're a bit of an odd group, but I'm sure it will go well."

"Tell me about Anne Tripper. She says the most awful things on television. Is she that mean in person?"

"We didn't speak for long," I said, reluctant to criticize

a colleague, although in truth I hadn't found her the most pleasant person. "Stella Bedford was very friendly. In fact, she insisted we take a photograph together. She's going to send a print to me, and her manager promised Grady a copy, too. I'll ask her to autograph it for you."

"That would be great," Donna said. She raised her voice to be heard in the kitchen. "Speaking of Grady, I see Mr. Fletcher has been making his special concoction."

"And I didn't forget you," Grady said, bringing a glass for Donna into the living room.

I waited until he was seated next to his wife to ask, "Grady, did you ever speak with Daniel Howerstein?" I turned to Donna. "The producer asked him to call."

Grady laughed. "He didn't actually ask," he said. "He passed me a note, like we were in high school, telling me to call him this afternoon. He's a tough man to reach, but I finally got through on my way home."

"What did he want?" Donna asked.

"Strange. He just got back from working on a shoot in California, and he said his crew didn't get paid on time. California has a law requiring that the production company pay the crew at the same time they pay their office staff. If not, the production company, in this case Eye Screen, can get fined."

"Who's supposed to pay them?" I asked.

"We are," Grady said. "That's why companies use payroll services. Big production companies like Howerstein's shoot all over the world. That's complicated enough. They don't want to have to contend with all the different regulations in every state or country. With us, they don't have to. They just give us the time cards for the crew. We do all the processing, make sure to account for pension and welfare, and whatever other requirements there are, and write the checks. Of course, we don't send them out until Eye Screen sends us the money to cover the payroll."

"Did they forget to do that?" I asked.

"I don't know," Grady said, downing the last of his Fletcherita, "but I'll look into it tomorrow. Are you ladies ready to go to dinner?"

Grady had made a show of seeming unconcerned, but there was something in his expression that told me the news was worrisome to him.

"I'm ready," Donna said, putting down her drink. "Where's Frank?"

"The boys are upstairs," Grady said. "Mary invited Frank to stay for dinner, and I said all right. Hope you don't mind."

"As long as Aunt Jessica is okay with it." She cocked her head at me.

"He was so excited to have dinner there, I didn't want to spoil his fun. I'll be back next week and we can spend a little time together then. Grady's going to bring him to the set."

"I know. Frank's been telling everyone," she said. "He can't wait."

"I hope he won't be bored," I said.

"I don't care if he is," said Grady. "I like the idea that he'll get to see how a commercial is made."

"Why is that important?" I asked.

Grady looked at Donna. It was clear that they had discussed this before.

"Kids are bombarded with ads and commercials," Donna said, "not only on television, but on every computer site they visit. Even outside. Wherever we go, there are ads—in the stores, on talking billboards at the subway station. The buses are covered in ads, inside and out."

"As adults, we can tune them out," Grady put in, "but kids are attracted to them. They can't always make the distinction between what's the truth and what's simply a sales pitch. Sometimes I can't either."

"So you're hoping that if Frank sees how commercials are made, he won't find them so intriguing," I said.

"Or at least he'll understand that the purpose of a spot is not just to entertain him," Grady said, "but to try to sell him something."

"Well, I'm glad I'm not doing an ad for a product that appeals to children," I said.

"We are, too."

Chapter Six

MINDBENDERS NEW YORK SHOOTING SCRIPT—"JESSICA FLETCHER KNOWS PERMEZZO"

PRODUCTION COMPANY: EYE SCREEN; ADAM AKMANIAN, DIRECTOR

SLATE: © PERMEZZO

Low lighting—an eerie feeling—CU of Fletcher in library setting—copies of her books on shelf behind her.

FLETCHER: Hello . . . I'm Jessica Fletcher. . . . It's no mystery why I always carry my Permezzo card when I travel to do research for my novels. . . .

Wider shot—Fletcher in front of green screen—foreign locales play behind her.

> My work takes me across the country and
> around the world.... But whether it's famil-
> iar places or exotic lands ... I know that with
> my Permezzo card I'll be welcomed wher-
> ever I go, and under any circumstances....
> (*Chuckle from Fletcher.*) And believe me,
> I've found myself in some pretty unusual
> and challenging circumstances.

Medium shot of Fletcher back in library.

> Permezzo's no-limit charging and expert
> concierge service is the best in the business,
> always ready to help me land a reservation
> at a popular restaurant ... change my flight
> at the last minute ... or find a special gift
> for a favorite person.... Well, I'd better get
> back to work.

*She turns to her computer keyboard—looks back at camera
over her shoulder.*

> I carry only one card when I travel ... and
> that's Permezzo.

Fade on Fletcher working at keyboard.

vo: Jessica Fletcher knows Permezzo. You should,
          too.

"I don't like that line about Permezzo being the 'best in
the business,'" I said.

"Why not?"

"Well, I don't really know if that's the case. Is it the best? I don't want to say anything that's not truthful."

Robin Stockdale, a drama teacher at the high school and a frequent director for Cabot Cove's regional theater group, had agreed to go over my lines with me so I would be able to return to New York prepared for the filming. For the last half hour, we'd been sitting at my kitchen table in Cabot Cove, dissecting the script, analyzing the lines, and discussing how best to say them.

"Jessica, this is a commercial," she said, circling the problem copy. "No one expects you to have done comparative research on the veracity of the client's claims."

"I understand that," I said, "but the agency must believe that people will trust what I say—or else why would they want me to make their commercial?"

"Exactly! I'll bet they were thrilled when Grady suggested you. I doubt he could have talked them into it if they'd been resistant. Not that Grady isn't persuasive, but these are advertising professionals, Jessica. Mindbenders is an established agency. You have to assume they know their business. You have to trust them."

"I do. But still . . ." I trailed off.

"Is there another problem with the script?"

"Well, Permezzo is not the only card I carry when I travel. I would rather not say that it is."

Robin laughed. "Jessica, I have never seen you so unsure of yourself."

"It's not that I'm unsure of myself," I said, getting up to turn off the stove when the whistle on the kettle began to sing. "But my name is going to be out there. I don't want to make a statement about a product if I don't believe in it." I opened a cupboard and took down two mugs and the box of tea bags.

"If you don't believe in Permezzo, why did you agree to do the commercial in the first place?"

I sighed and gave Robin a sideways look.

"Okay, don't tell me. Grady, right?"

"I couldn't let him down," I said, shaking my head. "He's doing well in this job and I wanted to help him. And it's not that I don't believe in Permezzo. I've been using the card for years, before I ever heard about the commercial."

"Well, let's talk about that. That can help you with your motivation. If you don't know why you're saying something, you'll never be able to pull off the line. A good actress believes what she says. When the camera zooms in on you, we'll know by looking in your eyes if you're speaking from the heart. So, tell me in your own words: What do you like about Permezzo?"

"They have a very attentive and efficient concierge service," I said, smiling at a thought.

"Why are you smiling?" Robin asked.

"You'll probably think I'm old-fashioned," I said, setting our mugs on the table next to a plate of sugar cookies I'd baked that morning. "What I like best is that their telephones are always answered by real live people. I prefer to talk to a person without having to wade through multiple voice prompts and menu choices delivered electronically."

"You mean a person actually picks up the phone when you call Permezzo?"

"Yes."

"That's certainly unusual," Robin said, dunking a cookie into her tea.

"It is. And there's another thing. When you're traveling overseas on business, you need someone who can serve as a travel agent to help you rearrange your plans when something unforeseen comes up. Permezzo does that."

"I thought you had a travel agent."

"I do. Susan Shevlin, the mayor's wife, has been my travel agent for years."

"Can't she help you when you're on the road?"

"She often does," I said. "It was Susan who suggested I get the Permezzo card. While I would hesitate to call and wake her up in the middle of the night to reticket me if I missed a connection in Tokyo—which happened once—I have no such compunctions when it comes to calling Permezzo. They're open twenty-four hours a day. And I'm assured of getting someone who will be able to understand my problem, and work with me to fix it."

"Why don't you rewrite the commercial to say just that?"

"I don't think that would make me very popular with Betsy Archibald."

"Who's she?"

"The creative director. Besides, I'm not even sure I could say all that in sixty seconds. That's a special skill, fitting a lot of information into a short period of time. And I hesitate to rewrite someone else's copy unless I'm asked. It would be disrespectful."

"Well then, what are you going to do?"

"Learn my lines, and when the time comes, raise my hand to object."

There was a knock at the back door. I waved in Seth Hazlitt, my old friend and one of Cabot Cove's preeminent physicians. Seth had chuckled when I'd telephoned from New York to tell him that I was going to appear coast-to-coast in a commercial for Permezzo.

"I hope they're paying you well," he'd said.

"More than well," I'd replied. "I'm going to donate the money to charity."

"Assuaging your guilt?" Seth had said. "I thought you never wanted to endorse a product. Seems to me I might have heard that over the years."

"Your memory is too good," I had said before hanging up.

"I hope I'm not interrupting," Seth said as he came through the door, settled in the seat next to Robin's, and helped himself to a sugar cookie. "Had a feeling I might find one of these here."

"We were just finishing up," Robin said. "If you don't need me anymore, Jessica, I have to check in with the theater group. They're meeting this afternoon to decide what the spring play should be."

"Of course, Robin. I hope I haven't kept you away," I said, escorting her to the door. "Thank you so much for your help."

"It was nothing. You'll do beautifully. You're a natural actress. Anytime you want to join us, we'll find a part for you."

"That's very kind, but I'm afraid my travel schedule makes it too difficult to make any long-term commitments."

"You've used that excuse for years," Seth said after Robin had left.

"Now, don't you start," I said, going to the sink to wash our mugs.

"Just remarking on the obvious. I've managed to find a little extra time in my busy life to contribute to raising the cultural level of my fellow citizens."

"And I've enjoyed watching you onstage. I make a much better audience member than I would an actress." I dried the mugs and returned them to the cupboard.

"So you say."

"Have another cookie," I said. "You can't criticize me with your mouth full."

Seth took a second cookie and chewed it thoughtfully.

"Would you like some tea?" I asked, drying my hands on a dish towel. "I'm fresh out of coffee. I'm out of just about everything. That's why I asked you to give me a lift to the grocery store."

"Got any milk?"

"I think I can squeeze out half a glass," I said, taking the bottle from the refrigerator and emptying what little was left into a glass.

"Sit down, woman. You're making me crazy with your nervousness."

"What am I doing?" I asked, taking the chair I'd abandoned a few minutes ago.

"If you wring out that dish towel any more, it'll be nothing but shreds."

I looked down at the coiled mass of cotton in my lap and carefully spread it on the table, smoothing out the wrinkles I'd twisted into it.

"What's on your mind?" Seth asked softly. "As if I didn't know."

"It's Grady."

"Thought as much."

"He has so much going for him, Seth. He's smart and personable, and knowledgeable in his field. Donna says he's the sharpest accountant she knows."

"And she would know, being an accountant herself," Seth said.

"Just so. Grady has a wonderful home, a wonderful marriage, and a wonderful child. I'm so proud of him."

"Yet he seems to have a knack for picking the wrong company to work for. Has he done it again?"

"I'm not certain, Seth, but I'm worried that might be the case. A producer complained to him about a payroll issue. Grady was concerned and told me he was going to see what he could find out. I called him at the office before I left for the airport, but he was in a meeting. He hasn't called me back."

"You're probably worrying for nothing, Jess. A man with a job and a family doesn't always have time to chat on the phone with his aunt."

I looked up, startled, but then I laughed. "You always know what to say to put me in my place."

"You don't need to be put in your place," Seth said, leaning over to pat my arm. "But I do think you're making a mountain out of a molehill."

"Why do you think he didn't return my call?"

"He probably needs to do a little more investigating, like a certain relative of his, and doesn't want to draw a conclusion until he's sure of the facts. I'd say that's a responsible way to approach the problem."

"You're right, of course. Now, why didn't I think of that?"

"Must be the influence of the city. Fogs the brain. Grady will get back to you in good time. If I know my Fletchers— and I think I do—he'll wait until he can speak to you in person before he spills out whatever it is he finds."

"That won't be until I see him next week."

"True. So I suggest, madam, that we take your mind off this conundrum by making a visit to the local supermarket, where you can stock up on coffee. That way, the next time I have one of your sugar cookies, it will be accompanied by the proper beverage."

"Doctor, you always prescribe the best medicine. I'll get my coat."

Chapter Seven

A bouquet of flowers and a split of champagne in a silver ice bucket greeted me when the Waldorf-Astoria bellman escorted me into my room. I went to the desk and picked up the card leaning against the vase: "Welcome back to New York. I look forward to seeing you on the set." It was signed "Antonio Tedeschi," but I was pretty sure it had been sent by Betsy Archibald. She had been a tad less than cordial when I'd called to ask about accommodations for the out-of-town "talent" who were in the commercials.

"No, it's not a problem," she'd said on a long sigh. "I have to make a few phone calls, get the producer to issue a new call sheet, alert the car service. Just don't change your mind again, please. I don't want to hear tomorrow that you prefer to stay in a more modern place downtown. The director drove me crazy insisting on a hotel in the Meatpacking District. He wanted a hipper neighborhood than Park Avenue. I don't suppose you need a hip neighborhood, do you?"

"Park Avenue is perfectly fine for me," I'd rushed to say, having had my fill of the city's more avant-garde lodging. I've never thought of myself as "hip" and knew I'd be more comfortable in what I considered a "grown-up room."

"Then we'll have a reservation for you at the Waldorf," she said before hanging up. "A car service will pick you up in the morning. You have an eight a.m. call. That's when you have to be at the location. Don't be late."

I had sent Grady an e-mail telling him where I would be staying, and thanking him and Donna for their gracious offer to have me room with them. I would be happy to take them up on their hospitality another time, but not when I needed to be rested and clear thinking for the morning's work.

I took a moment to take in my surroundings. My room was spacious and freshly decorated in a classic style, featuring a queen-sized bed covered in a quilted ecru silk, which matched the paint of the walls and harmonized with the buff carpeting accented with small blue medallions. The soothing color scheme was enlivened with an armchair in a muted red and white floral and, at the large windows, red and blue striped drapes. There was more than enough room for my toiletries in the marble bath, and I was delighted to find a plush terry-cloth robe hanging behind the door.

As I always do, I unpacked my things and put them away in a cherrywood armoire, which also held the television. Even if I'm staying in a hotel for only one night, I prefer to hang up my clothes in a closet or put them in a drawer rather than to live out of a suitcase.

I was meeting Matt Miller later, and had a little time to relax before changing for dinner. I hung up my suit, put on the robe the Waldorf had provided, and curled up in the armchair to look through the materials in the Eye Screen folder once more. On the front cover was the company logo, an ice-cream cone with an eye where the ball of ice cream usually is. On the back cover was their tagline: "We all scream for Eye Screen!" An echo of my days in the school yard when as children we chanted "I scream, you scream, we all scream for ice cream." I wondered if children still did that.

I had my lines memorized by now, as well as those of the others whose scripts were included in my folder. I reviewed the call sheet, which listed all the crew members. There were at least forty people named, eight of them production assistants. I gathered that the key prop was the person in charge of the prop crew, but what did the key grip do? And the gaffer? In addition to their roles on the set, the sheet listed the names and telephone numbers of everyone associated with the shoot. Sure enough, I found my name and cell phone number under the TALENT section, together with Matt Miller's phone number under AGENT. We had an eight a.m. call, and the next column said CAR SVC, which I already knew. I was to be bright-eyed and bushy-tailed and downstairs in the lobby by seven fifteen for the ride to the set.

As far as I could tell, no detail was left off the call sheet.

There were the names, addresses, and phone and fax numbers of the hotels where certain important people were staying—the director was at the Gansevoort—and lists of people representing the agency, the client, and the editorial company, even though all of them probably wouldn't attend the shoot. Betsy Archibald would be there, of course. Her name was under AGENCY, as well as the names of several other Mindbenders staff. The company phone numbers were listed but not Betsy's cell number. I wondered if she preferred not to be called directly. Antonio Tedeschi's name stood alone under CLIENT. The commercial was being shot on location at an office building north of the city. At the bottom of the page was the name and address of the local hospital, something I hoped we wouldn't need.

I sifted through the papers, scripts, driving directions, and storyboards, and sighed. There was no more to learn from these pages. All my questions would be answered in the morning.

"Jessica, I'd like you to meet Kevin Prendergast. He's one of the principals of Mindbenders."

Matt Miller stood next to a slim man of medium height, not handsome but with pleasant features and arresting light green eyes. His long black hair was pulled back into a ponytail, and he wore a button-down yellow shirt and navy slacks. The sleeves of a blue cashmere sweater were looped around his neck.

"So nice to meet you," I said, shaking hands.

The waiter pulled out the table and I slid onto the banquette. "You don't look old enough to run an advertising agency," I said.

"Looks can be deceiving," he said, smiling. I had the feeling he had heard that observation before.

"Kevin is my neighbor in Southampton," Matt said. "Since we're both in Manhattan tonight, I figured you might like to meet each other."

Matt's wife and daughters lived in a charming Victorian house on the East End of Long Island, where many people in the advertising and entertainment industries keep second homes. Matt's house was his family's main residence, however, and his children went to school in the village. He maintained an apartment in Manhattan in addition to his office, commuting back and forth on weekends by helicopter when he could hitch a flight from one of his wealthier neighbors, or by train or jitney when he couldn't.

"And by the way," Matt said to him, "thanks for the referral of my new client."

Prendergast shrugged. "You're the only literary agent I know."

"Not exactly a ringing endorsement," Matt said, "but I'll take it."

That's interesting, I thought. *Was that "new client" Anne Tripper? Did Kevin Prendergast know Anne Tripper before she was hired for the ad campaign?*

Kevin turned to me. "I understand you're going to be in one of our spots tomorrow," he said, leaning his elbows on the table and playing with string attached to a pair of frameless glasses that dangled in front of him. "How did we get so lucky?"

"I haven't quite figured that out," I said, laughing. "My nephew works for the production company's payroll house. Somehow, my name came up when he was talking with the producer, and before I knew what was happening, I was agreeing to do a commercial for Permezzo."

"However it came about, we're delighted to have you on board," he said. "My creative director has put together a good group, very different types and interests. It should appeal to a wide audience. I think it will serve us well. Perhaps I'll stop by tomorrow to see how you're getting on. I know for a fact that Tonio was absolutely tickled when he heard that you'd agreed to be in his spot."

"That's very nice," I said, noting that he referred to Antonio by a nickname. "Have you known each other for a long time?"

"He and my father served on a board of directors together in Milan. One of the big leather companies. I've been to his house many times. When he decided it was time for Permezzo to break into the U.S. market, I convinced him that Mindbenders could handle the rollout and all the marketing details. And that's what we're doing."

"Makes it sound simple, doesn't he?" Matt said to me. "Didn't you trot half your New York staff to Italy to pitch him, Kevin?"

"Only the key people."

"I'll bet one of them was that gorgeous redhead from Toronto. Who could resist her?"

"I use all the weapons in my arsenal," Kevin said, smiling. "Tonio has a crush on Betsy. I knew she'd convince him to take us on. He only knew me as a friend of the family. I had to make him aware that my agency was sophisticated enough to handle his account. I couldn't take anything for granted. Since we got his business, we've opened an office in Milan to service it."

"How's that working out?" Matt asked.

"A little slow. I'm thinking of sending Betsy over there to head up our Italian office. I want to start picking up more accounts in Italy, and in particular I want to take over Permezzo's European advertising as well. I think she could do it."

"That would be quite a coup," I said.

"It would," Kevin said, putting on his glasses and opening the menu. "It would also cut back on my business travel. My girlfriend is not happy. Unfortunately, she also travels for business, so we don't see each other very often. We just leave each other notes in the kitchen."

"That must be difficult," I said.

"Sacrifices have to be made when you're building a company," Kevin replied mildly.

I thought of Grady's response when Betsy Archibald said the agency was open around the clock. It wasn't only Mindbenders' owner, however, who had to make sacrifices to build his company. His staff did as well.

"Well, what are we going to have?" Matt asked. "They have great escargots, of course, if you can handle the garlic, although it looks like tonight's version is made with truffles."

Truffles!

We were dining in L'Absinthe, a French brasserie on the East Side of Manhattan, a good hike but a short cab ride from the Waldorf. The last time I had been there with Matt was just before I'd left for France on an extended holiday. It became a working holiday, as it turned out, when the chef of a cooking school where I was taking classes was found with one of his own knives sticking out of his chest. Still, I had wonderful memories of the country, the food, and the truffle market in France, and was fond of this New York French restaurant, too.

"I think I'll have the skate," I said to the waiter.

"And I'll have the Maine sea scallops, in your honor, Jessica," Matt said, closing his menu.

"I'll have the venison and foie gras pie," Kevin said. "And I'd like to see the wine list."

Two hours and three bottles of wine later, the men had moved to the bar for cognacs while I made my excuses, citing an early call and my hope to get some sleep before it. I thanked Matt for dinner, declined his offer to hail a cab for me, shook hands again with Kevin, and left the restaurant, taking a deep breath of the cool air as the glass door closed behind me. There was no way I could keep up with Matt and Kevin as they consumed glass after glass of wine, nor did I want to. My one glass had been sufficient, although they attempted to top it off several times as they regaled each other with the antics of their Hamptons neighbors, looking for my reaction to the outrageous stories.

"You could write a book," Matt had said.

"Someone already is," Kevin said, chuckling.

"Is that what it's about?" Matt asked. "She wouldn't tell me."

"She wouldn't tell me either. She's very secretive, even

rented an apartment on the West Side, just to use for writing. She says that way I can't read her pages when she's out of town."

"Is that Anne Tripper's book you're talking about?" I asked.

Matt winked at me, but ignored my question. "What I don't get," he said to Kevin, "is how you two got together. You're the classic bleeding-heart liberal, and she's gotta be right of Attila the Hun."

"She has her charms," Kevin had replied.

I figured the Waldorf was less than a mile as the crow flies, if there are any crows in New York City. There are plenty of pigeons, of course, but I wouldn't be seeing them tonight. It was already dark. Several taxis slowed as I stood in front of the restaurant buttoning my coat. I waved them off. A leisurely stroll to the hotel was what I needed to work off dinner, especially the warm apple tart Matt had insisted I try. It was worth every calorie. Years ago, I wouldn't have attempted to walk back to my hotel, but the city is much safer now.

As I started down the street, I replayed that last conversation in my head. Although they hadn't mentioned her name, it seemed clear to me that if they were leaving messages for each other at breakfast, Anne Tripper was Kevin Prendergast's live-in girlfriend. It began to make sense now. As neighbors, it would have been natural for Kevin to have talked to Matt about having Anne Tripper in a commercial for Permezzo. Perhaps Matt took the opportunity to suggest me for the campaign as well. When we'd sat at the City Bakery, he certainly seemed to know a lot about

Permezzo's marketing plans. If Kevin had mentioned me to Betsy Archibald, it was not so surprising that she would have jumped on it when Grady raised my name. Leave it to Matt not to tell me that he'd put a word in at the beginning. My participation didn't hurt his relationship with his neighbor. In fact, it put them back on equal footing. Kevin had done Matt a good turn by providing him with a new client with lots of bestseller potential, and Matt had returned the favor by encouraging me to be in a commercial for Kevin's client. Very neat.

I ambled over to Lexington Avenue and headed south. It was only nine o'clock, but traffic was heavy and there were still many people on the street, window-shopping, walking dogs, or spilling out of the myriad restaurants and bars. Many, like me, seemed like out-of-towners. As I knew from my days as a city resident, there is no time of year when New York is without a sizable tourist population.

I was halfway to the hotel when I felt my cell phone vibrate. I had turned off the ringer before dinner, so as not to be rude to my dining companions. I know I'm in the minority, but I still cling to the notion that people who talk on cell phones in restaurants are displaying terrible manners. Not only are those conversations usually loud enough to disturb people at nearby tables; they also send a message to whoever is unfortunate enough to be sitting with the phone wielder that the person on the other end of the call takes precedence over present company.

I paused in front of a bus stop and answered my phone.

"Grady! I was just thinking about you."

"I can't talk long, Aunt Jess. I'm sorry I didn't get back to you earlier. It's been a crazy time."

"May I call you later? I can barely hear you with the noise of the traffic."

"No, that's okay. Just wanted to let you know I'm afraid we have a scandal brewing. I don't like what I'm hearing."

"What are you learning?"

"Huh? I'm not turning anywhere."

"Learning. I said, what are you learning?"

"Can't hear you. Was that a bus?"

"Yes. I'm on the street. Oh dear, here comes a fire engine." The loud siren had me covering my ears. "Grady, you still there?"

"Sorry, Aunt Jess. Gotta go. When I see you tomorrow, I'll explain everything."

Back at the Waldorf, refreshed and unfortunately wide-awake, I set my alarm clock for five thirty, dialed the operator for a wake-up call, and arranged for breakfast from the twenty-four-hour room service. *That's like having a belt, suspenders, and a balloon to hold up your pants,* I thought. But there would be no chance I'd sleep late and miss the car. I pulled out my large shoulder bag, tucked the Eye Screen folder inside, checking it first to make sure my script was the first paper on top, placed it on the desk next to the unopened champagne, and climbed into bed.

As relieved as I was to have heard from Grady, I still wondered what was making his life so crazy, and what scandal could possibly be brewing. I hoped it wasn't as bad as he suggested. If it was, would he still be taking the time off to bring Frank to the set?

I was eager to see Frank again. *It's going to be such fun for him,* I thought. He'll get to watch his great-aunt act in a commercial, and I'll get to enjoy seeing the production from the perspective of a nine-year-old boy. *We'll have a wonderful time,* I told myself. *Won't we?*

But as I drifted off to sleep, a thousand thoughts swirled through my mind, and a line from Shakespeare came to me. It was from *A Midsummer Night's Dream,* and in my dream, I heard Puck say to the fairy king: "Lord, what fools these mortals be!"

Chapter Eight

"Ah'm so glad they put us in the same limousine." Stella Bedford drew out the word "glad" until it had two syllables instead of one. "You know the others insisted on cars just for themselves. Now, that's just wasting fuel, if you ask me. In these days of global warming, you shouldn't do that. We could certainly have fit more in here. Lookit all this room."

"Count your blessings, Cookie," Jimbo Barnes said from the passenger seat next to the driver.

We were on the West Side Highway heading north out of the city. The Hudson River was a gray white strip to our left, a mist hovering over the surface. Across the water on the New Jersey side, the windows of apartment buildings lining the Palisades reflected the early-morning sun as it edged out from behind the clouds. On the southbound side of the highway, cars were already stacking up as the rush into New York City from its suburbs had begun.

Stella pulled up the sleeve of her white sweater, held out her right arm, and rocked her hand from side to side, admiring the gold-and-diamond ring on her third finger, and the matching bracelet. "Got these at Tiffany's with Antonio's card. Ain't they nice?" she said. " 'Course, I had to add a bit to get them both, but I think it was worth it. Don't you?"

"They're very pretty," I said.

"I think so, too," she said, tugging down her sleeve. " 'Course, I won't wear them when I put on the overalls for my commercial. I'd be tempted, but I won't. Got to keep up the image people expect." She sighed heavily.

"Just remember those overalls made your career," Jimbo reminded her.

"Ah know. It's just too bad I couldn't cook and still wear my diamonds. Paula Deen does. No one criticizes her."

"When you're as famous as Paula Deen, we can talk about it," Jimbo said. "You're not quite there yet."

"But I surely will be." She grabbed my arm and lowered her voice. "We just picked up a whole passel of local affiliates in addition to the cable network. Pretty soon my name will be as familiar as Wolfgang Puck's. Jimbo and I are looking at two locations in Dallas for my next restaurant. Everybody loves barbecue—I'm partial to my pulled pork myself. Umm. Ummm. There's nothin' I love more than my pulled pork on my special bread." Her eyes became dreamy. "Anyhow, I'm working on a new menu that's healthy but still authentic. That's what you have to do these days. Figure out a way to make fatty foods healthy. Keep 'em delicious at the same time. And that ain't easy, let me tell you."

How she was going to come up with healthy pulled pork was a mystery to me.

"Is your handsome nephew goin' to be there today?"

"He is," I replied. "He's bringing his son, Frank, my grandnephew, with him. We're going to show Frank how a commercial is made."

"How old is Frank?"

"Nine."

"Oh, that's a sweet age, old enough to appreciate things but not old enough to have a smart mouth yet."

"You sound as if you're speaking from experience. Do you have any children?" I asked.

"Did," she said. "I had a son. Lost 'im in Afghanistan."

"I'm so sorry," I said. "That must be very difficult for you."

"It's nice to hear you say that in the present tense," she said, taking my hand. "So many people think because some years have passed that I don't mourn him anymore, but that ain't true. I think about him every day."

"I'm sure you do."

"He was a hell-raiser for sure, drove his mama and papa crazy. Homer thought the military might give 'im a chance to sow those wild oats and get 'em out of his system. We encouraged him to join. We never figured we'd lose him." Tears filled Stella's eyes, but they didn't spill over. Lost in her thoughts for a moment, she put down my hand and patted it. "You're a good listener, Jessica."

"Thank you, Stella."

"No thanks needed. It's just the truth. I think we're gonna be friends. So you just go on ahead and call me 'Cookie.' It's what my friends call me."

"I'm honored to be considered a friend, Cookie."

"You may change your mind when you get to know her better, Jessica," Jimbo growled from the front seat.

"Oh, him," Cookie said with a laugh. "Ain't he too much?" She leaned forward in her seat. "You better be nice to me, Jimbo, or I'll tell your wife you was cattin' around in New York."

"That's not true," he said, indignant.

"I know that, but she doesn't. And she'll be a daylight nightmare for you till I set her straight. So watch your step." Cookie straightened up in her seat, took a compact from her purse, powdered her nose, put the compact away, and brushed imaginary lint from her sleeve.

Jimbo twisted around and gave me a wink. "I don't care what you tell her," he directed at Cookie. "Just don't show her them diamonds or I'll never hear the end of it."

"Ooh, they are nice," she said, and settled back, admiring her jewelry. "I just hope Homer don't think some secret admirer is givin' me diamonds. He'll turn greener than a cactus." She shifted her gaze out the window, a small smile playing on her lips.

When we pulled into the parking lot of the office building that was to serve as our location, there was a line of trucks blocking the entrance, and a crowd of crew members emptying them. Huge cases on wheels were rolled up to the door. Skeins of rope and cable were slung onto shoulders. Lights and stands and toolboxes and what appeared to be enough equipment to kit out a construction site were hauled from the truck beds and bays and scattered temporarily on the driveway before being dragged into the lobby.

Our driver dropped us off at another door some distance from the busy entrance. Several people were standing around an open rectangle of folding tables, from which breakfast was being cooked and served. All the kitchen equipment needed for a luncheonette was there—coolers, toasters, griddles, gas burners, and coffeemakers—as well as baskets of baked goods, cereals, bowls of cut fruit, berries, and nuts, and plates of sliced cheese and deli meats. The only thing missing was places to sit.

"I'm famished," Cookie said, taking a paper plate and reaching for a doughnut.

"Ms. Bedford?" A production assistant with a clipboard cocked her head at Cookie. "I'm Alice Evans. Whenever you're ready, I'll need you to follow me. We have to check into the production office, and I'll show you where wardrobe and makeup are."

"Jimbo, hold that for me, please," Cookie said, handing her plate to him. "I'll be back."

Jimbo put down the plate, wrapped the doughnut in a napkin, and hurried to catch up with her. "See you later, Jessica," he called over his shoulder.

"Mrs. Fletcher?" It was Jason, the production assistant from our meeting the previous week. "I'm supposed to bring you inside to meet the second AD. Would you like something to eat first?"

"I'm tempted," I said, leaning over to examine the selections. The Waldorf's room service had delivered coffee and toast shortly after I was awakened by the alarm clock and the hotel operator. It was not a large meal and my stomach was starting to grumble. "Those omelets look wonderful." I shook my head. "I already had a bite at the hotel. Perhaps later."

I followed Jason inside, down a long empty corridor, and into an open space with cubicles on both sides. Waist-high counters separated the work areas, which were buzzing with activity. There must have been thirty people milling around. Two were emptying trunks filled with clothes in a small room; another wheeled two clothing racks across the aisle. A pair of tall director's chairs, one occupied, faced large mirrors. A young woman perused a suitcase of makeup, and chose an assortment of brushes, placing them on a nearby table, on which were several head forms bearing wigs in blond, brunet, and red. The woman in the chair, I realized, was Anne Tripper. She wore a cape to protect her clothing, and a headband to hold her hair off her face. She spoke to a man standing next to her, her head swinging, her hands gesturing, and her many rings twinkling in the lights surrounding the mirrors.

"She is just the pits," I heard her say. "I don't know why you put up with her. She wouldn't know the truth if it hit her in the head. And let me tell you, I was very tempted to do just that. I was fit to kill. If I didn't want the name of my book to get out there, I would have told her to shove it. She was lucky I wasn't wearing my gun."

I couldn't hear the man's reply, but when he moved to face her, I recognized Kevin Prendergast, the agency head. *Oh dear,* I thought, *something isn't going well.*

"Mrs. Fletcher?"

I swirled to find a woman aiming a Polaroid camera at me. A flash went off, leaving me with a yellow circle in my line of vision. "Thanks so much," she said.

The photographer handed Jason the white square that emerged from the camera and had yet to develop, and we continued across the room. We passed a group of men squatting over a floor plan, one pointing with a thick finger to something on the drawing. People darted around us and hurried off to somewhere else in the building. The overall impression was one of controlled chaos. I had no idea what was going on, but everyone else seemed secure in their duties and in a rush to accomplish them.

Lance Sevenson, trailed by his assistant, hailed me as he passed in the opposite direction. "Where are you going?" I asked.

"To get some food," he said. "I had to get out of there. The atmosphere was toxic."

"What was wrong?"

"That woman! I'm doing her a favor and she acts as if I owe her. If I had a rose quartz with me, I'd give it to her. She needs something to cool her temper. But I'm not going to stay if she keeps this up. I didn't sign on to be abused."

"Who?" I asked, but he didn't wait to answer my question. He strode toward the exit, his assistant trotting behind in high heels, taking three steps to his every one.

Jason opened a door and ushered me into an area of relative calm where two women sat behind desks, laptop computers open before them, Bluetooth cell phone headsets plugged into their ears. "Here you go," he said to a man in a green T-shirt and jeans. "Bye, Mrs. Fletcher. See you later."

"Dave Fitzpatrick, Mrs. Fletcher," the man said, extending his hand. He was very tall and broad and sported a bushy mustache. He wore a padded down vest over his shirt and a baseball cap on his head, to which was affixed a campaign button saying I DIDN'T VOTE FOR HIM. "I'm the second assistant director on the shoot," he said, smiling. "I'll be taking care of you today."

It struck me as a strange thing to say. It sounded as if he were about to give me a massage, or perhaps take my blood pressure, or serve me a cup of soup. He flipped open his cell phone and spoke into it, simultaneously passing what was now my photo to a disheveled young woman behind the first desk. She fingered through a box of cards, extracted two, stapled my picture to one, made a note of the time on the other, and asked me to sign it. Tucking a stray lock of hair behind her ear, she hung the first card up on a piece of board that already contained the cards and photos of a scowling Lance, an unsmiling Anne, and a laughing Cookie. I looked startled in my photo, not surprising given that no one had told me I was about to have my picture taken. While Dave talked on the phone, I took a moment to study my "costars." The cards presented not only our faces but also our clothing and shoe sizes, with spaces left empty for height and weight.

Noticing my interest, the young woman said, "These are the casting cards. They go to wardrobe so they know who you are and what you need when you come in. I'm Susan, by the way, production supervisor. That's Jennifer talking on the phone. She's the production manager. And our PA, Lily, is around here somewhere."

"I'm back here counting the petty cash," Lily's voice said from behind a cubicle wall. She appeared a moment later, carrying a strongbox, which she put on the desk at Jennifer's elbow.

"You can leave your shoulder bag with us if you want, Mrs. Fletcher. We'll be here all day," Susan said. She pointed to the cubicle from which Lily had just emerged. "There's already a couple of them there. Put yours wherever there's room."

Four bags had been left on a shelf. I put mine at the end next to the quilted red bag I recognized from the agency meeting as Anne Tripper's, and returned to where Susan sat pulling on a band that had loosely secured her hair in a ponytail. Holding the band between her teeth, she shook her head, tipped it back, finger-combed her hair, and re-made her ponytail. "I never had a chance to dry my hair this morning," she said, making a face. "We had a six-thirty call and I live an hour and a half away. The alarm went off at three thirty." She linked her fingers and stretched her arms over her head. "This is my third cup of coffee—or is it the fourth?" She frowned at a Starbucks container, the large size.

"What do you do here?" I asked.

She opened her arms. "This is the production office."

"What does the production office do?"

"Everything! We're the center of it all. If the production is a body, we're the nervous system," she replied. "We keep everything running."

"I would have said the brains," Lily added.

"And the director is the heart," Jennifer said, joining in the metaphor. It was hard to tell whether she was still on the phone or talking to us, but her eyes locked on mine, so I assumed she was addressing me.

"And the agency creative director is . . . ?" I said.

"A pain," Susan said.

Jennifer raised her brows.

Susan grimaced. "Sorry," she said.

"We track expenses," Jennifer said, waving a piece of paper. She picked up another. "We put the call sheet together. We make sure everything at the location is set up properly."

A cell phone on Susan's desk barked and she lifted it to her ear without the headset. "The director wants another latte," she said to Jennifer.

"He's going to float away."

"Can I go this time?" Lily asked. "I'm dying to get some fresh air."

"I guess," Jennifer said, opening the petty cash box. "Take someone with you who knows where Starbucks is."

"Mrs. Fletcher, would you like a latte, too?" Lily asked.

Dave, who was still on the phone, gestured with his left hand, pointing at his chest.

"None for me, thanks," I said. "I'm keyed up enough as it is."

"Get five or six," Jennifer said. "Someone else is going to want it as soon as you walk through the door."

With Lily out on the coffee run, and Dave finally off the phone, I thanked Susan and Jennifer for watching my shoulder bag and walked with Dave to makeup, where he introduced me to Maya. "We've got two in rehearsals upstairs," he said, squinting at his watch. "I'm supposed to bring you up in an hour, but if you want to see your set, I can take you there as soon as Maya finishes your makeup."

"I *would* like to see the set," I said, climbing up into the makeup artist's canvas chair. *And I'd like to find Grady and Frank,* I thought, assuming they had arrived.

"I'm going ten one hundred," he said to Maya. "Be back in ten." To me, he said, "We also need to check in with wardrobe."

"Where's he going?" I asked.

Maya smiled. "That's code for the bathroom," she said, whipping a vinyl cape over my clothes.

"I don't know why he needs to escort me to wardrobe," I said. "It's right over there." I indicated a cubicle across the room. "I can just walk over when I'm finished here, can't I?"

"The second AD always handles the talent. He has to make sure you get to 'talent holding' in time," Maya explained. "When they want you on the set, he's the one they call. He doesn't want to lose track of you."

"Ah, I see. I promise I won't wander around and make him look for me."

"He'll appreciate that," she said. "By the way, welcome to the Vanity Department, Mrs. Fletcher. Are you wearing any makeup this morning?"

"Not very much," I replied.

"Well, we're about to fix that."

Chapter Nine

An hour later, made-up in heavy pancake and more eye shadow than I would ever use, and wearing a different jacket and blouse from those I'd arrived in—"This one looks more authorish," the wardrobe lady told me (*Authorish?*)—I followed Dave up the stairs to where the shoot was taking place. Grady was there and I introduced him to Dave.

"We've already met," Grady said. "Frank and I got here early."

"Where is Frank?" I asked.

"Aunt Jessica!"

The young man in question flew down the hall, deftly skirting a pile of electric cable. The laces of his sneakers were untied, and the pockets of his pants were bulging; a white wire dangled from the right one. "You've got to see this," he said, breathless. "There's a guy sitting in a cor-

95

ner and he's got all this equipment around him, and he can hear what they're saying even though he can't see anything. And the other guys have televisions on sticks and we can see everything that's happening in the room. And the cameraman let me look in his camera, and Ricky, the grip—he's really a carpenter—he let me try out his nail gun even though Dad didn't think I could do it. And look, they gave me my own earphones to wear. I brought my walkie-talkie, but these are even better. See, it's got a number one on them, and they're red. That's the best color. They have four channels. . . ."

"Whoa, sport," Grady said, putting his hand on Frank's shoulder. "Take a breath and give your aunt Jessica a second to look around."

"I will," Frank said, "but you have to see this, Aunt Jessica." He took my hand and dragged me down a corridor of cubicles filled with lights and stands and rolling carts containing all manner of construction material. Over the tops of the cubicle walls, I could see bright lights illuminating another part of the office.

A voice called out, "Quiet, everyone. Settle down, please. Okay, roll tape, roll camera."

Frank came to an immediate stop in the hallway. He put his index finger over his lips, his eyes wide as he looked at me. I nodded and put my finger over my lips, too.

Another voice: "Rolling, rolling, rolling. Quiet, please. We're locked up. Ready? And action."

A third voice: "Permezzo, five-oh-one, take eight. Mark!"

Frank let go of my hand and tiptoed slowly down the

hall, carefully stepping over the coil of cable and dodging a light stand and toolbox in his way. He leaned forward to see around the corner, turned back to Grady and me, and waved his arms to indicate we could come forward.

I smiled at Grady, who rolled his eyes and smiled back. Dave motioned us forward and we walked gingerly, making sure not to trip over the equipment and wires that Frank had so skillfully avoided.

"That's a cut," we heard. "Reset, please."

Frank let out the breath he'd been holding, and whispered to me, "They're shooting the barbecue lady in the kitchen, but she can't remember her lines and the other lady with the red hair is mad."

I looked around the corner to see a kitchen with white cabinets and stainless-steel countertops. Cookie, looking like one of her cookbook covers in blue overalls, a checkered shirt, and a straw hat, was standing next to a butcher-block-topped island on which were various-sized mixing bowls and an assortment of bottles that could probably be found in most kitchens: ketchup, mustard, oil and vinegar, and some others, the labels of which I couldn't see. Arrayed around the island, but out of sight of the camera lens, were at least twenty people, most wearing earphones. One man held a boom microphone over Cookie's head.

"You see, the problem is, I wouldn't use a word like 'cuisine.'" She pronounced it "coozine."

"The problem is, you never looked at your script until you got on the set," Betsy Archibald said to her. In contrast with her elegant attire at the agency, she wore jeans and tennis shoes, and a baseball cap with her red ponytail pulled through the gap at the back. She looked like a little girl, an angry little girl. She turned away from Cookie, a look of exasperation on her face. "I can't believe this. How simple can it be? Any idiot could have learned those lines by now."

Cookie continued talking to her back. "And another thing. I'm a cook. I cook barbecue, basic stuff." She held up a bottle and made a face. "There ain't no bottles of champagne and cilantro dressing in my kitchen. This just isn't authentic at all."

"Authentic! This is a spot for a credit card," Betsy exploded. "It's not your ridiculous cooking show. It doesn't have to be authentic. It's just for atmosphere."

"Now, see here." Jimbo jumped up. "You're not to talk to her that way." He pointed a finger at Betsy. "You give Mrs. Bedford your respect."

"I'll give her respect when she acts like a professional," Betsy shouted back.

Cookie put her fists on her hips. "Jimbo, I can handle this."

"Don't interrupt me, Cookie. She has no right to abuse you."

"Abuse?" Betsy shrieked. "I'm the one being abused. All these people are being abused. You're wasting our time." Betsy smacked the rolled-up script on her leg, then aimed it at Jimbo. "You tell her to learn her lines, the way they're written. This isn't amateur hour. I'll be waiting." She stomped off the set and threw herself into a chair, crossing her arms and her legs.

Cookie pushed a fuming Jimbo to the far side of her set, away from Betsy.

The man behind the camera that was aimed in her direction waved at Cookie. "Mrs. Bedford, no one will be seeing the label that says champagne-cilantro dressing, I promise you. It's just a nice-shape bottle. You can come over here and look through the lens if you want."

"But Ah don't like to have something that would never be in mah kitchen on this here counter," Cookie said, pounding her fist for emphasis.

"Props!" called a man in a canvas chair sitting in front of a monitor. "Eighty-six the bottle." He ran a hand over his shaved head.

Another man took the bottle from Cookie's hand and put a jar of molasses in its place on the counter.

"Now, that there's much better," Cookie said, smiling.

Betsy's eyes rose to the ceiling and she flapped her arms in irritation. "That there's much better," she mimicked in a Southern accent.

"Howerstein, you tell her to watch her tongue or this shootin' party is over." Jimbo's face was very red. "We're not taking any more cheap shots like that."

Cookie stamped her foot. "Jimbo! Cut it out."

Dan Howerstein stepped forward and spoke to the man with the shaved head. "Can we take five, please, Adam?"

"That's Akmanian," Grady whispered to me, indicating the man in the chair.

I nodded. "The director."

"And that one"—Grady pointed to a man wearing earphones and standing next to the director—"is the first assistant director, or AD."

The first AD raised his voice. "All right, folks," he said. "Take five, but no one go very far, please."

Howerstein guided a furious Betsy around the corner and out of sight, but not out of earshot. We could hear her complaining loudly as she walked away.

"Would you please keep your voice down," he said.

"Don't touch me!" she growled.

"I'm not touching you," was Howerstein's irritated reply.

Jimbo walked back onto the set and threw Cookie's script on the counter. "I told you, you needed to learn them lines. Even so, I'm not lettin' her talk that way to you."

"Now, you just calm down. I can learn them lines easy," Cookie said. "I just don't like that one word, Jimbo. I don't wanna hafta say something I never would."

"You shoulda raised that flag earlier, Cookie. It's too late now."

"Ah know it's late. But if my viewers hear me talkin' about 'coozine,' they'll think I've gone all fancy-pants on them. You go talk to her, but you talk nice, now, ya hear. I know you can do that. No yelling."

Jimbo stalked away.

"You tell her we're a down-home show," Cookie called after him, then muttered "and I'm not changin' who I am for that little . . . little stuck-up witch."

"You don't have to, Mrs. Bedford. We'll change the line." The speaker was Kevin Prendergast. I hadn't noticed him in the crowd until he spoke up.

Antonio Tedeschi was at his side. "Yes, yes, of course,"

Antonio said. "Our Betsy, she is a very passionate woman. It is good. But you can say the line how you like, just so you say how wonderful is my Permezzo."

"Antonio!" Cookie said, her eyes lighting up. "I didn't see you there. Just wait till you set your eyes on what I got with the card you gave me." She patted her pockets. "Now, where'd I put my diamonds?"

"Excuse me," Kevin said. He pointed at the director. "I'll talk to Betsy. We'll take care of this right now."

"Yes. I will talk to her, too," Antonio said.

"There's no need, Tonio."

"I will like to talk to her."

Akmanian waved his hand, taking in all those standing around the room. "Take as many people as you want. They can *all* talk to her. Whatever. I got paid in advance. My time is yours." He looked at the floor around his chair. "Where is my latte?"

A production assistant leaned forward and put the cup into his hand.

Cookie said, "Well, if you're all goin' off, Ah'm gonna get me a doughnut."

Five minutes passed and then ten, but none of the combatants returned. The crew was standing around waiting.

"Is the number two set ready to go?" the director asked.

I felt a tap on my shoulder. "Mrs. Fletcher?" Dave Fitzpatrick said. "Would you like to see your set now?"

"Ooh, can I see it, too?" Frank said.

"Of course," I replied.

Grady, Frank, and I followed Dave back the way we'd

come and down a different corridor with offices on both sides. We could hear a loud argument going on in one of them. As we approached, I recognized the voices of Howerstein and Betsy.

"Where's the money, Betsy? I had to lay out a fortune for Akmanian. And I got a crew to pay."

"Stuff it, Daniel. You get paid when the client pays us. Not before."

"If I find out you're cheating me . . ."

"What'll you do? Leave? You're easily replaced. There are dozens of production companies that would jump at the chance to work with Mindbenders, even if they never got paid."

"Not this one!"

"I don't have time for this." Betsy stalked out of the office, slamming the door behind her. An ironic expression bloomed on her face when she saw us. "There's always oodles of drama on a production," she said, forcing a smile. She strode down the hall in the direction we'd come from.

Frank hugged Grady's side as we continued down the hall to a book-lined library at the end. "She sure yells a lot," I heard him whisper to his father as we entered the room.

"Grown-ups don't always behave like grown-ups should," Grady replied. "Let's forget about her and see what Aunt Jessica's set is like."

A large walnut table that I assumed usually occupied the center of the room had been pushed to one end, and its chairs wheeled in a bunch next to it. In their place, a desk, surrounded by light stands, had been set up in front of a bookcase. I noticed a row of my books on one of the shelves. On the desk, a laptop computer sat on a blotter framed in brown leather. Lined up neatly at its side were a brass pen and pencil set and a stack of lined paper pads. Three books—a dictionary, a thesaurus, and a book of quotations—stood between a set of marble bookends in the shape of lions' heads. Warm light from a desk lamp shone down on a small bowl of flowers. It looked like a very pleasant place in which to write.

"This looks cool, Aunt Jessica," Frank said. "When did you get a new desk?"

"It's not mine, Frank. It's just the suggestion of my working space," I explained. "It doesn't have to look ex- actly like my desk at home, but we'll pretend that it does for the commercial."

"Is that allowed?" he asked.

"I think for this purpose, it's allowed. But you should keep in mind that a lot of things you see in commercials on television may not be portrayed the way they actually are in real life."

"Oh."

"Do you like it, Mrs. Fletcher?" Dave asked.

"It's lovely," I said.

He pulled up his sleeve and looked at his watch. "Your spot has been moved back to this afternoon. We're plan- ning to shoot you at the desk, and then do some of your lines in front of a green screen we have set up in another room," Dave said. He looked at Frank. "Do you know what a green screen is?"

Frank shook his head.

"It's a neutral background, and it's really colored green," Dave told him. "I'll show it to you later. When we take what we've filmed in front of the green screen, we can insert any kind of picture behind your aunt. We can put her in front of the Eiffel Tower or London Bridge, or we can show her standing in a jungle."

"Awesome!" Frank said.

"Are those the backgrounds you're going to use?" I asked.

"I don't think it's been decided yet, but they'll probably ask you if it's okay to use whatever they pick."

"I'm sure whatever they choose will be fine," I said.

"How did you get this office building?" Grady asked.

"And where are all the people who work here?" Frank added.

Dave laughed. "We had a bit of luck. An insurance company went under and left this place just as you see it. Since it's unoccupied, our location scout was able to get a good deal from the landlord to let us shoot here."

"So it already had a kitchen," I said.

"Yes, ma'am. Kitchen, library, offices. We're using their satellite-conferencing setup to mimic a news studio for Miss Tripper's spot. And we found a great room for Sevenson. It's got wallpaper with stars on it. He's the famous new age guru, right? It's the perfect background. I just hope he doesn't figure out he's in a day care center."

"He would love that," I said, thinking the opposite.

"The toys are gone, so I doubt he'll know what the room was used for. At least I hope so."

"Well, you can be assured I won't tell him," I said.

Jason poked his head in the conference room. "Dave, Howerstein wants you back on number two. That guy Sevenson is threatening to leave."

"Speaking of the devil," Dave said.

"He says he doesn't care what kind of paper she has—she can't treat him that way."

"Aw. C'mon. A contract's a contract." Dave excused himself and hurried from the room. Frank ran after him.

"Frank!" Grady called. "Come back here."

"It's okay, Dad. I'm just going down the hall. I can't get lost."

"You better stay out of trouble. And don't get in the way."

"I won't."

Grady looked at me. "Just as well. I want to talk to you about something."

"Are you sure he'll be okay?" I asked.

"Oh yeah, everybody's been looking out for him this morning. They've been great. He's like their mascot. Besides, everything takes place on this floor. He can't go far."

"If you're sure," I said, but I was uneasy at leaving a nine-year-old boy unsupervised.

"Can you believe that argument between Betsy and Howerstein? I don't want to be responsible if his company goes under."

"How could you be responsible?"

"Because of that problem he asked me to look into. Remember? We may have a bit of trouble with that."

"Who's we?" I asked.

"My company. I checked with the California office and

it seems we've been late on a lot of crew payments lately. We don't have the money to cover them."

"But I thought the production companies had to give you the money in advance for their payroll. Aren't they doing that?"

"The problem is, they *are* giving us the money."

"Then why are the payments late? Where is the money going if it isn't going to pay the crew?" I asked.

"I wish I knew. The office is sending out the checks, but not on time. It doesn't make sense."

"Is it possible the company overextended itself, spent more money than it had?"

Grady scratched the back of his head. "The big brass made a number of acquisitions lately, buying up smaller companies. I thought we were growing awfully fast."

"Could they have used some of their production companies' payroll money to pay off those purchases?"

"That's what I'm afraid of. If they've been scrambling to cover the checks, they may be taking money from the next company to pay the crew of the last company. At that rate, they'll always be behind."

"If you're right, Grady, that means your employer is in financial trouble. It's bound to catch up with them sometime. Is there anything you can do?"

"I'm not sure. I don't want the production companies I work with, like Eye Screen, to lose their payroll money. I've worked hard to learn their business and I know they trust me. But at the same time, I don't want to accuse my company of doing something unethical, or even illegal, unless

I'm really sure that's what's happening. If I'm wrong, it could ruin my reputation, never mind cost me my job."

"Can you speak with anybody about this?"

"My boss is out of town right now, but I'm going to bring it to his attention as soon as he gets back."

"Good idea," I said. "And, Grady, please let me know if there's anything I can do to help."

"I will, Aunt Jess. Thanks."

"Now, let's go find that boy of yours."

Chapter Ten

W e found Frank wearing a different set of ear-phones, the red ones he'd been given earlier looped around his neck like a collar, in imitation of other crew members. He was standing next to the soundman, who had commandeered one of the cubicles for his equipment and himself. He was close to my age, gray and slope-shouldered, practically an anachronism on a set where the next-oldest person was probably in his or her forties. He leaned back in an office chair behind an array of decks with as many dials, buttons, and meters as he would have if he were sitting in an airplane cockpit. A cardboard sign, taped to the back of one of the components, said CLIFF'S CAVE—KEEP OUT!

"Now, you listen to me, kid," Cliff said to Frank. "Experience means never having to move. If you know what you're doing, you don't have to see what's going on. You can hear everything and make adjustments from this seat without ever having to get up. Look at this."

Frank leaned closer so he could see the dials to which Cliff pointed.

"I hand-massage the sound," Cliff said. "It goes through my ears and into my hands." He reached out a gnarled finger and twirled a dial. "Hear the difference?"

Frank nodded. "What's that banging sound? It sounds like bowling balls."

"I can't see her, but this is what I'm thinking: They put the microphone on her collar and she's wearing some kind of necklace. Every time she turns her head, the beads click together and that's what you get."

"Wow! They're loud."

Cliff turned down the volume. "Now, you go around the corner and see what she's wearing. Then come back and tell me if I'm not right."

Frank took off the earphones, handed them to Cliff, and put his red ones back on. He rounded the corner of the cubicle intent on his task.

"Slow down, sport," Grady said as Frank passed us. "And tie your laces or you'll trip."

"No, I won't," Frank called back.

"Sharp little guy," Cliff said to us when we introduced ourselves. "Might just make a good soundman one day."

We heard an enormous crash, followed by a scream.

Cliff shuddered. "That's not a good sound," he said, but he didn't get up.

Grady and I glanced at each other and ran in the direction Frank had gone. He was kneeling on the floor, an enormous light lying next to him, its glass bulb in shards scattered on the carpet. Several other light stands had toppled over, making it difficult to reach him.

"You little brat! What are you doing here? See what you've done. Get out! Get out! Get out!"

Grady jumped over the poles to reach his son. "Are you all right?" he asked, helping Frank to his feet.

Frank nodded, but his face was ashen. "My earphones," he said, picking them up where they had fallen. "Are they broken?"

"Never mind your earphones," Grady said. "How did this happen?"

Frank pulled the earphones around his neck. "I don't know, Dad."

Betsy was standing in the doorway of an office. Behind her, Anne Tripper sat at a long counter that looked as if it were part of a newsroom. Clocks on the wall were set to four different time zones. A bank of television monitors tuned to CNN and MSNBC was off to one side.

Betsy was fuming. "You, there. Look what he did. This is a professional set. He doesn't belong here. Those lights will cost us thousands." Her voice rose as she vented her fury on Frank. "What were you thinking, you clumsy idiot? Didn't you see the lights? This is expensive equipment. Where are your brains?"

"Don't talk to him that way," I said. "He's only a child."

"A child has no business being here, especially not a stupid one who doesn't look where he's going."

"Now, just a minute," I said, getting angry. "It's not necessary to call him names."

Grady shook his head. "Please, Aunt Jess." He looked at Betsy. "I'm really sorry, Betsy. He didn't mean it."

"Sorry doesn't cut it. What are we supposed to do now?" she said, chopping off each word.

"Calm down, Betsy," Howerstein said. "Leave the kid alone."

"Leave him alone? He's created a disaster. I promised our client we'd come in under budget. We're on a tight schedule here, and he's just set us back hours, maybe days."

"No, he hasn't," Howerstein said. "We have other lights." He tried to put his arm around her shoulder, but she shrugged him off.

"And what are you all staring at? Standing there with your mouths gaping open. Get in here and fix this," she raged at crew members who'd stood frozen in place while she yelled at Frank.

Six people jumped forward and began righting the light stands, and picking up the slivers of glass. No one said anything. When a path had been cleared, I stepped around the crew to Frank and Grady's side.

"Is he injured, Grady?" I asked.

Frank hung on Grady's arm. "Dad, I didn't do it," he said, his eyes filling with tears. "I promise. I was just standing here."

"It's okay, son. We'll pay for any damage."

"You better believe you'll pay for the damage," Betsy said.

"No! It's not fair. I didn't do anything," Frank said, the tears rolling down his cheeks.

"You must have done something, son. How else did the lights fall down?"

"I don't know, but it wasn't me. I swear."

"He's lying," Betsy yelled. "Who told you that you could bring him here?"

"You did," Grady said, his face getting red. "And my son is not a liar. If Frank said he didn't do anything, he didn't."

"Oh, come off it. Next you'll be telling me kids never lie. I have another leg. You wanna pull that one?"

"Grady, let's get him out of here," I said softly. "We need to make sure he's not hurt."

"You're just trying to get out of paying for this." Betsy's voice was nearing hysteria. "But you won't get away with it. I'll take you to court."

"Betsy, shut up." Kevin Prendergast stepped forward and grabbed her arm.

"Let go of me," she screeched, wresting her arm away. "I'm not the one who ruined this shoot."

Prendergast signaled to Dan Howerstein, and Howerstein whispered to another man, who called out, "Lunch break. Be back at oh one thirty."

The crew hastily melted away, leaving only a few of us behind.

"We can do another day, no?" Antonio said, clearly unnerved by Betsy's breakdown.

"No!" Betsy said, trying to tamp down her anger. "We

cannot. We have a schedule to keep. Every second costs us money. Your money."

"But I pay everything already," Antonio said, waving his hands back and forth. "No more. I don't give any more."

"What did you say?" Howerstein yelled. He glared at Betsy.

Kevin forced Betsy to turn toward him and spoke to her in low tones I couldn't hear.

"Don't tell me to calm down," she said, shaking him off. "I know what it takes to get this done better than you do. . . . Don't threaten me, Kevin. If it weren't for me, you wouldn't even be here. I know all your secrets. Do you want me to start talking to Antonio?"

"What?" Antonio said. "What should you talk to me on?"

"Shut up or you're out the door," Kevin ground out, pushing Betsy to get her to move away.

"Oh, really? I'd like to see you try it. And I know what your little girlfriend is up to. Do you?"

In the office behind them, Anne Tripper sat serenely on her set. She was flipping through a magazine with one hand, while the beringed fingers of her other hand toyed with a strand of large beads. Her legs were crossed, and she casually bounced one foot up and down, the pointed toe of her patent leather shoe catching the light. She seemed to be unaware of or uninterested in the scene outside in the corridor, but she must have heard what happened. Did I detect a slight smile on her lips?

I leaned over Frank and put a hand lightly on his shoulder. He winced and I pulled my hand away. "Did one of those stands hit you and knock you down, Frank?"

He sniffled and shook his head. "I'm all right, Aunt Jessica," he said. "I didn't do anything." There was a hitch to his voice and I knew he was trying not to cry anymore. "You believe me, don't you, Dad?"

"Of course I believe you, sport, but I think it's time to leave."

"Nooo. It's not fair. I'm being punished and I didn't do anything."

"You're not being punished," I said. I felt terrible that Frank had been yelled at, and that Grady felt they had to leave, but I also wasn't happy that Grady and I had let Frank wander freely, only to get into trouble. As mature as he may be for a nine-year-old, he's still only nine. And most important, Betsy was right. He didn't belong there; a production is no place for a child. There are so many potential places where someone can get hurt, even for an adult accustomed to the fast pace and knowledgeable about all the equipment. For a boy who is quick and curious, it takes only one misstep to set a dangerous chain of events in motion. Add to that the high-strung nerves of the agency creative director. I agreed with Grady. They should leave.

"The kid can stay." The speaker was Akmanian, the director. He was sitting on his canvas chair, a Starbucks cup in his hand. "It's my set. I say who gets to stay and who has to go, not her."

"That's very nice of you," Grady said, "but I think we've seen enough for one day."

"Please, Dad, please. I want to stay."

"We can't take a chance, sport. I don't want to have to watch you every second."

"But I didn't knock down those lights."

"He's telling the truth," Akmanian said.

"What are you saying?" I asked.

"I saw one of the PAs clip the big stand," he said, cutting the air with his hand. "They went down like dominoes."

"See, Dad? See? We can stay now."

"Why didn't you say anything when Betsy was yelling at Frank?" I said, feeling my anger rise again.

"She was full into her tirade," Akmanian said, tipping his cup back to get the last drops of coffee. "I figured she wouldn't listen anyway. She certainly is entertaining when she's in a rant, isn't she?"

"Not when you're the nine-year-old victim of it," I said.

"You're okay, boy, aren't you?"

Frank knuckled away the tears from his eyes and nodded at the director.

Grady sighed. "Thank goodness I'm not working for her."

"Oh, yeah. We all say that," said Akmanian. "She's quite the drama queen. That's why I make sure the money's in the bank before I work with her." He glanced at his watch. "We should be ready for you by two this afternoon," he said, looking at me. "Got your role memorized? If you do, you're the only one."

"I know all my lines," I said with a sigh. "However, I have a problem with two of them. I'd like them changed, but I don't want to set off another outburst."

"Give me the Fletcher script," he said to the production assistant sitting next to him.

She had anticipated the request and had pulled it from the pile of papers in her lap. She put the script in his hand.

Akmanian cocked his head at her and smiled. "I've got two words for you, kid." He paused. "Light and sweet." He handed her his coffee cup.

The PA, who'd sat up straight in her seat expecting praise, collapsed like a punctured balloon. Her face paled, then flooded with color.

"Don't take me so seriously," the director said to her. "We'll keep you for the next shoot." He tapped her on the head with my script.

Akmanian read over the lines with me and I showed him the problem areas. We agreed on alternative language, and he said he'd take responsibility for making the changes.

"I'll tell her it was awkwardly worded," he said. "That should send her into a tailspin." He laughed.

"Please. I don't think my heart can take any more excitement today."

"Tell her I wrote it," Frank piped up, joining in on the joke.

"Don't be fresh, sport," Grady said, but he was hard put not to smile.

Dave Fitzpatrick escorted us to where lunch was being served. Three buffets had been set up in a series of rooms on the first floor. Luckily we managed to avoid seeing Betsy. We filled our plates and found seats next to Cookie and Jimbo, who were sitting with Antonio Tedeschi.

Cookie ruffled Frank's hair. "Heard about your little tiff this morning. We both heard the lioness roar today. You okay?"

Frank nodded vigorously as he stuffed a forkful of spaghetti into his mouth.

"Betsy's got more snap than a mousetrap," she said to me in a low voice, looking over to see if her manager was listening. "Ah thought Jimbo was 'bout to bust a gut when she turned that harsh tongue on me. He was that mad. I think he still is, but he's holdin' it in. They're gonna try to fit us in later, but if not, we gotta come back tomorrow to finish the shoot. Ah think I should know my lines by then." She winked at me.

Antonio got up to leave and came around the table to apologize for Betsy's behavior. "I am sorry for the . . . the—" He strove to find the right word, finally settling on, "She was not so nice to you." He pressed Cookie's hand. "And to you." He looked at Frank. "She has the brilliant ideas but is not such a diplomat. No?"

"Ah wouldn't recommend the UN use her in the Middle East," Cookie said.

"Still. Very smart, very creative, very passionate about her work," Antonio said.

"Can't argue with that," Cookie said.

Antonio pressed his lips together and shook his head. "But perhaps I shouldn't go with her," he said softly. "Maybe not such a good idea."

"Go where?" I asked.

"You can go anywhere you like with her," Cookie said. "Just keep her away from me."

"Yes, of course." Antonio forced a smile, bent forward in a brief bow, and walked away, a worried expression on his face.

Before we finished lunch, several crew members stopped at our table to ask after Frank, who was delighted by all the attention. He recounted the tale of the light stands falling around him, embellishing a bit each time he told the story, but was careful not to say anything about the tongue-lashing he received from the angry agency creative director.

As we cleared our plates and cups and dropped our napkins in the garbage can, Frank lingered by a big fishbowl that was filled with candy bars. It was a youngster's Halloween dream. Crew members on their way back to work plunged their hands into the bowl, grabbing a few bars to go.

"Did you see what they have, Dad?" Frank asked, his eyes wide. "I didn't have hardly any dessert, and they have Snickers. Can I have one?"

"You may have one, no more," Grady said. "And grab one for me."

Father and son munched on their treats as we made our way back to the library set.

At first it was quiet. I sat at my make-believe desk while the assistant cameraman held a meter up to my cheek, checking the light levels, and someone ran a wire inside my jacket for a microphone. The gaffer, who turned out to be the head electrician, directed the crew adjusting the lights. The fluorescent bulbs in the ceiling fixtures were removed and replaced with a large flood lamp, draped with black material.

The wardrobe lady came in to check my jacket, pinning the back to make it appear more formfitting in the front, and inserting a piece of rolled-up painter's tape under my lapel to hold it in place.

Maya, the makeup woman, refreshed my lipstick, powdered my face, and sprayed my hair to within an inch of its life. "The light picks up every stray hair," she said, snipping one off with a scissors she drew from her pocket. "If they see it in the final print, it can drive them crazy. They can fix it in postproduction, of course, but that costs money. And if word gets around that I let it happen, they'll stop asking for me by name."

The camera was delivered on a dolly pushed by the grips, who, I learned, are the general technicians on a set, moving, rigging, and building things.

Akmanian arrived with the director of photography, and all of a sudden there were dozens of people around me. The director sat behind a monitor and pulled on his headphones.

A script supervisor sat next to the director. "Let's talk camera direction," she said. "Where are you going to put her?"

"I like her just where she is," the cameraman replied. He adjusted the lens and ordered changes in the lights. "Waste it to the left, please," he called out. "That's no good. Let's try the other eyebrow on the camera. Did anyone bring in the inky snoot?"

Grady and Frank had taken chairs on the side of the room. Antonio slipped into the room and sat next to Grady. I caught Frank's eye and winked at him. He bounced up and down in excitement until Grady threatened to escort him from the room if he didn't sit still. I could tell it was tough for him, but he gave it a good try.

"Let's go, guys. Today, she's a-burning."

"Where's the gaffer?"

"I'm right here."

"We've got a chance to wrap it by six, and save a bundle."

"Quiet on the set. Let's go from the top."

"Quiet, please. Randy, raise that boom."

"We're rolling. Rolling, rolling."

"Permezzo, five-oh-three, take one. Mark!"

"Action!"

"Hello . . . I'm Jessica Fletcher. It's no mystery why I always carry my Permezzo card when I travel to do research for my novels."

The shoot went smoothly, but even though I knew my lines, the taping took a surprisingly long time. Altogether, we did twenty or thirty takes—I lost track—including a "reverse" with the camera looking over my shoulder, and a stand-up in front of the green screen. Each change of camera direction or placement necessitated time to relocate and adjust the lights, focus the lens, raise some part of the set decoration using what they called "apple boxes," double-check the sound, smooth my jacket, powder my nose, and respray my hair, which was feeling more and more like a helmet by the moment.

Betsy Archibald never came to the set, so my concerns about her reaction to changes in the script were for naught. I didn't see Howerstein either. By the time Kevin Prendergast poked his head in the library, we were finished.

Cookie walked up to me on the set as one of the crew

was unhooking my microphone. "Ooh, Jessica. You're gonna put me to shame," she said. "You are such a pro."

"Thank you," I replied. "Have you been here all this time? I didn't see you."

"Oh, Jimbo and Ah was hiding in the back."

"You were?" I laughed. "Where is Jimbo?"

"He was just here." She craned her neck to look for him. "Must've gone to the little boys' room. I better go find him. That producer said they probably gonna want us to try again."

"Tonight?"

"Well, now is as good a time as any, I always say. You were such a wonderful inspiration, I'll be sure to do better. Now that they put the right bottles in my kitchen. Your set is looking very authentic. I want mine to be, too. Ah better get over there, just in case. See you later."

"She certainly can talk a blue streak, can't she?" Grady said, taking my arm as I walked off the set.

"I think she's a little nervous about doing her spot."

"Not everyone is as smooth as you," Grady said. "You were great, Aunt Jess. Wasn't she, Frank?"

"I liked the green-screen part best," Frank said. "I want to see what they put behind you."

"Me, too," I said, tweaking his chin.

"Akmanian told me you were a real pro," Grady said. "I knew all along you'd be the best one."

"Oh, I don't know about that," I said. "But he was very gracious."

"He was thrilled," Grady said, grinning. "Did you have a good time?"

"I must admit it was fun, and I didn't think it would be."

"See?" He laughed, then lowered his voice. "Probably because a certain someone wasn't here to carry on."

"That certainly helped."

Frank, who'd been trailing the crew as they moved to the next set, returned to us. "They're doing the man next, Dad. Can I go watch?"

"You just sat through a whole commercial being made. Wasn't that enough?"

"Please?"

"I think your mother wants us home for dinner," Grady said.

Frank jumped up and down. "Five minutes, that's all. I just want to stay five more minutes."

"Okay, sport, five more minutes. But I don't want you to complain when I come to find you."

"Make it ten, then," Frank said.

"Get out of here," Grady said, giving Frank a soft swat on the behind. "And make sure you stop in the bathroom. You haven't gone all day."

"I will."

"And tie those laces."

"Grady, are you sure?" I said, thinking I didn't want to hear what Betsy had to say if she saw Frank on the next set.

"He wasn't responsible, remember? We'll give him a couple of minutes up here, and then go. What do you need to do now?"

"I have to get my own clothes and return these to wardrobe, and collect my shoulder bag from the production office. I can't wait until I'm back at the hotel to remove the makeup and wash my hair."

"That should be enough time for Frank," he said as we walked to the stairwell. "Did I tell you, you look very glamorous in all that makeup?"

"No, you did not, and it's just as well. That's the last time you'll see this much paint on me."

Downstairs, some of the crew were stowing equipment that wouldn't be needed for the spot shooting upstairs; they were rolling it out to the trucks in fiberglass carts. The makeup stands had been folded, the lights and mirrors dismantled for the day. Maya waved to us as she hunted for a missing wig. The wardrobe mistress was packing the trunks, her assistant breaking down the clothing racks. I returned my "authorish" costume and retrieved my own clothes, as well as my shoulder bag from the production office, where the ladies complained about being on the phone all afternoon, arranging for the next production. We made our rounds and were back upstairs in the promised ten minutes, but when we looked in on Lance Sevenson's shoot, we didn't catch sight of Frank.

"Let's ask if anyone's seen him," I said.

"I don't want to disturb the crew while they're working," Grady said. "He probably went looking for us back on your set. Let me check and I'll be right back. If he shows up, have him wait here with you."

Grady returned in minutes, but without Frank. "I don't know where he could have gotten to. He said he wanted to watch this shoot."

"Maybe to see the soundman," I said.

We found Cliff in his cave, but he said he hadn't seen Frank since before the accident. "If you see him, please tell him we're looking for him," I said.

We walked back to the kitchen set that was being used for Cookie's commercial. They must have rescheduled it for the next day. The bottles had been removed from the butcher-block island, and the lights were off. We hurried down a dim corridor to find the room that had served as a set for Anne Tripper. No Frank. We raced back to the Sevenson set in case he returned to where he'd said he'd be.

"Try video village," said a grip I stopped in the hall. He directed us to a room with lounge chairs around a table and a lineup of monitors along one wall. The table was littered with empty coffee cups, soda cans, and doughnut boxes, but no one was there.

"He was wearing his earphones," I said to Grady. "Let's get someone to page him and tell him to get back to the set."

"Aunt Jess, you're a genius. Of course. Why didn't I think of that?"

We retraced our steps to the Sevenson set, which was between takes. Lance was sitting on a stool in an empty room, the walls of which were covered in royal blue wallpaper with a random pattern of tiny foil stars. The movie lights gave the stars a twinkling effect. A different makeup lady was powdering Lance's brow. He looked a little uptight. You'd think he'd never been in front of a camera before.

A grip with a line of clothespins attached to the placket of his shirt was winding a cable over his shoulder. Two others were removing ceiling tiles to accommodate an overhead light. Akmanian directed another to shift around light stands while he stood on top of a ladder, peering through the camera lens.

I found Dave Fitzpatrick and explained our problem.

"Sure, Mrs. Fletcher. What channel was he on?" he asked, donning his own earphones.

"I'm not sure. Can we try them all?"

"Don't see why not. We're not shooting at the moment." Dave pulled a receiver from his belt, pressed a button, and spoke into the microphone. "Frank Fletcher, if you're on channel one, your dad is looking for you. Please come to the Sevenson set immediately." He repeated his message on the three other channels.

Grady and I sighed with relief and stood up tall to spot Frank when he would come bounding onto the set, as we were sure he would. But five minutes passed, and then ten, and Frank did not show up.

"I'm going to kill that boy when we find him," Grady said, exasperated. "Just ten minutes. That's what he promised. And look—" He glanced at his watch. "It's been almost three quarters of an hour. He's in big trouble now. He's going to hear from me, but good."

"And I'll be next in line," I said. "Grady, where else did you go with him before I met up with you this morning? He was all excited about the different things he'd seen. And he was talking about a carpenter."

Grady slapped his forehead with the heel of his palm. "Right. We were with the guys building pieces of the set. One of them let him try the nail gun."

"Where was that? Was it on this floor?"

"Yeah," Grady said, looking around. "I think it was this way." He grabbed a passing grip by the elbow. "Where did you guys set up the carpentry shop again?"

"Down that way," the man said, pointing to a dark hallway. "But it might be locked. I think they're packed up for the night."

"We want to check anyway," Grady said.

"Then hang a left at the end and it's two or three doors down on your right. Flip on the hall lights as you go."

"Thanks," Grady said.

We took off at a jog.

"He'd better not have tried that nail gun again," Grady said, his voice tight. "I told him it was a dangerous tool, but he was so fascinated by it. Oh God, Aunt Jess, you don't think he's hurt, do you? I'll never forgive myself."

"Let's not borrow trouble. We have to find him first. Then you can berate yourself. But if he's not here, Grady, I think we should get help."

We followed the grip's directions, switching on the overhead lights in the hall as we went. At the end of the corridor, we turned left. All the doors on the right were closed. Grady turned the knob of the first door. Thankfully, it was unlocked. He pushed it open. The room contained several light stands, but was otherwise empty. There was nothing at all in the second room. The third room was dark, but filled with equipment. I wondered why so much had been stuffed into the one room when there were two others that could have been used as well. Grady groped along the wall for the light switch. Only a single fluorescent came on. The bulb next to it flickered and went off.

"Frank, are you in here?" Grady yelled.

No answer.

He looked at me uncertainly. "He's not here, is he?"

"I hope not," I replied, "but let's look around anyway."

The room was crammed with light stands, dollies used to move the cameras, giant clamps, reflectors, ladders, and at the rear lines of rolling carts, piled high with lumber and other building supplies. The floor was littered with wood chips and sawdust. I skirted the standing pieces, moving some and inching sideways around others to reach the first carts. I was afraid to look and afraid not to. There were rolls of screening and black fabric. I pushed them aside in case there was a small person inside. Grady tried to peer behind the carts for his son, but there were too many and not enough room to maneuver them.

"Let's roll some of this into the hall," I said. "We can get help putting it all back if he's not here."

Grady had to drag several stands into the hallway before he had room to move out one of the carts. He backed up, pulling it toward the door, stopped, and ran around the other side. "Oh God," he said, stooping down.

"What? What is it?"

He held up a pair of red earphones, dusted with flakes of wood. I could see a sticker on one of the earpieces. It was the number one. "These are his, Aunt Jess. He must be here," Grady said, his voice cracking.

Frantically, we began pulling all the stands and carts out into the hall. One by one, we moved them, pausing only briefly to check inside each cart. The farther back in the room we went, the dimmer the light. It was getting difficult to see. I thrust my hand into my shoulder bag to search for my flashlight. Kneeling on the floor, I leaned down to look under the carts, aiming the light in a wide arc.

"Do you see anything?"

"I think I do," I said. What I didn't say was that I thought I saw the soles of a pair of sneakers, and a loose lace. "Let's get these moved quickly."

The carts in the back row had been wedged in together. We pulled one, our arms straining against the weight. "Look at this, Aunt Jess," Grady said, tears coursing down his cheeks. He pointed inside the cart to where someone had stowed a nail gun. "You don't think—?"

Together we pulled on the cart, but it wouldn't budge. The weight of its contents, plus the pressure from carts on either side, made it too difficult for us. Pieces of metal and wood were packed standing up. A coil of orange electric cable had been stuffed in the side, along with a nail gun and its compressor. Grady began emptying the cart, taking out the nail gun, the compressor, and the heavy cable and flinging them to the side of the room. He tried to lift a metal pole, but it was stuck.

"We need help, Grady," I said. "Maybe the sawdust is keeping the wheels from moving freely."

"No!" he yelled. "I'm not giving up." He yanked on the side of the cart, pulling so hard his face turned scarlet and the veins in his temples stood out. "Move!" The wheels squealed. Grady struggled to catch his breath, then gasped. A small arm had fallen to the carpet from behind the cart. From our position, we couldn't see the body to which it was attached.

"Please, God," Grady whispered.

I squeezed around the cart and knelt beside the arm, placing my trembling fingers on the delicate skin of the wrist, feeling for a pulse. Steeling myself, I pointed my flashlight behind the cart, the beam bouncing before I could steady my hand. The light landed on a face. A moan escaped my lips.

"Oh no," Grady whimpered. He fell to his knees and covered his face with his hands, his body racked with tremors. "My baby, my boy."

"No, Grady, no," I managed to say, my voice breaking with emotion. "It's not Frank."

"What? What do you mean? Who is it?"

"It's Betsy Archibald."

Chapter Eleven

Dan Howerstein paced back and forth in front of two uniformed officers guarding the door of the conference room. "We have to finish tonight," he said. "We had the opportunity to come in under budget. I don't understand why you had to shut down our entire operation. You've got guards at every door. We're all trapped here. The least you could do is let us complete the one spot."

One of the officers coughed into his palm and wiped his hand on the side of his pants. "I told you, Mr. Howerstein," he said, sniffling, "I have no jurisdiction over this. I just do what I'm told. The detective in charge said no one is to leave this room." He pulled a handkerchief from his jacket pocket and honked into it. "Stupid cold," he said to his fellow officer.

"Just don't breathe in my direction, Sam," his colleague

said. "I don't want to get sick again. My six-year-old catches everything."

"It's ridiculous," Howerstein said, bringing the conversation back to the matter at hand. "Why do you have to close down the whole building?"

"It's a crime scene, sir," Sam said, wiping his nose. "A murder took place. Statements have to be taken."

"Well, I was on the set. There have to be thirty people who'll vouch for my whereabouts. And I have a meeting to get to tonight. I can't keep wasting time like this."

"We understand that, sir," said the other officer, "but we have procedures that have to be followed. Just take a seat and we'll get to you as soon as we can."

"Unbelievable," Howerstein grumbled, flinging himself into a chair against the wall, legs splayed and fists shoved into the pockets of his jeans.

The police had responded swiftly to my 911 call. They immediately rounded up all the remaining production crew and agency personnel—those who hadn't already left for the day—and confined us in several rooms while they launched their on-site investigation.

The news of Betsy's murder had swept through the building. Grady and I couldn't be positive, but we surmised that she'd been killed by the nail gun, which we'd found in the cart that was pressed against her body. We had made a mess of the crime scene by moving the equipment and carts. It couldn't be helped, of course. We'd had no idea the room had been the scene of a murder until we found the body. Waiting for the police to arrive, I tried to reconstruct what little I could. There were footprints in the sawdust on the side of the room and near the body. Someone wearing a shoe with a pointed toe. They weren't mine or Grady's. They weren't Betsy's either; she was wearing sneakers.

Whoever had killed her had tried to delay discovery of the body by piling up equipment in front of it. The shoot was scheduled to go several more hours, and pick up again the next day if necessary. If we hadn't been looking for Frank, Betsy's body might have remained hidden the whole time.

I stayed with the body until the ambulance and first police officers arrived. While the emergency medical technicians ascertained that Betsy was indeed dead, I explained the situation to the officer in charge, stressing that while the murder was certainly important, my grandnephew was still missing. I requested that they issue an Amber Alert.

Meanwhile, Grady had gone in search of Frank again, enlisting the help of crew members to comb every cubicle and room that had been used by the production. But that search ended when the police arrived and ushered Grady into another room. I tried to follow but was stopped.

I sat back in the upholstered chair and closed my tired eyes. The realization that it was Betsy's wrist I had held— when I had feared the pulse I was seeking was Frank's— had overwhelmed me. As sorry as I was that Betsy was dead, I had sobbed in relief that it wasn't Frank behind the rolling cart.

Despite Frank's disappearance, I tried to force myself not to panic, to think positively, but my mind was spinning out of control. *Surely he's all right,* I reassured myself. But those optimistic thoughts were assailed by the reality that my precious grandnephew was out there somewhere, away from the love and protection of his family. He was an intelligent little boy. Still, he was only nine, certainly not old enough to think and reason like an adult. Perhaps he'd been afraid that Grady would be angry with him for dawdling, and had decided to hide to avoid being punished. A youngster might do something like that, mightn't he?

Had he witnessed the murder and run away? That possibility was frightening. We knew that he'd been in that room at some point; we'd found his earphones at the scene. Could he be somewhere in the building right now, in a secret hiding place, too petrified to disclose his location in case the murderer was looking for him? I closed my eyes and shuddered at the notion. No child should ever be made to experience such intense fear.

I desperately hoped that he was still nearby. Should we suggest to the police that they bring in a dog to help find him? Frank loved dogs. I pictured a proud German shepherd or Doberman sniffing around until it discovered him in his sanctuary, and his whoop of joy and relief as he ran into the protective and welcoming arms of his father.

I took comfort from that happy-ending scenario, but knew it was purely an invention of my overactive mind. The alternative was too horrible to contemplate. Yet I did. Had Frank come upon the murder as it happened, and been kidnapped by the killer? If so—and I prayed it wasn't—it meant that Frank was in mortal danger.

Where was Grady? I wondered. They'd spirited him away to another room in the building. He should be out here coordinating the search for Frank. The situation was becoming nightmarish. I hoped Donna had been notified. Maybe Grady was speaking with her on a phone, trying to come up with ideas between them as to where Frank might have gone.

I was in the midst of these jumbled thoughts, my eyes pressed shut, when the crew's second assistant director, Dave Fitzpatrick, snapped me back to reality. "Are you the one who found her, Mrs. Fletcher?" he asked.

I opened my eyes and looked around. I'd blotted out everything, including the fact that there were others in the room with me. Fitzpatrick and I were two of approximately a dozen people, some of whom I recognized as being members of the crew, but whose names I didn't know. Several people were standing by the window talking in low tones. Others were sitting at the table, some napping, some not. Two were playing hangman on a pad of paper. None of them had seen Frank. Under other circumstances, I would have been making the rounds of the room, talking to all potential witnesses who might be able to tell me something about Betsy and who might want to kill her. But consumed with Frank's disappearance, I'd pushed Betsy's murder to the back of my mind.

What was it Dave had asked? Oh, yes, was I the one who found her? "I was," I said, turning to face him.

He smoothed his mustache with his thumb and forefinger. "I heard she was killed with a nail gun," he said. "That so?"

"That's what we think it might have been," I said. "There was a nail gun in the cart that was pushed up against her."

"How did you happen to, um, discover where she was?" he asked.

"Grady and I were searching for Frank when we found her."

"I can't say I really liked her, but I hate to see something like . . . well, you know." He stopped.

"Of course," I said, surprised that it even occurred to him to say that. "No one deserves to be murdered."

"She sure ripped into him, though, didn't she?"

I straightened in my seat and frowned at him.

"He must've been pretty scared of her," he said.

"What are you suggesting?"

"I'm not saying he might have done it on purpose or anything like that, but if she pounced on him again the way she did this morning, I could see him, you know, trying to defend himself."

"Are you saying that you think my nine-year-old grandnephew might have killed her?" I was working hard to control my voice, not terribly successfully.

"Whoa," he said, raising his hands. "I didn't say that. But he *is* missing, isn't he? You asked all of us if we'd seen him. Maybe he got scared by what he did and ran away."

"He could have gotten scared for a number of reasons," I said angrily. "I can't believe you would even think such a thing. He's only a boy. I hope you're not starting any rumors."

"It wasn't me. I didn't start anything."

"Oh? Then who is saying it?"

"You know, some of the guys who were on the set this morning."

I glanced around, but while they couldn't help over-hearing our conversation, the people in the room were studiously looking in another direction. "And they're accusing Frank of killing Betsy?"

"No. No. They just said if she'd yelled at them like she did at him, they could see themselves . . ." He trailed off.

"This is outrageous." I pushed back my seat and stormed to the door. "Officer?" I said, squinting at his name badge: M. LASKER. "Officer Lasker, I'm Jessica Fletcher. I insist on speaking with the detective in charge. It's urgent."

"Take it easy, lady," the other officer said. "The detective's going as fast as he can."

I turned to look at the speaker's nameplate. "You're Officer Rubins?"

"Yes, ma'am, but we can't get the detective for you. Everybody has to wait their turn. These things take time. Now . . . now . . . ah . . . ah . . ." He sneezed.

"Bless you."

"Thank you," he said from behind his handkerchief. "Please take your seat again, and wait until you're called."

"You don't understand," I said. "There's a dreadful rumor going around that we absolutely must put a halt to immediately."

"Yeah, there's always rumors," Officer Rubins said, punctuating his comment with a cough.

"Please listen to me," I said. "This is very important. My grandnephew is missing. He's only nine years old. And now, people—" I shook my head. I couldn't bear it that anyone would think Frank capable of murder. "People are suggesting he ran away because he . . . they're saying that he might have inadvertently hurt Miss Archibald. It's completely ridiculous, of course. Frank would never do any such thing. And the sooner we find him, the faster we can clear this whole thing up."

I was met with blank stares.

"Who is the detective in charge?" I asked.

"His name's Chesny, Detective Chesny. But we can't interrupt him. He's questioning witnesses. Sorry."

I could see I wasn't going to get anywhere with these two. I craned my neck trying to see into the hall beyond them. The door to the next room opened and a tall, African-American man in a brown pin-striped suit emerged.

"Hey, Detective, this lady says—"

I stepped in front of the officer. "Detective Chesny?" I called out. "Detective Chesny, I need to see you now."

"Come on, lady, don't make trouble," Officer Lasker said as he took my right arm and tried to push me back toward my chair.

"I'm sorry, but I must speak with Detective Chesny!"

"What's going on here?" the black man asked in a deep voice. "Let go of her, Officer."

"We're sorry, Al, but she started making a scene."

"I can hear that."

"Thank you, Detective Chesny," I said, shaking off the two officers and rushing to the door. "I'm Jessica Fletcher," I said softly, trying not to be overheard. "My nephew, Grady, and I were the ones who discovered Betsy Archibald. I really need to speak with you right now. It can't wait."

"All right," he said. "Come with me, Mrs. Fletcher."

He returned to the door through which he'd just come,

and I quickly followed. I didn't dare glance behind me because I knew there must be consternation on the faces of the two officers, who would now be concerned that others in the room might make a similar fuss. Sure enough, I heard Dan Howerstein speak up. "Do I have to do that to get any attention around here?"

Chesny motioned for me to take a chair across a small table from another empty chair. He was a middle-aged man with a touch of gray at the temples and deep pouches under eyes that were, at once, keenly perceptive but not unkind.

"You're the mystery writer," he said flatly.

"That's right."

"They told me you were involved."

"I'm not sure I'd use that word."

"Suit yourself. You know who did it?"

"Well, no, not yet. I mean, I haven't even thought about that. You see, my grandnephew—"

"Yeah. Yeah. I know."

"It's not as if I wouldn't be glad to help you. It's just that—"

"I hate to disabuse you, Mrs. Fletcher, but our police are perfectly capable of solving crimes without your help. However, as long as you're here, I might as well get your statement."

"All right," I said, "but first I have something to ask of *you.*"

He sighed and said, "Look, Mrs. Fletcher, I'm beat, and I don't have a lot of patience. I've had a long day, been in court since early this morning, and now I catch this case, so I'd appreciate it if—"

"I know," I said.

"You know *what*?"

"That you were in court today."

Quizzical creases dominated his face.

"Oh, I'm sorry," I said. "You'll have to forgive me. My mind is going in a dozen different directions at once. I noticed the wrinkles on the back of your jacket, and I know that officers spend a lot of time in courtrooms testifying, sitting around, and if you'd been in your office, you'd probably have hung up your suit jacket before sitting—but in court you don't have that luxury, so I assumed the wrinkles came from—" I shook my head. "I am sorry, Detective. As I said, my mind is a roller coaster since this terrible thing happened. Yes, of course, take my statement. But before you do, there's the matter of a missing nine-year-old boy, Frank Fletcher—he's my grandnephew—and he's gone and I think finding him should take precedence over anything else you and your officers do. Please! His father and I are worried sick about him."

"His father is Grady Fletcher. Right?"

"Yes, that's right. Where is he?"

He ignored my question and took the chair opposite mine.

"Are you doing anything to find Frank?" I asked.

"We have an APB out."

"An all points bulletin?" I was indignant. "Frank's not a suspect."

"He's a person of interest."

"What about an Amber Alert? He may have been kidnapped."

He shook his head. "We can't do that yet. We don't have confirmation of an abduction. And we don't have a description of a kidnapper or a vehicle. The law is very specific about when we can use an Amber Alert. But his mother is bringing up a photograph we can distribute to the officers searching for him." He looked at his watch. "I expect her any minute."

Poor Donna. She must have been devastated when she learned Frank was missing. Did Grady call to tell her? Or did she have to hear it from a police officer? How terrible either way. She must be miserably unhappy, driving alone, not sure where she's going, not knowing where her child is, or even if he's alive. I hoped she and Grady would be able to comfort each other and not allow recriminations to push them apart at such a distressing time.

I took a deep breath. "Thank you," I said on a sigh. "Have you searched the building already?"

"Some of my men are doing that now, and I've requested backup to lend a hand."

"That eases my mind a bit."

"But we haven't found him yet."

"If he's still somewhere in the building, you will. I pray that you do."

"In the meantime," he said, "mind if I ask you a few questions?" He pushed a button on a small tape recorder on the table.

"No, of course not."

"Tell me what happened today, Mrs. Fletcher. You said you and your nephew found the body."

"That's right."

"And how did Miss Archibald die?"

"I imagine the medical examiner will determine that."

"But I'm asking *you*, Mrs. Fletcher."

"I didn't see any external wounds—and there wasn't any blood on her sweater—but there was a hole in her blouse, and we found a nail gun nearby. We thought someone might have used it to kill her."

"Where was this nail gun you found nearby?"

"In the cart that blocked our view of her body."

"You didn't see her and yet you knew the body was behind the cart?"

"We saw her hand, and then we moved the cart."

"And you found Miss Archibald. What made you suspect she was dead if you saw no blood?"

"It's not unusual for there to be no blood. If she was killed instantly, her heart would have stopped pumping, and there wouldn't be any blood. But I imagine that's not news to you. As a detective, you—"

"Sounds like you looked at the body pretty carefully, Mrs. Fletcher."

"Well, a little. I think she might have been dead for a while. Her jaw—"

"Oh? You're also a coroner?"

"Of course not." I waited for him to interrupt me again, and when he didn't, I went on. "I'm an author of mystery books, but you already know that."

"Does that make you an expert on time of death?"

"Not at all. But I've learned quite a lot over the years."

"Talk to me about that when you have a medical degree. I don't want to hear your opinion otherwise."

"Very well."

He stood and paced the floor in front of me. "I understand Frank got himself into quite a bit of trouble today," he said.

"That's just it, Detective Chesny. He didn't. He was wrongly accused."

"Wrongly or rightly, Miss Archibald believed he caused a lot of damage to the production equipment, didn't she?"

"Yes. She was very upset."

"From what I hear, 'upset' is putting it mildly. I'm told she was livid."

"I suppose that's an apt description of her demeanor."

"And she attacked Frank in front of a lot of people."

"Verbally, yes."

"And you came to his defense."

"Of course. He's nine years old. He couldn't defend himself. She was being abusive, and as it turns out, he didn't cause the damage at all. Someone else did."

"But you were pretty angry at her, weren't you?"

"I was."

"Angry enough to confront her later on?"

"Had I seen her later on, I might have been. But Frank seemed to have weathered the incident well and was acting normally, so probably not."

"Then you're saying you didn't meet up with her again."

"No."

"How did you happen to be in the room in which Miss Archibald died?"

"Grady and I were looking for Frank. The two of them had been in that room earlier in the day. It had been used as a carpentry shop. We were trying to think of where Frank might have gone and were retracing all of his steps for the day."

"So you just happened to be in that room and discovered the body."

"I told you, we didn't just happen to be there. We were looking for Frank."

"And Miss Archibald was there."

"Yes."

"Are you sure she wasn't alive when you entered the room?"

"I suppose it's possible, but I don't believe so. When we found her, she was already dead."

"You're telling me she wasn't alive when you entered the room?"

"As far as I know."

"Why don't I believe you, Mrs. Fletcher?"

"I don't know why you don't believe me, Detective Chesny. I'm telling you the truth."

"You know what I think the truth is, Mrs. Fletcher? I think it's possible that Betsy Archibald was very much alive when you found her, and that you and Mr. Fletcher got into an altercation with her, and that one of you picked up the nail gun and killed her."

"I assure you, that is *not* what happened."

"We have the nail gun, and we're checking it for fingerprints. Any chance I'll find your prints on it, Mrs. Fletcher?"

"I doubt it. But Grady took the nail gun out of the cart."

"Why did he do that?"

I knew it was going to sound ridiculous, but I said it anyway. "To help lighten the load. The cart was too heavy for us to move, and he—"

"I can't believe he thought the weight of a nail gun would make a difference. Did *you* think it would make a difference?"

"He took out the compressor and the electrical cable, too."

"Heavy. Heavy."

"I don't appreciate your sarcasm, Detective. I'm trying to explain what happened."

"You might also be trying to make up a story to cover what you and your nephew did. We now know that his fingerprints are likely to be on the nail gun. And we know that he was angry at Betsy Archibald, possibly angry enough to kill her. Are you trying to cover up for him?"

"No!"

"I think you are, Mrs. Fletcher. And it will do you no good."

"What do you mean?"

We both turned at the sound of the door opening.

"This is the mother of the missing kid," an officer announced. He stepped aside to allow Donna to enter.

I jumped to my feet and Donna ran into my embrace.

"I can't believe this is happening," she said between sobs. "Where can Frank be? And the police won't let me see Grady."

"The police are doing all they can, Donna. They're searching the building, and they've put out alarms. I'm sure he'll be found safe and sound any minute."

She looked past me to the detective.

"This is Detective Chesny, Donna. He's in charge of the murder investigation."

"The *murder* investigation," she said. "A murder? And now Frank's missing. Oh, Aunt Jessica." She ended on a wail.

"Please, sit down," I said, leading her to my chair. She took it, and I knelt next to her, holding her hand in hopes of calming her.

"Where's Grady?" she asked no one in particular.

I looked up at Detective Chesny. "Yes, where is my nephew?" I said, rising. "He should be with his wife to comfort her. Please, can't you bring him in here?"

"I'm sorry, Mrs. Fletcher, but I'm afraid that's impossible. He's not in the building at the moment."

The look on my face and on Donna's reflected our confusion.

"Where is he, for heaven's sake?" I asked.

"We brought him down to headquarters."

"Why?"

"He's being held for questioning in the murder of Betsy Archibald."

Chapter Twelve

The police were located in a building that housed the Department of Public Safety for a small suburban city of New York, only a half hour out of town. We drove by a series of chain stores and low-rise buildings on either side of the highway that led to it. But as we entered the downtown area, we passed many taller buildings with more under construction. Office complexes, shopping malls, and residential high-rises dwarfed the older homes and other low buildings from the municipality's earlier days, and echoed its much larger neighbor to the south.

At headquarters, we found our way to a tan brick wall, behind which were the police dispatchers. Only a glass window that didn't open allowed communication with the officers in the back. Donna and I went to the window and waited to be acknowledged. A series of notices taped to the glass directed visitors to go to Records for copies of all reports, and for fingerprints (ten dollars for the first card, five dollars for each additional card). There was a list of towing companies on duty for the month, and another list of bail bondsmen with their telephone numbers. A card leaning against the window said NO VISITING WITH PRISONERS. Someone had added another sign next to it as an afterthought: THANK YOU. I didn't know if Grady was considered a prisoner, but I intended to talk with him no matter what.

"Aunt Jessica, I don't feel so well," Donna said, slumping against my side. She had been very brave when Detective Chesny told us that Grady had been taken in for questioning, and had managed not to break down when she'd handed the detective a photo of Frank to be distributed to officers searching for him. And she'd held it together when Chesny had allowed us to leave, and while she drove us from the office building where the commercials were being filmed to the police headquarters. But the stress of a missing child, and a husband in custody, were taking their toll on her. One look told me her nerves were frayed, her muscles knotted, and her stomach was churning.

"Let's get you sitting down over here, Donna," I said, assisting her to a line of plastic chairs bolted to the wall. "Do you need some water?"

She slumped in the seat. "I think I have a bottle in my bag."

"Are you dizzy? Put your head between your knees." I found the water bottle in her shoulder bag, opened it, and pressed it into her hand. "Here, just take a few sips. You should feel better in a minute. This is a lot to handle in one day."

I sat beside her and rubbed her back until she was able to sit up. Her face was very pale.

"Oh, Aunt Jessica, what are we going to do?"

"Now, listen to me, Donna Mayberry Fletcher. We're going to make a plan right now, that's what we're going to do. I don't know if Grady will be able to leave with us tonight, but if not, we'll go back to the apartment right away. We have a lot to do. We may need to call a lawyer for Grady. But most important, we should call the news media to put the word out about Frank. We'll get everyone in New York looking for him."

"If someone found him, they could be calling the apartment right now," Donna said, her voice shaking, "and I'm not home to answer the phone."

"But didn't you give the police your cell phone number?" I asked.

"I did, but what if it isn't the police who call? What if whoever took Frank calls w-with ransom demands, and we're not there?"

"Let's not assume the worst," I said. "Frank is going to be fine. I'm sure of it."

"But there was a murder."

"That may have nothing to do with Frank."

"Do you really think so?"

I didn't, but she needed me to be confident, and I needed to feel that way, too. "Frank is such a curious child," I said. "It's possible he just lost his way. It's a big building, and there must be lots of corridors. He could have wandered down the wrong hall and not been able to find his way back. The police could call at any minute to say they've found him."

"But what if the police don't call me? What if they call the apartment instead? We might not hear the message for hours."

"Is there someone in your building who has a key to your apartment?"

"Mary does. She's Michele's mother. You haven't met her. She's very nice. We've become good friends. She's been such a big help to me in learning the neighborhood. There's so much to know when you move someplace new. She's the one who showed me where the nearest bookstore is, and told me which grocery has the fairest prices, and where to find a good hairdresser, and which cafés don't chase you out in twenty minutes if you only order a cup of coffee. Did I tell you how the boys met? It was in the laundry room." She stopped. "I'm babbling, aren't I?"

"That's all right," I said. "You have a lot on your mind. Are you feeling a little better?"

She nodded.

"Why don't you sit here and give Mary a call. Tell her what's happening, as much as you want her to know, and find out if she would be willing to wait in the apartment until we get back. And ask her to answer the phone in case someone calls, and to write down any messages."

With a task to accomplish, Donna took a deep breath to steady herself, and dialed.

I went back to the glass window and waited while the police officers answered phone calls and conferred across the room. Eventually, a uniformed officer came to the window. "May I help you?" he said. Even though there was a small opening at the base of the window used for passing papers back and forth, I was barely able to hear his voice through the thick glass.

"Yes. I understand my nephew, Grady Fletcher, was brought in this evening for questioning. Detective Chesny told me I might find him here."

"Who?"

"Detective Chesny."

"You're looking for Pressley?"

"No," I said, "it's Chesny. C-H-E-S-N-Y."

The officer fumbled with an intercom button. "Did you say Chesny?" he asked. The intercom made his voice sound tinny, but at least it was audible.

"Yes."

"He's out on a case."

"I know. He sent me here. I'm Jessica Fletcher. My grandnephew, Frank, is missing and his father, Grady Fletcher, was brought in for questioning."

"What was it, a custody battle?"

"No, Officer. I'm sorry if I didn't make myself clear. Detective Chesny said he has his officers out searching for Frank." I wasn't going to raise the issue of the all points bulletin. "We need to speak with Grady. That's his wife over there." I gestured toward the seats. "Do you know how long he'll be here?"

"Are you his lawyer?"

"No. I'm his aunt. Why would he need a lawyer? Has he been charged?"

"I have no idea, lady. I've been working in here all night."

"Then may I see him?"

He pointed to the sign that said NO VISITING WITH PRISONERS.

"But he's not a prisoner," I said. "He's only being questioned."

"If we're holding him, it's as good as. Does he have a lawyer?"

"Does he need one?"

"If you have to ask, he needs one. Do you want a list of local lawyers?"

"No, thank you. I'm sure he'll have someone he wants me to call. How can I speak with him?"

"You can't."

"But, Officer, a child is missing." I lowered my voice so as not to upset Donna even more. "He may have been kidnapped. It's urgent that I speak with the child's father."

"Do you want to complete a missing-persons report?"

"Yes, of course, but is that really necessary if you already have the police looking for him?" I had the feeling he was trying to put me off by having me fill out forms. "If I can speak with my nephew for just a few minutes."

"Sorry, lady, no can do." He pointed to the sign again.

I straightened up and tugged at the hem of my jacket. "Then may I speak with the watch commander?" I was going over his head.

"He's going to tell you the same thing."

"I'd still like to speak with the watch commander, please."

"Okay. Wait over there." He pointed to where Donna sat.

"Did you reach Mary yet?" I asked when I took the chair next to hers.

"Yes," Donna said, dabbing at her eyes with a tissue. "She said she'd go downstairs right away. Are they bringing Grady out?"

"Not yet," I said. "I've asked to speak with the watch commander, and—"

The door swung open and the man in question stepped into the foyer. "Mrs. Fletcher?"

"Yes," Donna and I said together.

"Which one of you is Mrs. Fletcher?"

"We both are," I said, standing and extending my hand.

He shook it warily.

"I'm Jessica Fletcher, and this is my niece Donna Mayberry Fletcher."

"I'm Commander Willoughby. What can I do for you?"

"You see, Commander, we were over at the office building where the commercials were being filmed and we had my grandnephew, Frank, with us—he's this Mrs. Fletcher's son. He's only nine years old and he's missing—and he was watching one of the commercials, but when we went to find him, he wasn't there. And then when his father and I were searching for him, we came upon the body. And the detective said the police brought him here. And now we really need to speak with him—"

"Okay, ladies, come into my office and give this to me

in little pieces." He pulled out a magnetic card and held it up to a box on the side of the door. We heard a click, and he pulled open the door and ushered us into his office.

We spent the next ten minutes explaining the situation to him. Thankfully, at the end of my story, he agreed to let us have five minutes with Grady in an interview room.

"There will be two officers in there with you," he said. "It's routine. You'll have to leave your handbags in here. They'll be safe. I'll lock the door."

We quickly agreed, and Commander Willoughby took us to an empty office where he asked us to wait. Donna paced back and forth in the small space, while I made an effort not to look at my watch. Frank had been missing for more than two hours. It was dark outside. If we didn't find him soon, he would spend the night alone, or so I fervently hoped. It was worse to think of him in the hands of a kidnapper—or killer. How long would it be before we found him? How many hours? I couldn't bear to think it might be days. When he was a baby, Frank had been afraid of the dark. Was he still? It was not a question I would ask Donna.

The door to the office opened and two uniformed officers brought Grady into the room. His wrists were handcuffed behind him. Donna rushed to him and threw her arms around his neck. The officers stepped back and stood at either side of the door, but didn't move to unlock the cuffs.

"Oh, sweetheart," he said, but he couldn't hold her with his hands tied. "Did you find him?" His eyes sought mine over Donna's shoulder.

I shook my head, and he dropped his face into Donna's neck.

Donna stepped back and put her hands on Grady's cheeks. "We'll find him, Grady. I know we will. Are you okay?" She kissed him gently.

"I won't be okay until we find Frank. You were right, Aunt Jess. I never should have let him go off by himself. He didn't need to see another commercial being made." He looked at his wife. "It's all my fault, Donna. I should have taken him home after the lights fell down. I never should have let him convince me to stay. It's all my fault. And now he's gone. I'll never forgive myself."

"Grady Fletcher," Donna said sternly, "I don't want to hear you talk like that. Of course we'll find Frank. I'm sure of it. You did nothing wrong, you hear? You're a loving father. You are not to blame. And you know how Frank can wheedle us to get what he wants."

They gave each other a small smile.

"We're going to find him," Donna continued. "You'll see." Her voice dropped to a whisper. She glanced at the two policemen guarding the door. "Will you be able to come home with us tonight?" she asked in a small voice.

Grady shook his head "I don't think so."

"How long do you have to stay?" Donna asked, deflated.

"I wish I knew."

"Why are they holding you, Grady?" I asked. "What did they say?"

"They said I had motive and means. Some of the crew had told them about Betsy's meltdown. They think I killed her in retaliation for her attack on Frank. It's stupid. I wouldn't do that. But they think I did. And there's another problem."

"What's that, Grady?" Donna asked.

"My fingerprints are on that nail gun."

"We'll get you a lawyer and I'm sure you'll be out by tomorrow," I said. "Is there someone specific you want us to call?"

"We don't really know any criminal lawyers," Donna said.

"We can find one," I said. "And I know who to call for recommendations."

"If they ask for bail, we'll have to take the money out of our savings account," Grady told Donna.

"We used up most of the money to buy the apartment. How much do you think it will be?"

"I don't know, sweetheart."

"But, Grady, what if we don't have enough?"

"Don't worry about the bail," he said. "Look, I'm not the important one here. Frank is the only thing that matters. Even if I can't leave here, you've got to keep looking. Are the police still searching for him?"

I told Grady the police had Frank's photograph and were scouring the building and the surrounding area. I didn't use the initials APB. I didn't want to upset him even more. An APB is issued when the police are looking for a suspect in a crime. I didn't know if Grady knew that, but I wasn't taking the chance. He had enough to lose sleep about without worrying that the police might suspect Frank of murder.

"Aunt Jessica suggested we go to the news media and have them put Frank's picture on television and in the papers," Donna told him.

"You think that would work?"

"It was my idea," I said, "but I think I'd like to run it past Detective Chesny before we do anything. The police are the experts in missing children. If someone took Frank, we don't want to do anything to aggravate a kidnapper."

Donna looked at me accusingly. "You said you thought he was lost," she said.

"I'm hoping he's lost," I said. "But I don't want to rule out any possibility."

"How can we know for sure?"

"We can't," I said. "The critical thing is for us to get Frank back safe and sound."

"Don't get upset with Aunt Jess, sweetheart," Grady said. "She's doing her best for us, and there's no one better to look for Frank." He looked at me. "Please find Frank for us, Aunt Jess. I'm counting on you. I know you won't let us down."

"I'll do everything in my power," I said.

Chapter Thirteen

Detective Chesny was coming into the station house as Donna and I were exiting. Donna went to get the car, which she'd parked a few blocks away, and I took the opportunity to question Chesny about whether it was prudent to give the media Frank's picture. And if so, which media? I reminded myself that while Frank lived in New York City, we had been filming in its outer reaches. We would need to alert media in both places, since we had no idea in which direction a potential kidnapper might have taken him.

Chesny didn't think the timing was right. "I recommend you hold off for a day," he said. "If the boy *was* kidnapped, seeing his face in the paper might spook whoever took him. And I have to tell you, there are crazies in this world who would call the posted number just to give you a hard time, to tease you. Wait a day. Let's see if he shows up, or if you get any ransom calls. If not, we can revisit the idea of distributing his picture to the press."

I was glad Donna was not with me when I asked the detective, "If Frank witnessed a murder, would his kidnapper, presumably the killer, make a ransom call?"

"Probably not," he said. "But I think it's more likely the kid is hiding."

"Is that your professional opinion?"

"It is, Mrs. Fletcher. If he finds his way out of the building, we have every available cop looking for him. I know you're worried about Frank, but I'm sure he's fine."

"How can you be so sure?" I asked. "Can you guarantee that he hasn't been kidnapped?"

"You know I can't."

"Then why not issue an Amber Alert, or at least put Frank's picture where the public can see it?"

"Mrs. Fletcher, I told you before, the law is very specific about under what circumstances an Amber Alert can be distributed."

"But a child is missing. A nine-year-old. Isn't there anything else you can do?"

He heaved a great sigh. "I tell you what. I'll call your precinct in Manhattan and arrange to have them monitor and record calls on your niece and nephew's telephone so that if—and I doubt this will happen—so that if any calls from a kidnapper come in, they'll have it on tape and possibly be able to trace it."

Detective Chesny was as good as his word. By the time Donna and I pulled up in front of the building, a police

van was parked outside and a uniformed officer was coming out the front door. For an instant, I thought Frank had
been found. Donna's thoughts echoed mine. Her face immediately brightened, but fell as quickly when we learned
that the officer had just installed a tap on their home
phone. No calls had come in so far.

Mary was in the living room when we came in. She rose
from the sofa and enfolded Donna in a hug. The emotions
that my niece by marriage had held in all evening came
flowing out in Mary's embrace. It was heartbreaking to
hear her sobs. She was under such emotional pressure—
the fears, the mourning for a missing child even though
we held on to our hopes that Frank was still alive, the misery at not having Grady to share the grief, the worry about
her husband's situation, and always, always the terrible
uncertainty of it all.

I put down my bag and went into the kitchen to make
a pot of tea, my panacea for all that ails me, even though
I knew tea would offer little solace to Donna. She needed
some food in her stomach. I put the water up to boil,
searched their refrigerator for something for her to eat,
and made a plate of fruit and cheese and crackers, slic-
ing up the last of the apples I had brought to them. Mary
joined me as I was pouring water into the teapot.

"She's lying down in Frank's room," she said, "holding
on to his teddy bear."

I nodded. "She needs the rest."

"My son is in Donna and Grady's bedroom watching
TV. I hope you don't mind that I brought him down with
me. I didn't tell Michele what's happening, but he knows

something is wrong. He told me he wishes Frank would come home." She fought to hold back the tears.

"Of course I don't mind. I hope he gets his wish—and soon." I carried the food to the table. Mary followed with the teapot and mugs.

"Donna told me everything," Mary said, "about Grady being arrested, and Frank seeing the murder and being kidnapped. It's all so awful. I can't comprehend it."

"I think Donna was communicating her worst fears," I said. "We're not sure yet if Frank saw anything. We only know that we found a pair of earphones he was using in the same room where we found the victim's body. And while it's true that Grady is being held, the good news is that he hasn't been charged with any crime. At least not yet. I have the feeling he's being held more as a person of interest—that's a police term—than as a definite suspect."

"That's a relief."

"Yes, it is. However, I have to find a lawyer for him, and it's been a few years since I lived here in the city."

"My husband is traveling right now, but when I speak with him later tonight, I'll ask if he knows a good one."

"Thank you, and I'll be making a few calls myself. My agent or publisher will certainly be of help. I'll use my cell phone so I don't tie up Donna and Grady's line."

"Is there anything more I can do for you or Donna or Grady? Would you like me to stay the night? It's not a problem. We can bring down sleeping bags."

"That's kind of you, but it's not necessary. I'll stay here until Grady gets home, and however long they need me after that. I have a friend at my hotel who can pack up my belongings and send them down here."

"Why don't I get Michele and give you a little privacy to make your calls. Donna has my phone number, but I'll write it down for you in case she's sleeping and you need me. We're only upstairs. I don't plan on going anywhere this evening. Please call for any reason, at any hour."

"I certainly will, Mary. Thank you."

She walked down the hall to fetch her son, and I placed two quick phone calls. One was to Cookie, who was probably out to dinner; I left her a voice message asking that she send my things to Grady's apartment. The other was to the Waldorf's front desk, informing them that I would be checking out, and requesting that someone give their guest Stella Bedford the key to my room when she returned this evening.

Michele covered up a yawn with one hand as he followed his mother into the living room; the other hand held his walkie-talkie, which was making loud static noises. My thoughts flew again to Frank—they were never very far from him—and I knew he must be tired, too. Michele would get to sleep in his own bed that night, but where would Frank sleep?

Donna wandered in from Frank's room, red-eyed and exhausted. "I can't lie still," she said. "My mind is just a jumble of thoughts. Are you leaving, Mary?"

"I was, but I'll come back any time you ask."

"You've done more than enough. Thank you so much." She placed a hand on Michele's shoulder. "How are you, Michele? You're Frank's best friend. Do you know that?"

"We go to the zoo when my father is home," Michele said. "Frank wants to see the *elefante*, and I want to see the *leone marino*."

"That's the sea lion," Mary said, smiling softly at her son.

Donna's eyes met mine. She dropped her hand. "That's nice, Michele," she said. "I'm sure the two of you will have a wonderful time." There was a hitch in her voice.

"I went once to the zoo," Michele said. "I tell Frank, he will like the *elefante*."

The static sounded on his walkie-talkie, drowning out his last words. Mary leaned toward her son. "Why don't you turn that off now? We're going upstairs for dinner."

Michele held up the walkie-talkie and shook his head, but on Mary's insistence, he turned the knob, stopping the sound of the static.

"We'll see you later," Mary said.

Donna walked them to the door. I watched as they stepped into the hall. Something was bothering me, but what was it?

"Wait!" I said, rushing to stop them before they left. "Mary, would you come back inside for a moment, please."

They returned to the living room and Donna closed the door. "Aunt Jessica? What is it?"

I put my hands on Michele's shoulders and looked earnestly into his eyes. "Michele, did you speak to Frank on his walkie-talkie today?" I asked.

Michele shrugged one shoulder and shook his head.

"Why do you ask, Aunt Jessica?" Donna put her hand

on my arm. "Frank didn't have his walkie-talkie with him today. I told him not to take it. I was afraid it would get lost."

"Do you know where it is?" I asked.

"Yes. I put it in the top drawer of his dresser." She walked quickly to Frank's room and I heard the drawer being opened. "Here it . . . no, it's not here."

I smoothed down my hair and cocked my head at her. Obviously, Frank didn't always listen to his mother. "Frank mentioned that he had it with him when I saw him this morning," I said. "I didn't see it, but it must have been in his pocket."

"His pockets are always full," she said, the second smile I'd seen that day making a fleeting appearance on her lips. "I have to be careful when I do the laundry to make sure he's emptied them."

I turned back to Michele. "Do you think Frank keeps his walkie-talkie on, like you do?"

He shrugged again and looked over his shoulder to his mother.

"You can answer Mrs. Fletcher, Michele."

But he looked at me with a worried expression and was silent.

"What are you thinking, Aunt Jessica?"

It was a long shot. After all, Frank was probably still somewhere outside the city. But a long shot is better than no shot at all. And Grady had said the walkie-talkies were long-range. Just how long-range I didn't know. "Michele, is Frank your good friend?" I asked.

He nodded.

"Would you do a big favor for him? Would you turn on the walkie-talkie again?"

Michele looked to his mother for approval.

"Go ahead," she said.

He twisted the dial until the sound of static filled the room again. "Please try to call Frank now," I said over the noise.

Michele shook his head.

"Michele," his mother said cajolingly, "please do what Mrs. Fletcher asks."

Michele shook his head and pointed toward the master bedroom.

Mary looked at me apologetically. "I'm sorry, Jessica."

"That's all right," I said, my eyes never leaving Michele. "Does the walkie-talkie work better in the bedroom?" I asked him.

There was a small nod and a smile.

"May we try it in there?"

Michele twirled around and skipped down the hall to the bedroom. He sat on the end of the bed and twisted the volume button to high. "Station two to station one. Come in."

There was a blast of static and then nothing. Michele pursed his lips, then moved to the window. He leaned on the windowsill and tried again. "Station two to station one. Come in, *per favore.*"

More static and then a tiny voice came through. "Station one to station two, I hear you."

Donna gasped. "Is it Frank?" she whispered.

"May I?" I asked Michele, putting out my hand for the walkie-talkie.

He hesitated, tipped his head to the side, his eyes on mine, smiled, and handed it to me.

I pressed the button to talk. "Station one, this is Aunt Jessica. Is that you, Frank?"

"You have to say 'come in' or he won't answer," Michele instructed.

"Oh. Thank you." I tried again. "Station one, this is Aunt Jessica. Is that you, Frank? Come in, please."

The tiny voice was marred by static, but I heard, "This is station one. Hi, Aunt Jessica."

Chapter Fourteen

Donna's hands were trembling when she took the walkie-talkie from me. "Frank, are you all right?" she asked, tears streaming down her cheeks as she fumbled with the talk button. "Can you hear me, Frank? Are you all right?"

"I'm okay, but are you coming to get me soon? I'm hungry."

"Y-y-es, sweetheart. As soon as we can," she said, wiping away the tears. "But we don't know where you are. Can you tell me where you are, Frank?"

"I don't know, Mom. You sound funny. Can I talk to Dad?"

"He's not here right now, sweetheart," Donna said, sniffling. She looked at me. "He doesn't know where he is. How can we find him?"

"May I talk with him again?" I asked.

"Aunt Jessica wants to talk to you, Frank. Hold on." She handed the instrument back to me. "How are we going to find him?" she whispered to herself again. "He doesn't know where he is. We have to find him."

"Frank, this is Aunt Jessica again. If you can't tell us where you are, tell me what you can see."

"Nothing, Aunt Jessica. It's dark and I can't see out the window."

"But you have a window where you are?"

"Yes, but it's on the other side and I can't get to it."

"What's keeping you from getting to the window?" I asked, fearful he would say that his hands were tied.

"There's a bunch of boxes and stuff, and I'm stuck behind them."

"Are you in a storeroom?" I asked, thinking that if he was still in the office building, I would get Detective Chesny back to the location as soon as possible.

"No! I'm in a truck."

"A truck!" Donna and Mary and I said at the same time.

Michele, who was sitting on the edge of the bed, bounced up and down gleefully. "He's in a truck," he said, laughing.

"Is anyone with you?" I asked.

There was a pulse of static; then I heard, ". . . left."

"Who left, Frank? Who was with you before?"

More static. ". . . icky."

"Was that Ricky? Did you say Ricky?"

"Yeah, he's . . . rip."

I remembered that Frank had told us about the grip,

Ricky, the carpenter, the one who let him use his nail gun. Was Ricky the murderer? Had he kidnapped my grandnephew?

"Did Ricky take you with him when he left?"

"Not exactly."

"What do you mean by 'not exactly'?"

"I was helping . . ." The static was getting louder and Frank's voice was fading.

"Frank, can you still hear me?"

I couldn't make out what he said.

"The battery must be going," I said to Donna. I tried pushing the call button again. "Frank, if you can hear me, we'll be there as soon as we can."

The static stopped. Michele's walkie-talkie was dead.

"Oh, no," Donna gasped.

"We can charge the battery," Mary said. "I have the charger upstairs. In the meantime, he sounds fine, Donna." She wound her arm around Donna's shoulder. "Just remember, he's all right. He's safe, he's sheltered. Nothing can hurt him. That's the important thing. We'll find him."

"But how?" Donna looked at me imploringly. "Aunt Jessica? We don't even know this Ricky's last name. And where is this truck? What if we can't find him? Frank will starve."

Michele groaned. Mary released Donna and knelt down in front of her son. "No, Michele," she said, taking his hands. "It's okay. Donna didn't mean that. Frank is fine. You heard him. We're going to find him. And we'll give him a big dinner."

"I'm sorry, Michele," Donna said. "I didn't mean to alarm you."

"Speaking of dinner," I said, addressing Michele, "we've kept you from yours. Why don't you go upstairs with your mother and have your dinner, and we'll call you as soon as Frank is home. And thank you, Michele. It was your walkie-talkie that will help us find Frank. You're a real hero."

Michele gave me a big grin. "I'm glad Frank is coming home."

"Me, too," I said.

After Mary and Michele left, Donna and I sat at the dining table, the telephone in front of us.

"We have to let Grady know," Donna said. "And I want Frank back here tonight. Can we do it?" Her tears had dried, and a fierce resolve had taken the place of her earlier misery.

"Why don't you call Detective Chesny?" I said. "Tell him what we know, and ask if he'll get word to Grady. Maybe he'll have some suggestions on what we should do next."

Donna rose from the table. "I'll take my cell phone into the bedroom so I don't disturb you. Who are you going to call?"

"I'm going to find out where this truck is," I said, opening my bag and pulling out the Eye Screen folder I'd been given for the shoot.

Donna bent down and gave me a kiss on the cheek. "You're the best, Aunt Jessica. Brilliant. I don't know what we'd do without you. I'd never have thought to try the walkie-talkies."

"It was a lucky break."

"I don't believe in luck. It's you. You're wonderful."

"You can tell me that when Frank is tucked in his bed," I said. "Go on. Make your call. We have a boy to find."

The bars on my cell phone were low. I attached it to its charger, which I plugged into an outlet in the kitchen. We might need it later, and I wanted to be sure it wouldn't run out of juice, as Michele's walkie-talkie had.

The call sheet I had examined so closely the night before held all the information I needed, the names and phone numbers of the crew. I ran my finger down the categories on the left until I found the names of the grips, and dialed the number for Richard Pepper, the only name I figured might be "Ricky." His voice mail answered, and I left a message telling him it was urgent that he return the call. I gave him Donna and Grady's number as well as that of my cell phone. Next, I looked under the EQUIPMENT section for the name of the company that provided the grip supplies. It was after business hours, but an answering service picked up. Again, I left my message and numbers, and requested an immediate return call.

I checked my watch. At this time of night it was going to be difficult to get in touch with anyone, but I intended to keep trying until I found a person who could help us locate the truck Frank was in. My next call was to Jennifer, the production manager I'd met that morning. Susan had said the production office was the nervous system that kept everything running. I figured Jennifer would know how to track down the truck if anyone would.

"Hello. This better be important. I'm right in the middle of dinner."

"Hello, Jennifer. It's Jessica Fletcher. We met this morning. I'm sorry to interrupt your meal."

"Oh, hi, Mrs. Fletcher. My apologies for the rudeness. Someone from the office is always calling me the second I lift my fork. What can I do for you?"

I explained the situation, that I believed Frank was locked in a grip truck and that we didn't know where the truck was parked.

"How did he get in the truck?"

I took a guess based on my brief talk with Frank over the walkie-talkie. "I think he may have been helping someone."

"Poor kid, he must be scared silly."

"He will be if we don't rescue him soon."

"That guy's in real trouble," she said.

"Who is?"

"Whoever he was helping. It's against union rules for anyone to load the truck except a member of the Teamsters, never mind a kid. Our insurance doesn't cover that. Let me make some calls and I'll get back to you."

I scoured the call sheet to see if there was anyone else who could help us find Frank. I debated calling Kevin Prendergast. He probably wouldn't know where the truck was parked, but he could put a fire under his employees to find out.

I was about to pick up the phone again when it rang, startling me. Evidently, I was jumpier than I let on. I picked up the receiver.

"All the trucks are in a secure lot on the West Side," Jennifer said without preamble. "If there's a watchman, he may have the keys, but I'll keep making calls to make sure. In the meantime, here's the address."

Donna, who'd hurried into the room at the sound of the phone, hovered over my shoulder while I jotted down the information. I told Jennifer to call back on my cell if she needed to reach me again.

We didn't bother with the car, which Donna had put in their garage, but hailed the first cab we saw and gave the driver the address of the parking lot. We held hands as the taxi raced across town. We passed busy neighborhoods with tall buildings, and many people on the streets, shopping, sitting in cafés, leaving a movie theater. Farther on, the buildings grew lower, and fewer people were about, a man walking a dog, a couple hurrying home. At last, we entered a part of the city with long, low buildings with walls of brick devoid of any windows, and empty lots surrounded by chain-link fences with rolls of razor wire on the top. A car dealership on the corner was lit up like a carnival with plastic flags fluttering in the wind. No one was on the street.

The cab pulled up to the address we'd provided, a concrete wall with a steel-bar fence across the only opening. A security booth was vacant and unlit. An empty police car blocked the driveway, its red light flashing and car radio blaring. The cab pulled up in back of the cruiser. We paid the driver, asked him to wait, and got out.

"Mrs. Fletcher?"

Donna and I both turned. A young policeman carrying a nightstick walked toward us.

"My partner went around back to see if he could get inside," he said. "The station is looking up the owner of the lot."

"Thank you, Officer."

"How did he know where to come?" Donna whispered to me.

"The police were tapping your phone," I said. "They must have overheard my conversation with the production manager."

We could see the vehicles in the lot through the gate. There must have been thirty of them, from small panel trucks to what looked like huge moving vans. This was not going to be easy.

The second officer turned the corner and walked toward us, swinging a large flashlight. "There's no access from the back," he called out. "The lot adjoins a building. This is it. We've got to get in here."

"I got an idea," his partner replied. He opened the trunk and pulled out a bullhorn. "What's your son's name again, lady?"

"Frank," Donna replied. "Frank Fletcher."

The policeman raised the bullhorn to his mouth and flipped the switch. "FRANK FLETCHER!" The sound was so loud, Donna and I jumped. "THE POLICE ARE HERE TO RESCUE YOU. WE'LL GIVE YOU INSTRUCTIONS IN A MINUTE. YOU HANG IN THERE AND WE'LL TELL YOU WHAT TO DO."

"What the heck is goin' on here?" An old man, his trousers unzipped and his flannel shirt hanging open over a T-shirt, climbed from a town car parked inside the lot. What hair he had must usually be combed over his pate; now it stood straight up from his scalp.

The policeman with the flashlight aimed its beam at his face. "Ain't you supposed to be on duty, old man?"

"Just takin' a little nap. What's the harm in that?" He smoothed his hand over his head.

"You're supposed to be guarding this place, not napping," the officer with the bullhorn said. "Come on. Open up." He banged his nightstick against the metal fence.

"Hold your horses. I'm coming." The old man zipped himself up, limped to the security booth, hoisted himself inside, and pressed the control for the steel gate. It rose up with a groan, the chains wrapped around the pulleys squealing in the silent night.

"That sound could wake the dead," Donna said to me, hands covering her ears.

The officer handed something to his partner, who went off into the darkness behind the first row of trucks.

The second officer approached. "Ladies, I'd appreciate it if you waited here. We may have to move some of the trucks if we can't find him right away, and I don't want to accidentally run anyone over."

"How are you going to look for him?" I asked.

The officer showed me what was in his hand. It was a doctor's stethoscope.

"What's that for?" Donna asked.

"We're going to knock on each of the trucks, and then put these up to the side and listen. I'm going to tell Frank to wait till he hears a knock on the truck he's in. Then he has to yell and scream and bang on anything he can, anything to make lots of noise. We should be able to hear him with two pairs of these."

I chuckled. "That's certainly clever."

He smiled. "When you're a cop, you learn how to jury-rig what you need. This is relatively high-tech for the department."

The police started with the back row of trucks, giving Frank instructions through the bullhorn and working from the outside in, hammering on the side of a vehicle and then listening. The work created its own tempo like a cacophonous piece of music: bullhorn voice, ten seconds of loud banging, and twenty seconds of silence. At each silent break, Donna and I would hold our breath, straining to hear an answering sound. At last, when one of them reached a blue panel truck with a picture of movie lights on the side, the banging yielded a muffled yell. The policemen whooped, "We got him."

Donna and I jumped up and down like kids in a playground, hugging and crying for joy. We ran to the back of the truck, calling out to Frank, while one officer went to find the security guard to see if he had the keys.

"Frank? It's Mom," Donna called out, pressing her ear to the side of the truck. "Aunt Jessica and I are here, sweetheart. Be a little patient and we'll get you out."

I heard Frank's voice answer from the inside. "Okay, Mom."

"We can break into the truck if we have to." The policeman with us patted the seam where the truck's rear doors met. "We've got crowbars. But we'd like to do as little damage as possible. Here he comes."

The second officer returned with the guard. His shirttail flapped in the evening breeze, but his hair was freshly combed. He was fingering through a huge ring of keys. He tried several on the rear-door lock until finding the right one.

"Yay," Frank called out when the doors swung open and night air filled the vehicle.

"Hang on, son. We've got to move some of this equipment before you can climb out."

The five of us worked together to lift out the light stands, C-stands, piles of boxes, and rolls of fabric that had been crammed into the rear of the truck. With equipment scattered around us on the ground, it looked as if we could start our own production right there in the parking lot. Eventually, enough space was cleared for the officers to climb aboard and joggle around the large carts that had been loaded first, carts similar to the one Grady and I had found pressed against Betsy Archibald's body. I shivered at the memory. But the thought flew from my mind when I saw Frank, a wide grin splitting his face. He was grimy and disheveled, and there were dark circles under his eyes to match his mother's, but he was ebullient. "Yay! Yay! You rescued me." He hopped to the edge of the truck bed. Donna put her arms up and he jumped into them, his weight carrying them both to the ground, giggling.

"You okay, lady?" One of the policemen offered his hand to help her up.

"Couldn't be better," Donna said, getting to her feet and brushing herself off, all the while hanging on to her son. "Thank you so much, Officers. You've been wonderful."

"Hi, Aunt Jessica," Frank said, grinning up at me from his mother's arms.

"Hi, yourself, Frank. You gave us quite a scare."

"I knew you'd find me. I just knew it."

"You did?" Donna said, releasing him but keeping a hand on his shoulder.

"Sure. But you took a long time. I got hungry. I found a Snickers in my pocket. I ate it for supper. Is that okay?" He looked to his mother for approval.

She just nodded and smiled. "We'll get you a big dinner when we get home."

Frank's smile died away, and his brow was knit when he turned to me. "I lost my good earphones, Aunt Jessica, the red ones. It's such a bummer. I looked everywhere, but I couldn't find them. That's how I got stuck on the truck. I thought I dropped them and I was looking for them when Ricky locked the door and then the truck took off."

"Your dad found your earphones."

"He did? Awesome! That is totally cool. Where?"

"In the carpenter's room. What were you doing in there?" I asked.

"You should have seen how much stuff they had in there, Aunt Jessica. Ricky said it was weird. He'd never seen it so full. I was helping him take some of it out to the trucks."

"Weren't you supposed to meet me and your father on the set where the shooting was taking place?"

"I would've, but I got locked in. I couldn't help it. I was yelling and screaming, but the guy had his music on so loud, he didn't hear me."

Frank's elation at being rescued was beginning to fade

away as he realized he might be in trouble for disobeying his father.

"Why didn't you use *your* walkie-talkie to call Michele?" Donna asked him.

"I forgot I even had it," he replied. "I guess I was too scared to remember anything." He glanced at his mother. "Anyway, I knew you would find me, so I just put on my iPod and waited." He dug into his pants pocket and pulled out the little device, raising his fist so we could see it, and dropping several other items at the same time. "Michele and I put in Aerosmith and Train and other stuff, so I had a lot to listen to." He retrieved the torn package from the Snickers bar that had fallen on the pavement, and pushed it back into his pocket with the iPod.

I bent down to scoop up another item that Frank had dropped. "What's this?" I asked.

"I found it on the floor."

"*Where* did you find it?"

"In the carpenter's room. Ricky and I were rolling stuff out to the trucks and I found it on the side of the room." He turned to Donna. "That must be when I lost my earphones. I thought I dropped them in the truck and I was crawling around on the floor in there trying to find them. That's when Ricky locked the door and—"

"Yes, dear. You told us that," Donna said, drawing him to her and patting him on the back.

Frank buried his face in his mother's shoulder. "I'm glad you finally came."

"Me, too," Donna said, kissing the top of his head.

"Can we go home now?"

I decided it was not the time to question Frank. He and his parents had been through a lot. We needed to get him home, fed, and to bed, and most of all we needed to call the police station to get word to Grady that Frank was alive and well—and home. Tomorrow was another day. Tomorrow would be soon enough to ask Frank to tell his story again.

I opened my fist and looked down at what he had dropped when he pulled the iPod from his pocket. It was a ring with a large black opal.

It was Anne Tripper's ring.

How did it get in the carpenter's room?

I didn't know, but now that Frank was safe at home again, I was determined to find out.

Chapter Fifteen

Grady, of course, was thrilled at the news that Frank was safe and sound. His news was good, too. He'd engaged a local lawyer with whose help he had convinced the police that he wasn't a flight risk. Grady had promised that he wouldn't leave the country, and the police had agreed to release him without bail the following day.

"I don't even want to leave the apartment," he told us. "And I'm not sure if I'm kidding."

"What time can we pick you up?" Donna asked. She was on the phone in the bedroom and I listened on the extension in the kitchen.

"I'll have to wait for Detective Chesny to get here, and then fill out some paperwork. If you get here by ten or eleven, that should be fine. Chesny wants to talk to Frank. It's okay with me if it's okay with you."

"What do you think, Aunt Jessica?" Donna asked.

"As long as he agrees to have you sitting with him during the interview."

"I can't wait for you to be home," Donna said, brushing away a tear, "to have the family together again. We'll see you tomorrow."

Earlier Donna had called Mary from the cab on the ride home from the lot where the police had rescued Frank from the truck. She'd left the number for Detective Chesny on her bedroom night table, so that call had to wait. Once back in the apartment—and after thankfully being allowed to speak with Grady to tell him the news of Frank's rescue—we fielded the callbacks from the messages we'd left earlier. Ricky Pepper was extremely apologetic. He thought Frank had already gone back inside the building when he'd locked up the truck.

"Please tell the little guy I'm really sorry this happened. He was a great helper. I'm glad he's safe at home."

We called Jennifer, who was thrilled that Frank was found, and we told the trucking company that the crisis was over.

We didn't explain to Frank the real reason why Grady wasn't there—we simply said his father had some business to attend to.

Frank was so exhausted he didn't question our explanation. Donna made him his favorite dish for dinner, macaroni and cheese. Halfway through the meal, Frank nodded off at the table. We got him into pajamas, and after a quick brush of the teeth, he fell into bed, asleep before we pulled the covers over him.

After breakfast the next morning, we told Frank about Betsy.

"Do you think God punished her for being mean to me?" Frank asked.

He was sitting on the sofa, his chin on his chest, legs dangling, feet several inches off the floor. Donna perched next to him, her back very straight. I sat across from them in an armchair.

"No. I'm sure not," I said. "Everyone has good days and bad days. If God punished all the people who behaved badly, there wouldn't be a lot of people left in the world, would there?"

"I guess not."

"You don't have to worry about that, Frank," I added. "You were not in any way responsible for Betsy's death. I hope you believe me."

Frank's nod was not convincing. He fiddled with the white iPod wire that was hanging from his pants pocket.

Donna put her arm around him. He rested his head on her shoulder, his fingers still busy with the wire. "Even if you were very angry at her for yelling at you," she said, "even if you wished at that moment that she would just drop dead—you know what?—you couldn't make that happen." She gave him a squeeze. "Wishes don't kill. We don't have that power. And it's a good thing, too. What would've happened to me when I grounded you for getting into that fight at school? You were very angry with me then, weren't you?"

Frank smiled, but it faded quickly.

"She wasn't very nice," he said, kicking one sneaker against the front of the sofa, "but I'm sorry she died."

Donna put her hand on his leg. "We are, too, sweetheart."

Frank looked up at her. "Are we going to her funeral?"

"No, dear. She wasn't a friend of ours, and we don't know her family."

"Since we were all in the building where Betsy died," I said, "the police want to ask us a few questions."

Frank sat up straight. "Mom wasn't there."

"That's true," Donna said. "But I'd like to come along to be with you. Is that all right?"

"Well . . . okay. Are those police guys from last night going to be there? They were cool. Will it be like it is on television? Are they going to tape me?"

"I don't think so, Frank," I said, "but you can tell us afterward what you thought of it."

"Awesome! I'm going to tell Michele." He hopped off the sofa.

Donna and I exchanged looks. Frank's upset at Betsy's demise had been short-lived, but I didn't fool myself that we'd heard the last of it. Children often take a while to process new information. We'd keep an eye on him and raise the topic again if he seemed affected by it.

"Do you recognize this object?"

Frank nodded.

"Tell the gentleman what it is, Frank," Donna said.

"It's a ring."

"Is it yours?"

Frank swallowed. "I . . . I found it on the floor in the carpentry room."

"Did you tell anyone you'd found it?"

Frank hesitated, a worried look on his face. Then his eyes brightened. "I told my mom and Aunt Jessica."

"What time was it when you found this ring on the floor of the carpentry room?"

Frank shrugged. "I don't know."

"No idea?"

Frank looked to his father.

"He doesn't wear a watch, Detective Chesny," Grady said.

The interview room was much nicer than ones I'd seen before where there were bare walls and few pieces of furniture, usually nothing more than a desk and a chair, and sometimes a computer. This room was painted a soft blue, and while there were no pictures on the walls, it was furnished like an executive office with comfortable seating, a desk, and a bookcase, the shelves of which held a few law-enforcement magazines. Grady and Donna occupied a sofa with Frank between them. Detective Chesny sat in one of the two chairs opposite them. I sat in the other. Behind him, on the desk, he had an array of items to which he could turn—a lined legal pad, pens, a tape recorder to back up the digital camera affixed to the wall, a paper evidence bag, and Frank's earphones. When we arrived, Donna had given Chesny the ring and explained that Frank had found it, but the detective asked us not to talk about the details until he had a DVD recorder running. He had been very careful in questioning Frank, but it was clear he wasn't sure how to handle a nine-year-old. Grady helped out.

"Frank, did you find the ring after we left the filming of Aunt Jessica's commercial, or before?"

"After."

Grady looked at the detective. "Aunt Jessica's filming was over around six," he said, "so Frank must have found it after that." He addressed Frank again. "Please tell Detective Chesny what the carpentry room looked like when you found the ring."

"Um, they were packing stuff up."

"Who was, Frank?"

"The grips. Ricky and Bob. Ricky was mad that some-one had moved his stuff. He said it wasn't fair for them to have to do all the loading, but Bob said there was more shooting tomorrow—um, today—so they could leave a lot of it in the room."

"And where was the ring?"

"On the floor next to the wall."

"And what did you do when you found it?"

Frank squirmed in his chair. "I was going to show it to Ricky, but he was pulling stuff out of the room to take to the truck and he dropped a clamp, one of those orange things. He asked me if I could get it and I did. I just put the ring in my pocket, and then, um, I guess—" He mumbled something.

"What was that, son?"

"I guess I forgot about it," he said softly, and hung his head.

"That's okay, sport. Detective Chesny will find out whose it is and make sure they get it back."

"I know who it belongs to," I said.

Chesny frowned at me. "You do?"

"Yes. It's Anne Tripper's ring. She was wearing it at the

meeting we had at the advertising agency last week. I didn't see her wearing it yesterday, but it's definitely her ring."

Chesny wrote something on a piece of paper and slipped the ring into a plastic bag. He looked at Frank. "Did you see Miss Archibald or anyone other than Ricky and"—he consulted his notes—"and Bob in the carpentry room?"

Frank shook his head.

"You have to answer, dear," Donna told him. "The tape recorder can't hear when you shake you head."

Frank nodded at his mother. "Um . . . I mean, okay. I mean, what was the question?"

Chesny repeated it.

"Uh-uh. We were the only ones there. We took some stuff from the room next door and then a few things from the carpentry room. And then . . ."

"And then, what?" Chesny asked.

"And then I had to go to the bathroom."

Chesny sighed.

"Frank, did you notice anything unusual in the carpentry room when you were there?" I asked. "Something that was different from the way it was earlier in the day?"

"You mean other than all the stuff that was in it that wasn't there in the morning?"

"Yes. Or anything else you may have noticed. Perhaps you remember something Ricky or Bob said."

"Well, when I got back to the room from the bathroom, I heard them arguing. Ricky was mad that no one had cleaned it up."

"What was supposed to be cleaned?" I asked.

"The floor. Ricky said he always swept it clean before

they packed up for the day. But whoever put the stuff away did a messy job. He was afraid he'd get blamed."

"Certainly someone to talk with," I suggested to Chesny.

"I have my whole team out questioning the crew," he replied, but he wrote Ricky's name on his pad. "Anyone they haven't spoken to yet, they can reach tomorrow. I'm releasing the scene so the production company can finish the shoot."

"You are?"

"We know who we have to talk to. It'll be easier having them all in one place."

"Who do they have left to shoot?" Grady asked me.

"Lance Sevenson, I imagine. He was in the middle of his shoot when we found Betsy. And Cookie never finished doing her commercial." I found it strange that the campaign would continue in the wake of a murder, but when money is at stake, practicality often prevails.

Chesny looked at Frank. "Anything else you can tell me, young man?"

Frank glanced at Grady before shaking his head. "No, sir."

"If you remember anything after you leave here, I want your word that you will report it to me." He handed Frank his business card, and gave another one to Grady.

Frank studied the card carefully before putting it in his pants pocket. "I will," he said solemnly.

Chesny pushed the button to turn off the tape recorder and stood, indicating the questioning of Frank was concluded. "I let them reopen on the condition that they have to have everyone who was there yesterday come back, even if they're not assigned work. And I'll want a list of whoever doesn't show."

"Frank and I were there," Grady said to Detective Chesny, "but I'd rather we didn't bring him back, if it's okay with you. He's missed two days of school already and I'd like his life to get back to normal."

"It's okay, Dad. I don't mind."

Grady put his hand on Frank's shoulder. "I do, son."

"We don't need him there," Chesny said, "but I reserve the right to question him again if I need to, and you as well."

Grady agreed.

As Detective Chesny escorted us out, Frank looked back longingly at the desk. "What about my earphones?" he asked.

"We're going to hang on to them a little longer," the detective replied. "But if you continue to cooperate with us, you'll get them back eventually."

"Awesome!" Frank said.

And on that note, we went home.

Chapter Sixteen

Grady's sigh of relief was audible when he entered the apartment. He and Donna looked exhausted, but happy. Frank couldn't wait to tell Michele how he'd been questioned by the police, and to show him Detective Chesny's business card. I decided to give them some space to process everything that had taken place, and to enjoy being back together as a family.

"Where are you going?" Grady asked as I prepared to leave their apartment.

"Oh, I don't know," I said, not being entirely truthful. "I thought I'd enjoy a stroll around the city, maybe do a little shopping. "Besides, you three have some catching up to do."

"Will you be back for dinner?" Donna asked.

"You go ahead without me," I said. "I may be a little late."

"We'll wait till you get home," Donna said. "You're an important member of this family and it will be wonderful for us to be together after all the upset."

I left the apartment and stood on the sidewalk. It was a little after one.

I'd had a message on my cell from Cookie the night before, telling me she'd arranged for my belongings to be brought to Donna and Grady's apartment from the Waldorf. "Jimbo and I are just devastated," she'd said. "Ah'm prayin' that that precious little boy is found safe and sound. No problem gettin' your clothing over to the apartment, and if there's anything else I can do for you, you just holler, heah? They're planning to start shooting the commercials again day after tomorrow. I know your spot is done—in the can, as I think they say—but Ah'm hoping you'll drop by. Hate to go back home without seeing you again."

That's funny, I thought. She never mentioned Betsy. Perhaps she didn't want to add to my upset about Frank.

I walked to the corner, hailed a cab, and gave the driver the address for Mindbenders. That represented my little white lie to Grady and Donna. The last thing I wanted to do was to go shopping. Now that Frank had been found, I felt compelled to make some rhyme or reason out of Betsy Archibald's murder. I could hear Seth Hazlitt's voice in my head as we drove through the city's clogged streets: *Here you go again, Jessica, pokin' your nose into where it doesn't belong.* He'd be right, of course. I'd given up years ago trying to rationalize my innate need to get to the bottom of things, especially when it involved a murder, to say nothing of my having been at the scene of one. It's in the genes, I suppose, embedded in my DNA.

Mindbenders, the agency at which Betsy had worked as creative director, was housed in a sleek but small building on Hudson Street in Greenwich Village. I wondered whether her death would have caused the agency to close, but that wasn't the case. It was open for business.

I'd become expert at coming up with reasons for, as Seth usually put it, my "snooping." In this case, I convinced myself that I was simply going there to give Kevin Prendergast my condolences. But when I asked for him at the reception desk in the building's lobby, I was told that he was not expected in that afternoon. It was not surprising. Perhaps he knew Betsy's family in Canada—Matt Miller had said she was from Toronto—and had gone to offer his sympathies, or to help arrange for her funeral, which was undoubtedly premature. The medical examiner's office would not have released her body yet, not in an ongoing murder investigation.

I thought about leaving, but when the receptionist turned away to pick up the phone, I took advantage of her distraction to join a group of people waiting for the elevator. I rode it to the third floor and looked out over the white pods, their black-clad office bees pecking away at their black laptops. I walked down the side of the pods, observing their occupants. No one seemed upset, nor did anyone respond to my presence. They were all working with great concentration. Halfway to the conference room where last week's meeting had been held, I spotted what might have been the only sign of mourning. Someone had left a black rose on one of the tables between a sofa and a chair.

I picked up the flower and twirled its stem between my thumb and index finger.

"That's mine!" someone exclaimed.

I looked up. It was the young man whose work Betsy had praised the last time I was there.

"Kip, isn't it?" I said.

"Yes," he said. "I left that rose for Betsy. No one here wants to make a fuss. They all want to go on with business as usual. It's disgusting. They're afraid if they acknowledge that she isn't here any longer, clients will start looking for a new agency."

I sat on the black felt sofa and returned the rose to where Kip had left it. "Business can be very cold," I said. "I barely knew Betsy, but I'm so sorry that she died. You must feel a terrible sense of loss."

"Yeah, I really do. Not that it means anything to them." He glanced over his shoulder at the other people hard at work.

"Sometimes people have difficulty expressing what they feel," I said. "And I imagine Betsy could be stern at times. But you seem to have had a good relationship with her. I wish I'd known her better. Can you tell me a little about her?"

He perched gingerly on the canvas chair. "Sure," he said, swallowing, his Adam's apple prominent in his thin neck. "She wasn't as tough as everyone says she was. She was pretty nice to me."

"No one is ever as bad as people make them out to be," I said. "How long have you worked at Mindbenders?"

"About a year."

"Do you know everyone here?" I indicated the expansive space with my hand.

"It's hard to know everyone. Some people only come in every once in a while. The teams, the ones you work with, those are the people you get to know, but everyone else . . ." He hesitated, then finished, "It's a fairly big agency."

"Did you work directly for Betsy?"

"Heck, no. I'm mean, she's the creative director. She's everyone's boss, everyone on the creative side, at least. Not the account managers. But come to think of it, sometimes she told them what to do, too."

"What is it that you do exactly, Kip?"

"I'm an assistant art director. That's low man on the totem pole. I'm not even up to junior art director yet. But Betsy gave me an opportunity to work on a new business project instead of just doing all the scut work that the art directors don't want to bother with. Of course I have to do that stuff, too. But she was very encouraging."

"Is that what you showed her last week when I was here?" I asked. "Something for a new business project?"

Kip nodded. "You saw that? Actually, it's kind of secret. I'm not supposed to talk about it."

"Not even now?"

He winced. "Yeah, I suppose you're right. No reason to be quiet about it now that Betsy's no longer here. It'll never get used anyway."

"What will never get used?"

"Her logo. I designed a special logo for her."

"Yes, I remember it now. It was very striking, very powerful. Did one of the *A*s stand for 'Archibald'?"

"Right. It's for a new agency she was planning. Like I said, no one was supposed to know about it, real hush-hush." He gave a short snort. "None of it matters now."

"I'd love to see it again," I said.

He went to a wall of file cabinets, unlocked one drawer, and withdrew the board I had seen him showing Betsy. He sat next to me on the sofa and laid it on his lap, carefully lifting the vellum cover sheet. Kip had designed two intertwining letters, capital *A*s, in a scrolling font, and beneath them in small block letters, it said ARCHIBALD ADVERTISING.

"I did another one with three *A*s, in case she wanted to add the word 'agency,' but she liked this one better."

"She was going into business for herself?"

"She never said, but if I had to guess, I'd say yes. It doesn't make much sense for her to create a separate agency within Mindbenders, but sometimes agencies will do that to specialize in something, like digital ads, or public relations, or whatever. But Betsy was, you know, kind of independent."

"Maybe she was planning to buy Mindbenders and change its name."

He sighed. "That would have been so cool. I could've come to work every day and seen my design on the door." He lowered the cover sheet. "I don't think so, but it's a nice idea."

"Why don't you think so? Because she gave the work to you?"

A rueful laugh escaped his lips. "Sure. If she was doing something for Mindbenders, she would have given the project to one of our big-shot art directors, not an assistant like me. Besides, I happen to know there's nothing in the files about it. I looked. Any papers she had on this she took home with her." He stood. "Anyway, thanks for looking at my work. I was pretty proud of it."

"You have a lot of talent, Kip. I'm sure another creative director will notice it, just as Betsy did."

He smiled. "You sound like my mom," he said. "I guess I'd better put this away and get back to work."

"Nice talking with you," I said.

"Same here."

Interesting, I thought as I left the building and looked for another taxi. Was Betsy secretly planning to leave Mindbenders to establish her own advertising agency? I didn't know how the ad business worked, but I couldn't help but wonder whether she intended to woo away clients from Mindbenders. Like Permezzo.

Had that been what Antonio Tedeschi was talking about at lunch yesterday—was it only yesterday?—when he'd muttered to himself that perhaps he shouldn't go with her? By "go with her," had he meant transfer his business to Betsy's new agency?

Betsy wasn't the nicest person I'd ever met. She was short-tempered, hard-driving, and probably manipulative. But would someone kill her just because she was nasty? There had to be something more at work, something in her background perhaps, something not easily seen on the surface—or something like planning to desert Mindbenders and take clients with her.

If Betsy was trying to steal away her current employer's biggest client, that could make some people at Mindbenders very angry. Angry enough to pick up a nail gun and pull the trigger? It was a potential motive.

I consulted the home address I had for Betsy from the package of materials we'd been given for the shoot, and gave it to a cabdriver. It wasn't far from Mindbenders' offices; we were there in less than ten minutes. My driver drew up next to a fire hydrant, the only space unoccupied by a car on the narrow, one-way block.

"I got too much traffic behind me to stop in front of the building," he announced. "They don't give you a break in this city. They press on the horn till you move. Drives me crazy."

"I don't blame you," I said, groping in my bag for my wallet.

"See where that girl is coming out of the building over there?" he said. "That's it."

My gaze followed his pointed finger to the front of a four-story, modern building. It looked to me as though someone had taken an older building in that space and applied a new facade to it, presumably renovating the inside, too. The girl to whom the driver referred was wearing jeans and a pink, zip-front sweatshirt with the hood pulled far forward. All I could see of her head was a pair of over-sized sunglasses, which covered half her face, and a fringe of red hair on her forehead. She jogged down the stairs, her arms wrapped around a manila envelope. I studied her back for a moment as she walked quickly up the block in the other direction.

"Something wrong, lady?"

"Oh, no. I'm sorry. What is it I owe you again?"

"It's right there on the meter."

I settled with the driver and exited the cab, taking a moment to admire the peaceful tree-lined street. The cabbie's complaints about other drivers notwithstanding, this was a quiet section of the city, at least at this time of day.

I walked to Betsy's building and debated with myself about being there. I'd come to New York on other business, and wound up taking part in a commercial for a credit card. That someone had been murdered during the production was tragic, to be sure, but no one had asked for my input. Not that that had ever stopped me before.

I climbed the front steps and perused the names and numbers on the building's directory of residents, finding the name B. ARCHIBALD next to apartment 4A. Because there was only one name, I felt safe in assuming that she lived alone, which meant that no one would be home to answer the buzzer. Instead, I looked in vain for a button for the building's superintendent. As I did, a mailman on his way out opened the door.

"Do you know which apartment is the superintendent's?" I asked.

"One C," he said, and held the door, allowing me to pass him to enter the vestibule.

The door closed with a loud *thunk*, leaving me standing alone on the black-and-white-checkerboard marble floor. A superstitious person might have said that I was meant to be there, that the mailman's timely appearance was a sign that it was all right to pursue Betsy's murderer, and that I was justified in coming here to try to learn more about her. But much as I'd like to believe that divine intervention had enabled me to gain access to the building, I couldn't fool myself. It had simply been a piece of luck. Had the mailman not arrived, I would have pushed a few buttons until someone answered and allowed me to enter.

Apartment 1C was ahead on the right. Across the way were the building's mailboxes, and beyond them an open staircase. The lobby was as sleek and modern as the exterior. I went to the elevator. A handwritten sign was taped to it: OUT OF ORDER UNTIL SIX.

I walked swiftly past the super's apartment and took the stairs, grateful for my regular exercise routine. By the time I arrived at the fourth landing, I was only slightly winded.

My heels echoed off the marble floor as I wandered down the hall, looking for a door marked 4A. I still intended to speak with the super, but first I would see if any of Betsy's neighbors were home and would be willing to share information about her. At the end of the hall, I found 4A, and was surprised to see that the door was slightly ajar. I used my bag to give it a push and it swung inward with a moan.

"She always meant to get that fixed," a voice behind me said.

I swung around to see an old woman standing in the doorway opposite Betsy's.

"My goodness, but you gave me a start," I said.

She had gray curly hair and wore glasses as thick as the bottoms of soda bottles. With one hand, she leaned on a cane. With the other, she tugged at the sleeve of a designer cardigan in a floral pattern of red and yellow. A Hermès scarf was expertly tied at her neck.

"What did Betsy mean to get fixed?" I asked.

"That squeaky door. I told her I always know when she gets home by that sound. Did she want me to know her business that much? She laughed and said she'd get it fixed, but she never did. Did you do that?"

"Did I do what?" I asked.

"Make that mess." She pointed at Betsy's open door with her cane.

I turned to see what she indicated. Someone had turned Betsy's apartment upside down. Clothes were strewn everywhere on the green patterned carpet, drawers left open. Books had been thrown off their shelf. The door to the bedroom was ajar. Through it I could see that the comforter had been stripped back and the mattress was tilted on the bed.

"Was Betsy a messy person?" I asked.

"Just the opposite. As fastidious as they come. Always wiping off the doorknobs, straightening the pictures. Neat as a pin, too. A snappy dresser, they used to say. She was a little thing, but she did like her clothes. Looked like she stepped out of the pages of a high-fashion magazine."

From the way she referred to Betsy in the past tense, I was confident that she already knew Betsy was dead. If I was wrong, I didn't want to be the one to give her the bad news.

She confirmed that she knew before I said anything else. "Cops all over the place here last night," she said, "making a racket. They knocked on every door, asking what we knew about Betsy. She wouldn't have liked it. She liked her privacy."

"Did Betsy's apartment look like this when the police arrived?"

"Nope. I was standing right here like I am talking to you when Mike—that's the super—opened the door and they went into her place. Looked like it always did."

I took a tentative step into Betsy's apartment and her neighbor followed. We stood quietly, looking at the damage someone had done to Betsy's belongings.

"Do you think the police might have done this?" I asked, knowing full well that they hadn't. The police are almost always careful not to disturb a scene containing potential evidence.

"Doubt it. Probably was the other one."

"What other one?"

"The young lady was here before you. Told me she was Betsy's sister and came by to get some things. From what I could see, she had red hair, just like Betsy's, but I didn't believe her. Looks like I was right."

"How did she get in?"

"Had the key."

"Could you give me a description of what this young lady looked like?"

"Couldn't see much, what with those big sunglasses she was wearing. I thought she was a teenager at first. That's how she was dressed."

"Pink hooded sweatshirt?" I asked.

She nodded. "That's the one."

I shook my head. "She was leaving the building as I arrived. I thought something was funny about her, but I couldn't put my finger on it."

"There was something funny about her all right. She was a thief, that's what she was." She cocked her head and squinted at me, and I had the feeling that she was trying to remember what I looked like so she could report it to the police in the event I was a thief, too.

I smiled. "Betsy and I worked together," I said. "We didn't know each other well, but I was part of the production on the location where she was killed."

She hobbled past me into Betsy's apartment. "Can't imagine why someone would do something like this." She used her cane to make an arc in the air. She sniffed. "I gave her this," she said, using her cane to flip over a large floral pillow that had probably been on Betsy's couch. Scattered on the floor beneath it were several books. One of them was a photo album with some of the pictures sticking out from between the pages. I picked it up along with the book underneath it.

The photos that had slid out of the album were pictures of Betsy leaning on a rail overlooking the ocean, obviously on a ship, on a cruise. I pushed them back into place. She looked younger, her red curls a nimbus floating about her face and catching the sunlight. She smiled warmly at the camera. Whoever had taken that photo must have found another passenger to take their picture together, because the next page showed Betsy with her arms around a man whose hair was longer than hers. She didn't mind being touched then, I thought, remembering how she'd avoided shaking hands. Betsy was smiling up into the man's face. It was hard to see what he looked like from his profile, but in another picture, his smile was directed at the camera. It was Kevin Prendergast, the head of Mindbenders.

"Do you know him?" I asked Betsy's neighbor.

"Let me see," she said, putting a hand on the book and squinting at the page. "Can't tell. It's too small. Come with me."

We returned to her apartment. I followed her into a living room decorated by someone who had a love affair with chintz. Flowered fabrics covered every piece of furniture, with more flowers on the carpet, drapes, and throw pillows piled on the sofa. Even several picture frames had been upholstered in the same design. The old woman hooked her cane over the back of a chair as she passed it and limped to a desk in the corner of the room.

"Let me see it again," she said, switching on the desk lamp and taking a silver magnifying glass from a tray.

I laid the photo album on the desk and stepped back. She leaned over the page, placing the glass an inch from the photo, and tipped her head from side to side. "Used to be her boyfriend," she said, tapping the picture with the handle of the magnifying glass. "He threw her over for some blonde. Don't they all? But she couldn't get rid of him altogether. Still sees him at work. Or did, anyway. She said he was going to be sorry. His new girlfriend would dump him once she got what she wanted. A gold digger, I say."

"Has she gone out with anyone since? Someone else you might have met?"

"Nosy one, aren't you?"

"Yes," I replied, smiling.

"Well, I know the type. Some people have called me the same. Guess Betsy won't mind now. Come have a seat." She waved at the sofa. "You want some coffee? I make it good, strong and hot. I'm Clara, by the way. It's actually 'Clara Belle,' but I dropped the 'Belle' when that puppet show was on the TV."

"*Howdy Doody?*" I said.

"That's the one. Didn't want the same name as the clown."

"I don't blame you, Clara. I'm Jessica."

"Have a seat, Jessica. You seem like a nice lady, not a thief. That's good, because I already called the police."

"You did?"

"Yup. Can't have just anyone barging in here like they belong. Besides, that girl lied to me. I don't like liars."

"It sounds like the police are here," I said, becoming conscious of the sound of heavy footsteps rushing up the stairs.

"Took 'em long enough. You could die several times over in New York before the police arrive. 'Course, they never listen to me. We'll talk to them provided they knock on the door and ask nice; then we'll have our coffee." She winked at me. "What's that you got there, Jessica?"

I looked at the other book I'd brought in with Betsy's photo album. "Looks like a high school yearbook," I said. "I didn't mean to take it."

"No harm done. You might as well keep it. Betsy won't be needing it anymore."

I laughed. "I do enjoy looking through old yearbooks. We change so much."

"Get old, you mean."

"Yes. That's what I mean. I will hang on to it for a day or two, but I'll see that it's returned."

"Suit yourself."

There was a loud knock. Clara took her cane from the chair where she'd left it and went to the door. I accompanied her.

"You let me handle this," she said.

Two uniformed officers were in the hall, one tall and thin, the other large, red-faced, and breathing heavily.

"You the lady called the cops?" the first one asked.

The panting officer eyed Clara's cane. "How the heck . . . do you . . . get . . . up those stairs?" he said.

"I don't leave the apartment when they're fixing the elevator," Clara said. "Mike, the super, lets me know ahead of time when it's going to be serviced." She shifted her gaze to his partner. "Yes, Officer, I was the one who called."

"Is this the thief you reported?" he asked, indicating me.

"No. This is my friend Jessica. We were just about to have a cup of coffee. Would you like one?"

The policemen exchanged glances. I could see they thought they had a kook on their hands. I remained silent.

"You reported a theft in progress, ma'am. Could you give us a little more detail?"

She pointed her cane at Betsy's door. "I reported a *thief* in progress," she said. "She made a muddle out of Betsy's apartment."

The first officer turned, pushed open Betsy's door, took in the disorder, and remarked, "My daughter's room looks a lot like that. She have a fight with her boyfriend or something?"

"Betsy's dead," Clara said. "Some crook came here pretending to be her sister and did all that."

"How did she get in?"

"She had the key."

"Are you sure . . . she wasn't really . . . Betsy's sister?" the portly policeman asked. He cocked his head to see around his partner's shoulder.

"Betsy didn't have a sister, at least not that I know of," Clara said.

"Is it possible she had a sister you didn't know of?" he asked, taking a deep breath.

"We were neighbors a long time. I never saw anyone before claiming to be her sister."

"And how old was this neighbor of yours? The one who passed away?"

I could see he thought that Betsy was Clara's contemporary.

"Somewhere in her thirties, I guess."

"Yeah, well," the tall one said, pulling Betsy's door closed, "we'll let the super know."

"May I?" I asked.

"Sure, go ahead," Clara said. "They're not listening to me."

"Gentlemen," I said. "Betsy Archibald, who used to live here, was murdered yesterday, and today someone claiming to be her sister ransacked her apartment. You may want to talk to the detectives who were here last night."

"Who were they?" the heavy policeman asked.

I looked at Clara.

"Never got their names."

"Okay, ladies, we'll make out a report." He looked at his partner, who shrugged. "We'll ask around the station house for the detectives who were investigating your friend's death. Okay? You go have your coffee. If they want to talk with you, we'll tell them where to find you."

We heard them descend the stairs, muttering to each other.

"You did the right thing," I told Clara, "calling the police. You never can be too careful."

"My thought exactly," she said. She shook her head. "What'd I tell you, Jessica? They didn't care a hoot about what I said. I bet they never listened to their mothers either. Let's have that coffee."

Chapter Seventeen

Kevin Prendergast lived in a sleek high-rise on lower Fifth Avenue. The doorman used the house phone to announce me and, after a long pause, directed me to the bank of three elevators with instructions to press PENTHOUSE B.

Kevin was standing in the doorway of his apartment when the elevator opened. His face was unshaven, his hair unbound, his feet were bare, and his button-down shirt was half-unbuttoned. "To what do I owe the honor of this unannounced visit?" he asked.

"I'm sorry to barge in on you, Kevin," I said. "I was just at Betsy's apartment, and I had a few questions."

"How did you get in there?"

"The door was open."

"Come on. That doesn't ring true. Did you bribe Mike?"

"I never actually met the superintendent, but I did wonder who else may have had the key to Betsy's apartment."

"And you thought it would be me."

"That thought did cross my mind. May I come in?"

He said no more but held the door open, sweeping his arm back in an overly dramatic gesture.

The apartment had a wall of windows with a jaw-dropping view of the city looking north, the spires of the Empire State Building and the Chrysler Building both silhouetted against the late-afternoon sky, together with other skyscrapers. Perhaps in deference to the tendency of New York City windowsills to collect soot, the custom-length sofa beneath the expanse of glass was a charcoal gray. Small decorative pillows in natural linen faced with silk-screened brown branches were placed at even intervals leaning against the back cushions. A mohair throw lay folded on one end of the sofa, its bright spring green color a surprise in the neutral surroundings.

In front of the sofa was a coffee table made of a long slab of thick glass set atop two chunks of burled wood. Newspapers were strewn on the table. Several sheets had fallen to the floor. One paper was opened to the story of Betsy's murder.

I glanced around at the modern open kitchen that overlooked the great room. To one side was an elegant table surrounded by low-backed, cream-colored, upholstered swivel chairs on a beige and pale blue Oriental rug, the rug defining the dining room in the open space. A long mirror on the wall next to the dining area reflected the windows and the breathtaking view. On the other side of the kitchen was an open spiral staircase leading to another floor.

"You're looking for . . . ?" Kevin said.

"I was just admiring the room."

"You came up here to talk about decorating?"

"No. I came to offer my condolences. Is Anne home? Anne Tripper?"

"I know who you meant. You're sure you're not moon-lighting for one of those rags?" he asked, pointing at the newspapers.

"I assure you I'm not," I said.

"Anne had an errand to run. I expect her back in a little while. Have a seat."

I chose to sit on a brown leather bench opposite the sofa. All the furniture in the room was low, allowing an unimpeded panorama of the spectacular cityscape from anywhere you sat or stood. I dragged my eyes from the view.

"Has the press been calling you?" I asked.

"Calling me, e-mailing me, dropping in on me, lying in wait for me. I stopped at the office this morning to talk to the staff and I had to leave to escape the reporters. We're going to have to get better security. If I hadn't had a car waiting, they would have chased me to the taxi stand." He sat on the sofa and picked up the stray pages of newspaper, folded them, and dropped them into a pile.

"The press can be very persistent," I said.

"You're lucky they never got wind of your nephew or you'd be hounded as well. I heard he was found. That was one piece of good news at least. Even so, I told Howerstein never to have that grip work on one of my productions again. How is your nephew?"

"Frank is my grandnephew," I said. "He's a little chastened by the experience, but I doubt it will dampen his natural good spirits for long. We told him about Betsy. He was very sorry to hear it. As we are, too, of course."

"Well, it had nothing to do with him, I'm sure."

"I'm happy to hear you say that," I said. "I don't think it had anything to do with him either. But I wondered if you had any ideas who it *did* have to do with."

He shrugged. "I have no idea. Why would anyone want to kill anyone? I don't know. Unless they were unbalanced. I guess that's a given."

"What's a given?" I asked.

He gave me a funny look. "That a killer is unbalanced," he said. "You don't see normal people going around killing other people."

"Sometimes emotions overwhelm even the most normal-seeming of people," I said. "But on the whole, I think you're probably right. Most of us can control the urge to kill even if we have a valid reason for our rage. I imagine you knew her better than most, so I thought I'd ask you who might have had a reason to kill her."

He was quiet for a long time, his eyes focused on an image in his mind. "She had a foul temper, as you saw. She was too much of a perfectionist. Stubborn as a mule. But a complete professional with a fabulous, creative way of seeing the world. She was a big factor in our success. I have to give her credit. She came from this little town in northern Ontario, from the back of nowhere. They don't even have cable TV. Yet she had big-city sophistication, and this quirky mind. She always knew the best way to get a message out, had perfect pitch when it came to hearing what people want. She could charm the pants off you when she wanted to." He shook his head. "I don't know what we'll do without her."

"Did Betsy have a sister?" I asked.

He shook his head. "Don't believe so. In fact, I'm pretty sure she didn't. I remember her telling me that she was an only child. Her father was a miner and her mother was a teacher. That's all I know."

"You must know more than that," I said softly. "You were her lover at one time, weren't you?"

"Who told you that? That biddy from across the hall? She just loves to gossip. You've been asking a lot of questions, Jessica. Now it's my turn. What were you doing at Betsy's apartment?"

"Who was at Betsy's apartment?" a voice said from behind me.

I turned to see Anne Tripper descending the spiral staircase. She was dressed in a red velour jacket and matching pants with gold slippers, and wore multiple rings on her fingers, as usual. She strode to the sofa, putting her hand out for Kevin's assistance as she stepped behind the coffee table. I wondered if she dressed on purpose to contrast with the muted tones of the room, to make sure she stood out, to compete for attention with the view.

"You changed?" Kevin said, rising to kiss her cheek.

"Some jerk bumped into me on the street and I spilled coffee all over myself," she said.

"Get done what you needed to?" he asked.

"Of course. I'm very efficient." She turned to me. "And how are you, Jessica? I hope the cops didn't keep you too late." She dropped onto the sofa next to Kevin.

I ignored her question. "How did you get in here?" I asked instead. "You didn't use the front door. Were you here all this time?"

"I rarely use the front door," she said. "We have another door to the upstairs. Saves me from traipsing across the whole apartment to get to the bedroom."

"The outfit you spilled coffee on," I said, "was it by chance a pink hooded sweatshirt?"

She laughed. "I haven't worn a hooded sweatshirt since high school," she said, "and maybe not even then. Why do you ask?"

"I saw someone coming out of Betsy Archibald's building today. She was wearing a hooded sweatshirt. I thought it might have been you."

"I wasn't anywhere near Sullivan Street today," she said. "But there have to be other tenants in Betsy's building who get visitors."

"I notice you're not wearing your opal ring," I said. "Did Lance's comments about it at the meeting spook you?"

She looked down at her hands. "I never listen to that jerk." She flashed an ironic smile at Kevin. "Sorry," she said to him, apparently not sorry at all. "I know what a big deal you made when Betsy got him for the campaign."

"He's got a big show. We wanted a big name."

"My name wasn't big enough for you?"

"C'mon, Anne. Let's not take up Mrs. Fletcher's time with our quibbles."

"My career is a quibble?" She was not about to let go of her irritation.

"The opal ring?" I asked. "It's very beautiful. Aren't you going to wear it again?"

"Well, I would, but I can't."

"Because of the bad luck?" I asked.

"Well, yes. It's actually quite bad luck. I lost it yesterday."

"The production company must have a lost and found," I said. "Did you ask the women in the production office?"

"As if anyone there would admit it. I left the ring in my handbag, which I left in the production office. One of them probably stole it."

"I'm sure it will be returned to you," I said.

Her face reflected her annoyance. "I doubt it," she said. She turned to Kevin. "I met the Barkers in the elevator. The couple from downstairs? They invited us to dinner. I said yes for us. I hope you don't mind."

He hesitated a moment. "That's fine," he replied. "Beats having to order in and have one of those reporters pretend to be a deliveryman from the Chinese restaurant."

"Can you be ready in a half hour?"

"I think so," he said. He rose and shrugged his shoulders at me. "I guess we'll have to put off the rest of this conversation, Jessica."

"That's all right," I said. "We can continue it tomorrow at the location."

"Will you be there?" Anne asked. "I thought your commercial was already finished."

"It was," I said, "but Detective Chesny has asked that everyone who was at the location yesterday be there again tomorrow. The only exception he made, I believe, is for my grandnephew, Frank, who has to be in school."

Anne made a *tsk*ing noise. "I can't wait for it to be over. I have so many other appointments to make. You'll excuse me, Jessica, won't you? I want to get ready for dinner."

"Of course," I said, thinking that if she knew she was going to change for dinner, why get dressed in this outfit?

Kevin opened the door and absently brushed his long hair behind his ear. "You might want to talk to Lance Sevenson," he said.

"Why?" I asked.

"Betsy knew him from Toronto. That's how she was able to get him to agree to be in the spot. She told me she called in some favor. He might know if someone had a grudge against her."

"But she was killed while the commercials were being made. Wouldn't that seem to indicate it was someone from your business, someone with a more recent motive for murder?"

"Then try Howerstein. She had a big argument with him, too."

"When was that?"

"After she got ticked off with the cook. He tried to calm her down and she blasted him. Then he went after her. Tonio and I practically had to pull them apart."

"Anyone else you care to accuse?"

"I don't know who, unless Stella Bedford's manager killed Betsy for yelling at his client. He's a pretty big guy, though. Given the opportunity, he probably would've punched her lights out instead. Too bad. That would have been a better outcome for Betsy. See you tomorrow." He shut the door.

I stood there perplexed. How could he make light of Betsy's murder? In one moment he was saying he didn't know how his business was going to go on without her, and moments later he joked about her death. I shook my head and rang for the elevator. I never got to ask him if he suspected that Betsy hoped to woo away his agency's clients for her new agency. I'd save that for tomorrow.

And Anne Tripper. Interesting that she was aware that Betsy's apartment was on Sullivan Street. I wondered if they knew each other before this commercial shoot, or if she knew where Betsy lived because she knew Kevin had dated her.

I got off the elevator at the lobby and the doorman opened the glass door to the vestibule. "Are the Barkers at home?" I asked him.

"The Barkers?"

"Don't the Barkers have an apartment here?"

"Never heard of anyone in the building named Barker," he said. "And I know them all. We've got a single woman named Baker, but she's away on a business trip."

"That must be it," I said. "I must have misheard the name."

"You want to leave a message for her?"

"No, thanks. I can try her again when she gets back."

It's been my experience that when people lie about small inconsequential things, they'll lie about big things, too. There was no need to pretend they had a dinner date to get rid of me. I was as happy to get out of there as they were to see me go.

Chapter Eighteen

"That was delicious, sweetheart. Nothing like a home-cooked meal."

Grady wiped his mouth with his napkin and looked around with satisfaction. A fleeting sad expression crossed his face, and I thought for a moment that he was going to tear up. But he blinked several times and smiled instead.

"Can I go up to Michele's, Dad?" Frank asked. "We want to put more songs on my iPod."

"Don't you have any work to do for school, sport? You've been out for two days."

"No. Miss Lyons said I can make up my reading over the weekend. Right, Mom?"

"Not exactly. She said you may have until Monday to catch up with your class, but that doesn't mean you don't have to start it tonight."

"Aw."

"Sorry, son," Grady said. "Schoolwork comes first; then you can play. But first, help your mother clear the table."

Frank sighed and made a long-suffering face, but obediently got up and began ferrying plates into the kitchen. I joined him and we had the table cleared in no time. Donna brought in a pot of coffee. I followed with our mugs. She looked at her watch. "If you finish reading the next chapter in your book, Frank, you may look online for another song for the iPod. But you'll have to tell Michele you can't see him until tomorrow. It's getting late and you have school in the morning."

"Okay! I'm a fast reader. I know just what I want to get, too." He excused himself and went to his room.

"He doesn't seem any worse for the experience," I said. "Has he talked about it at all?"

Grady laughed. "He must have told everyone in the building what happened by now," he said. "I think he looks on getting locked in the truck as an adventure, now that he's free. I can tell you, it sure took a couple of years off my life."

"Mrs. Cranford from the third floor stopped me in the hall to say how happy she is that Frank is all right," Donna said, suppressing a smile. "Most days, she barely says 'Good morning.' This afternoon, she told me how she had a nephew who got lost upstate in a snowstorm. The whole county turned out to look for him. They found him huddled in a hunter's cabin two days later. He lost a toe to frostbite, but was otherwise okay."

"Everyone has a story," Grady said. "I met Mr. Abbott

at the mailbox. He told me that he and his wife thought their kids had been abducted when they stopped in a shop in Gallup, New Mexico. They'd gone into a side room to look at Indian jewelry, and the kids were gone when they came out front. They found them back at the trailer, sitting on the car's bumper waiting for them. That was over thirty years ago, and he says when he heard about Frank, the memory and the fear came rushing back."

"The building is a little like a small town," Donna said. "Word gets around fast."

"Has Frank mentioned Betsy at all?" I asked.

Grady shook his head. "Not to me."

"Nor to me," Donna added. "I keep waiting for the other shoe to drop, but while he was excited about talking to Detective Chesny, the reason why seems to have slipped his mind."

"Speaking of shoes," Grady said. "Frank has already put in his birthday order. He'd like a pair of cowboy boots like Jimbo's." He looked at Donna. "I told you about Jimbo Barnes. That's Cookie—I mean Stella Bedford's manager. He wears these fancy tooled leather boots."

Frank poked his head out the door of his bedroom. "And they're this cool color, too. It's called turquoise," he said. "And he's always polishing them with this big red handkerchief. Even in the bathroom."

"Have you been eavesdropping on our conversation, young man?" his mother asked. "What did I tell you about that?"

Frank wandered out to the table. "I'm not trying to listen, but I can't help hearing your voices."

"It's easy to hear our voices when you leave your door ajar," Grady said. "Try closing it. Have you finished your chapter?"

Frank shook his head.

"Back to work," Grady said, pointing to Frank's room. "And shut the door."

"I just wanted to talk about the boots," Frank whined. "You're so mean."

"Go! And no fresh talk or there'll be no boots."

Grady gave me a wink. When he heard the click of Frank's door closing, he leaned forward and said in a low voice, "I hope I don't have to go all the way to Texas to buy kids' cowboy boots. You think I can find them here?"

"You can find anything in the world in New York," I said, "but finding it at a reasonable price is another story."

"Well, you went shopping today," Donna said to me. "Did you find what you wanted at a reasonable price?"

"Actually, I did a little investigating today," I said.

Donna glanced at Grady with a smile. "We figured that's what you were up to, Aunt Jessica."

"Dig up anything new?" Grady asked.

"Well, I did learn a few things I didn't know before, but I think I've raised more questions than I've answered," I said. "Would you mind if I used your computer for a while tonight?"

"Go right ahead."

"I won't be keeping Frank from doing his homework, will I?"

"No. He's got his book to read. You're welcome to use it."

"I won't be long. I promise. You two must be exhausted."

"Take your time," Donna said. "We're very happy to linger over our coffee."

"We've found a new appreciation for every opportunity to be together quietly," Grady said, "to be grateful for what we have." He reached out and squeezed Donna's hand. "You never know how much you have to lose until something happens that threatens your everyday life. All you want to do is to turn back the clock, to make your life exactly what it was before."

Donna gazed tenderly at him. "We're very lucky."

"Yes. We are."

Grady and Donna had set up their computer in a corner of the master bedroom so they would be able to monitor Frank's time online, and supervise the Web sites he visited. I pulled the chair up to the desk and clicked onto Google. Despite his obvious finger-pointing, Kevin Prendergast had given me a few ideas to follow up on.

I looked up information on Lance Sevenson. The phony British accent gave no clue to his origins, but Kevin had said Betsy knew him from Toronto. I thought back to when we'd been on a panel together years ago in Wisconsin. He'd bragged then about growing up on a military base in California and traveling all over the world with his parents, picking up his knowledge of crystals from Gypsies in Turkey, and honing his psychic abilities with Hindus in India. Was any of that true or had he made it up to bolster his image as a New Age guru? I remembered him as an insufferable snob who had refused to sign people's books if he didn't like the tone of their voice, or the way they looked at him.

I found the Web site for Lance's television show. The short bio on their popular star called him a citizen of the world with no reference to where he was born or raised.

On Amazon.com, information about the author of *Crystals in Your Life* was equally sketchy. I went back to Google and tried looking up Betsy Archibald, but other than articles on the ad campaigns she created that appeared in industry magazines like *Advertising Age*, *Adweek*, and *Shoot*, there was little data that I could find on Mindbenders' creative director.

"What are you doing, Aunt Jessica?" Frank peered over my shoulder at the listing of links on Google.

"Just doing a little research, Frank. Have you finished your chapter?"

"Uh-huh. I read ten pages."

"Ten pages, huh? That's terrific. You must be a fast reader."

"I am."

"And now you'd like to look up songs for your iPod, I take it."

"That's okay. I can wait till you're done. Can I look at this while I wait?"

"What's that?"

"I don't know. It's a book you brought home."

I turned to see what Frank had in his hands. It was Betsy's high school yearbook. I had left it in a corner of the room together with my shoulder bag and suitcase that Cookie had sent downtown from the Waldorf.

"It's a yearbook," I said, explaining to him that some schools publish books every year with pictures of the students, and that this one was from Betsy's high school. "Do you still want to look at it?"

"Sure," he said, opening to the middle of the book. "They had funny haircuts when she was in high school, didn't they?"

I glanced down at the page he was examining. "It didn't seem so at the time," I said.

"I'll see if I can find her," he said enthusiastically.

"You do that. I shouldn't be too much longer, and then you can have the computer back."

I continued my search for anything I could find on Betsy and Lance, even linking both names to see if it brought up any reference to Toronto, but the only articles where their names appeared together were ones about the upcoming Permezzo campaign.

"I found her!" Frank said. "Look! Look at this, Aunt Jessica. Isn't that her?"

"Let me see," I said, taking the book from him and propping it up in front of us.

Frank pointed to a very young woman with a head full of curls. Beneath her picture was the name Elizabeth Archibald.

"Very good, Frank," I said.

His face, which had been so full of excitement at recognizing the younger Betsy, suddenly became serious. He leaned into my shoulder. "It's sad that she's dead, isn't it?"

"Very sad."

"Now she won't see how your commercial comes out, will she?"

"That's true. She won't be able to see it. But the ads for Permezzo were all her idea, so if they come out well, and if people respond to them, it will be a kind tribute to her and her success in her field. Do you understand?"

"Kind of. People will like her idea and remember her?"

I put my arm around Frank and he rested his head on my shoulder. "That's right. And she probably had lots of friends who will remember her for other things."

"Like what?"

"Like that she was fun to be with, or perhaps because she did nice things for them. And maybe she had family who loved her and will miss her."

Frank nodded but didn't say anything.

"You know, Frank, we saw her when she had a bad day, but I'll bet she wasn't always like that. I'm sorry we didn't know her when she was being nice. Aren't you?"

Frank was silent for a moment. Then he raised his head. "How come she changed her name?" he asked.

"She didn't change her name," I said. " 'Betsy' is short for 'Elizabeth.' It's a nickname. Do you know what a nickname is?"

"Sure. Like 'Frank' is for 'Francis' or 'Franklin'?"

"Exactly."

"Except my name isn't 'Francis' or 'Franklin.' It's just plain 'Frank.' "

"Yours is a wonderful name," I said. "You were named for someone your dad and I loved very much."

"I know," he said. "You want to see who else I found in the book?"

"Who else did you find?"

He took the book back from me and turned several pages. "I saw him. I'm pretty sure it's him."

"Who, Frank?"

"The guy on television. The one who was in the room with the stars."

"Lance Sevenson?"

"But that's not his real name. He has a different name here, but it doesn't look like a nickname." He turned another page and put his index finger on a picture.

I took the book and studied the face Frank had pointed out. The name under the picture was "Laurence Stevenson." "I think you're right," I said. "Thank you, Frank."

"Why are you thanking me?"

"I've been trying to find out where Lance Sevenson grew up, and now I know. He isn't from California or Toronto. He's from a little town in Ontario, the same hometown as Betsy Archibald."

"I helped you out?"

"You certainly did." I closed the yearbook and placed it on the desk.

"Then, if you're done, can I use the computer now?"

I laughed and gave him a hug. "It's all yours," I said. "I have to make a couple of phone calls."

Chapter Nineteen

We had a nine o'clock call at the production location, but I convinced Grady to leave early so
that we would get there before the other talent
arrived.

There was a black-and-white cruiser in the parking lot
of the office building when we pulled in at eight fifiteen,
so I assumed the police were already inside. Whether Detective Chesny had preceded us remained to be seen. He
would be more likely to use an unmarked car. While I could
often spot unmarked cars on the road—they were usually
compact sedans of an older vintage—all the cars parked
at the location, presumably those of the crew, looked like
vehicles that might be used by the police.

I had requested a private meeting with the detective in
the hope that he would open his mind to the information
I had gathered, and the theories I was developing, and not

reject my help out of hand because I couldn't produce a degree from the police academy. I try never to step on the toes of the police officers I encounter, but I admit there have been times when their refusal to take me seriously has led to some confrontations. It was my intent to try to strike a deal with Chesny to accept my input in exchange for disclosing some of the evidence his department had collected. I could point to many cases in which my contributions proved useful, even critical, and led to an arrest. Even so, experience told me the authorities are often reluctant to share anything with an amateur, especially information.

Grady parked his car near the entrance where catering was setting up the breakfast station. I left him negotiating for pancakes while I made my way inside to the production office.

Jennifer, cell phone headset in place, greeted me with a smile. "So glad to see you, Mrs. Fletcher. How's the little guy?"

"He's fine," I said. "Back in school, which is where he belongs."

"That's great. We got the word not to take on Ricky again, but the police said he has to be here today, so I didn't waste money hiring another grip. Hope I'm not going to get in trouble for that. At this point, we want to keep it in the family and finish the job. Next time it'll be another story."

"I'm sorry if Ricky loses work over this."

"Hey, he broke the rules. That's the breaks. But it's not as if he's being blacklisted or anything. He won't work for

Mindbenders again, but I'll bet Dan Howerstein will include him in future crews for other agencies, knowing that there'll be no way in the world that Ricky will break the rules again."

"It's a tough way to learn a lesson," I said.

"Sure is," she said, putting up a hand to indicate she was getting a call. She looked at her watch. "No," she said to the caller. "Mrs. Fletcher is here, but the others haven't arrived yet. Want to get some breakfast before they do?" She pulled off the headset and left it on the desk. "I'm going to dash for a bagel," she said. "Can I get you anything?"

I shook my head. "Thanks anyway. I'll get something later. Do you mind if I wait here for a bit?"

"Not at all. Susan should be back any minute."

When Jennifer left, I went to the cubicle where several of us had left our personal items during the shoot. There was one handbag on the shelf, a blue leather pouch. I remembered it from the other day, and wondered if it had been there all this time. Was it Betsy's? Would the police have thought to look for her bag? Would the ladies of the production office have bothered to check if anything was left on the shelf? I doubted it. If the shoot was scheduled to continue for another day, the likelihood was that they'd lock up the production office for the night. There would be no need to check the cubicle before leaving.

I put my own shoulder bag on the shelf and pulled the blue one down. I don't usually go through someone's purse unasked, but if, as I suspected, this one was Betsy's, then Detective Chesny should add it to her personal effects. Plus, if her keys were missing, it might give us a clue as to how the woman who posed as her "sister" may have gotten them.

I moved quickly. Even though my motives were pure, I didn't want one of the producers to see me riffling through someone else's property. I pulled out the wallet and opened it. Just as I had thought, the driver's license was for Elizabeth Archibald. I studied the photograph for a moment. So many driver's license and passport photos are terrible—I know mine are not flattering—but Betsy looked lovely, the red hair unmistakable. I felt a pang for the loss, the waste of a life, the potential unfulfilled. Who could have done such a thing? And why?

I returned the wallet to the bag and swiftly checked the internal pockets, feeling around the bottom for a set of keys with no success. Perhaps she'd had them on her person. That was one of the questions I had for Detective Chesny. Where were Betsy's keys? It would have been easy for those of us who left our purses in the production office—or who worked there—to have access to Betsy's bag, or anyone else's for that matter. Since the cubicle was usually unoccupied and used only for storage, no one would have noticed had one of us slipped in and removed her keys. But if it happened that way, was it before or after she was killed?

Back in the main office, I wondered, *Was the office as secure as Jennifer and Susan assumed?* Anne Tripper intimated that someone had stolen her opal ring from her handbag. Of course, that was a convenient excuse if she didn't know where she'd lost it. Had she been in the carpentry room with Betsy? Had they continued whatever argument they'd been having at the meeting in the agency? Had she been jealous of Betsy? Jealous of her prior relationship with Kevin?

The woman who had turned Betsy's apartment upside down, the one I'd seen exiting the building wearing a pink hooded sweatshirt, could be someone other than Anne Tripper. Might she be someone from the production? If so, would that person know that Betsy's bag was still here? And would she try to return the keys sometime today?

I perused the talent board where my photo had been pinned along with the Polaroids of the others scheduled to be in the commercials. My picture had been removed— my shoot was completed—but the photos of the other three were still there. Were any of my "costars," as Betsy had called them, implicated in her murder? Or had this been someone she knew for a long time, perhaps someone she'd had a closer connection with? Kevin Prendergast fit that category. Did Antonio Tedeschi? And what about Daniel Howerstein? What had they fought over if it wasn't just Betsy's bad behavior? Again, so many questions. And where were the answers?

The door opened and Susan came in, juggling a large cup from Starbucks, with her backpack slung over one arm and a shopping bag on the other. "Hi, Mrs. Fletcher. I'm surprised to see you here. Didn't you finish up the other day?"

"I did," I said, "but I was asked to return with all the others."

"Oh, right. Wasn't that awful about Betsy? Everyone is freaking out. Wondering if there's a serial killer loose. Jen and I had a hard time convincing everyone to come back. There are going to be cops all over the place today. Not exactly a conducive atmosphere in which to make an effective sales pitch."

"Sales pitch? Oh, you mean the commercials."

"Yeah. I call a spade a spade. We like to think we're in the film business, making little movies of persuasion. But we're really in the sales business."

She pulled out her desk chair, dropped into it, and stashed her shopping bag and backpack in a large file drawer.

"Don't you put your bags in the back, in the cubicle?" I asked.

"Don't need to. This desk has a nice big drawer and I can even lock it if I want. That"—she flipped her thumb toward the cubicle—"is just for the talent and a few other muckety-mucks."

I laughed. "Who are the muckety-mucks?"

"Let's see. Who used it the other day? You, Sevenson's assistant, Lena—I think Betsy was the only one from the agency who did—also the chef, Mrs. Bedford."

"Anyone else?" I asked.

"Our intern, Lily, might have. She doesn't have a desk. Oh, and let's not forget Mr. Prendergast's girlfriend, the lovely Anne Tripper." This was said with a heavy dose of sarcasm.

"Not a fan of hers, are you?"

She grunted. "What a witch. Accused us of stealing her ring. Like I would wear anything of hers. She dresses like a sixties go-go girl. She probably lost her ring, and wants to claim it on our insurance. The talent always trusts us with their valuables. We're very vigilant and we don't let anyone else back there. Mrs. Bedford actually gave us a diamond ring and a bracelet to mind for her. She's so cool. She even said we could try them on. Naturally, we told her we would never do something like that." Susan's eyes lit up. "But of course, we did. She knew we would. After all, she told us we could." She laughed. "Boy, it would be nice to be able to afford things like that one day. Then again, if I had the money, I'd probably spend it on something else."

"We all have our secret desires," I said.

Jennifer returned with her bagel and donned her earphones.

"Who's up first?" I asked.

"Tripper hasn't done her green screen yet," she said, consulting her clipboard. "They want some extra footage on Sevenson. And Bedford has the whole shebang to do." She looked at her watch. "They're not due in for another fifteen minutes. Grab yourself some breakfast. They're all set up now."

"I think I will," I said. "See you later."

I found Grady sitting in front of a plate of pancakes and bacon, with a fried egg and toast on the side. "Having a healthy breakfast, I see," I said, setting down my fruit and yogurt.

"Donna never lets me eat this stuff," he said, taking a bite of buttered toast. "I'll be back on oatmeal and raisins tomorrow."

"In that case, I won't reveal your secret," I said.

"Oh, she'll know anyway. She says she can smell the bacon on my clothes. Find out anything yet?"

I shook my head. "I spoke with Mort Metzger this morning. He has a call in to some colleagues up north, but nothing so far. For good measure, I also called Detective Christian Marshall. I met him in British Columbia when I rode the Whistler Northwind train."

"That's pretty far away, don't you think?"

"You never know where people have connections. I thought it was worth a call."

"Look who's here," Grady said, indicating a couple who'd entered the room carrying plates.

Cookie spotted us and had a brief intense discussion with Jimbo before coming to our table. She sat next to Grady and batted her eyelashes at him. "Hiya, handsome."

He smiled, evidently used to her teasing now. "How are you this morning, Mrs. Bedford?"

"Mrs. Bedford," she mocked. "So formal. Well, I guess everyone is a little strange this morning, doncha think? To be back here after the murder. Gives me the willies, I tell you."

"Is Jimbo joining us?" I asked.

"Oh, him. He must've had a fight with his wife on the phone. He's been sniping at me all morning. Must've made me go over that script a hundred times. I'll be reciting Permezzo in my dreams. 'I won't be embarrassed again,' he says. As if Betsy yelled at him instead-a me." She leaned over the table, her eyes shifting right and left, then whispered, "Not to speak ill of the dead, but it'll be a lot easier today without her giving me the evil eye, if you know what I mean."

"When are you scheduled to shoot your spot?" I asked.

"Oh, listen to her. You got the lingo down pat, now, don't you? Ah'm not sure exactly. I have to go see those little girls in the production office. They'll tell me. But I wanted to eat. That's why Jimbo was annoyed with me. He wanted me to go there first. But they had grits this morning. Did y'all see that? Ah couldn't skip breakfast when they had grits. I got a great recipe for fried grits with onions and cheddar cheese. You will just die." She covered her mouth with her hand. "Oops, I better not talk that way today." She scooped up a forkful of grits.

"I think someone's looking for you, Aunt Jess," Grady said.

I followed his gaze to see Detective Chesny eyeing the crowd at breakfast. I raised my hand and he beckoned to me.

"Well, I have to see a man about a dog," I said, getting up. "Please excuse me. I'll see you later."

"Is she buying a dog?" I heard Cookie ask Grady as I walked away.

"I think she's getting a Chihuahua."

"Oh, they're so cute."

Detective Chesny escorted me to an empty office that must have accommodated small meetings when the office building had served its original purpose. There was a good-sized table surrounded by gray swivel chairs, and nothing else in the room except a whiteboard on the wall. Chesny's tape recorder was already set up. Also on the table was a laptop computer, a stack of lined pads, and a scattering of pens and pencils. At the far end was one of those new boxes that hold coffee, a sleeve of hot cups, a package of napkins, and next to that a box of doughnuts.

"Can I get you anything, Mrs. Fletcher?" he asked, waving at the coffee.

"No, thanks. I had my tea this morning." I pulled out a chair and sat, reaching for one of the pads and a pen.

He poured himself a cup and took a chair around the corner of the table from mine. "You have quite a few friends in law enforcement," he said mildly.

"I hope you weren't offended by their calls," I said. "I just wanted to communicate my credentials, and I also asked for a little help on one matter. How much or even *if* we work together is completely your call. I understand that."

"I hope you also understand that whatever evidence or information you've accumulated in the time since the murder is to be turned over to the department without any guarantee of a quid pro quo. I owe you nothing, and you owe me everything you have that pertains to this case. Do you accept that?"

"I'm disappointed," I said, "but if that's your preference, of course. I'll tell you everything I know."

He grunted. "Before we start, I have one question."

"What's that?"

"How is Frank doing?"

Chapter Twenty

Forty minutes later, Detective Chesny knew everything that I knew, and I knew a little more than when we'd started. I told him about the woman who pretended to be Betsy's sister. He consulted his list of Betsy's belongings and noted that it did not include keys. We were in agreement that her bag should stay in the cubicle in the event that whoever lifted the keys made an attempt to return them.

Setting up a hidden camera was too cumbersome and would draw too much attention for the limited time we had remaining. I suggested instead that Susan be designated to monitor activity in the cubicle by keeping a list of who came and went during the day. When Chesny hesitated about bringing the producers into our confidence, I reminded him that Susan, Jennifer, and Lily had alibis for the time when Betsy was killed; they'd been in the production office working on arrangements for the next commercial shoot. Cell phone records could confirm this. When I added that women who could be entrusted with Cookie's diamonds were not likely to be security risks, he acquiesced. But only for Susan. Jennifer and Lily were to remain in the dark.

He told me that the medical examiner had estimated the time of Betsy's death at around an hour or two before the body was discovered. That placed it directly during the filming of my commercial. Apparently, that news had served as exculpating evidence for Grady and Frank, since many people witnessed them in attendance during my shoot. The majority of the crew had been on hand as well, with the exception of those in the production office, and those charged with packing up any equipment or supplies that would not be left on the location for the next day's work.

According to Kevin Prendergast, Lance Sevenson and his assistant, Lena, had been in and out of video village, the conference room that held a bank of monitors that allowed those not on the set to keep track of the filming. Kevin claimed that he and Anne Tripper had been there all afternoon. Although they provided an alibi for each other, no one else could vouch for their continued presence in the room.

"Were you able to confirm that the murder weapon was the nail gun?" I asked.

Chesny nodded. "The murder weapon was *a* nail gun. The nail pierced her heart. Must've died instantly. Whether it was that particular nail gun remains to be seen. We haven't gotten the forensics back on it, but our tech said the safety mechanism was broken."

"Is that significant?"

"Depends on when it happened. You said your nephew threw it out of the equipment cart. It could have been damaged then."

"Have you checked with whoever may have used it that day?"

"Patience, Mrs. Fletcher. That's what we're here for today. My team has been compiling a list of questions. When we get the answers, we'll have a clearer picture of how Miss Archibald died."

"And why."

"Yes. And why. Manner and motive," he said, referring to the key elements police look for in a murder investigation, the manner in which the victim died—how he or she was killed—and the motive for the murder.

"Is your staff conducting background checks on anyone?"

"We checked on the victim, of course."

"Anyone else?"

An ironic smile crossed his lips. "We checked on you, Mrs. Fletcher."

Cookie was sitting in the makeup chair when I left my meeting with the detective.

"Ah'm gonna see if Maya can come work on my show. Look how pretty she made me look, Jessica."

Maya flashed a smile at me, then focused on adding blush to Cookie's cheeks. "You're pretty to begin with,"

Maya said. "It's easy when I have someone with such wonderful bone structure. I'm just gilding the lily."

"Ain't she sweet? Ah can't see without my glasses." Cookie raised a hand mirror so that she could examine the results up close. "Ooh! You're so good. But will it stay? Last time, under all those hot lights, I was afraid my face would melt."

Maya laughed. "I wouldn't have let that happen, Mrs. Bedford. I was right there in case we needed to powder your nose or fix your hair. I'll be there again today."

"Through the whole shoot?"

"Yes. Through the whole shoot, just as I did for Mrs. Fletcher."

"You did? That's just wonderful. Isn't she wonderful, Jessica?"

"She is," I said, remembering Maya had sprayed almost a can of lacquer onto my hair. "She won't let one lock of hair escape her notice."

"Gotta keep you looking perfect," Maya said, stepping back from Cookie to scrutinize her living canvas. She picked up a lipstick brush and chose a tube of lip gloss in a soft peach.

"By the way, Maya, did you ever find the wig you were missing the other day?" I asked.

Her eyes met mine. "I did. Funny you remembered. Lena brought it down this morning. You know, Mr. Sevenson's assistant? She said she found it upstairs on one of the sets. I can't imagine how it got there."

"Which one of these was it?" I asked, referring to the three Styrofoam head forms that stood on the table, each bearing a wig.

"The red one," Maya said without looking up from her task.

"May I look at it?" I asked.

"Help yourself."

Dave Fitzpatrick arrived to accompany Cookie to her set. "Whenever you're ready," he said.

"Two seconds more," Maya said, picking up the can of hair spray.

"Ah don't see you as a redhead, Jessica," Cookie said to me, shielding her face from the spray with her hands. "Ah like you as a blonde."

I took the wig from the stand and turned it over. There were several bobby pins attached to the webbing inside, used to secure the wig to its wearer. One of the pins had caught some strands of hair. I turned away from Maya and Cookie, took a tissue from my pocket, used it to pull the hair from the bobby pin, and put the folded tissue back in my pocket. "I think you're right, Cookie," I said, returning the wig to the form. "I'll stay blond for now."

"Psst! Mrs. Fletcher."

"You're Ricky, aren't you?"

"Yeah. How's the kid? How's Frank?" Ricky was a muscular fellow with a buzz cut and thick horn-rimmed glasses. Despite the chilly weather, he wore cargo shorts and a T-shirt, which showed off his tattooed arms.

"He's fine, thanks. He's back in school today."

"Your call scared the life out of me the other night," he said. "I swear to you, I never knew he was in that truck. I'm really sorry. He'd been talking about goin' to watch the shoot. When I didn't see him, that's where I figured he'd gone."

"Well, everything turned out all right in the end. He doesn't seem much worse for the experience, but I was told that he shouldn't have been helping you."

"I know. I know. Believe me, I got reamed out but good. But you know.... Stuff is going on.... You get distracted."

I tilted my head. "What stuff was going on?"

"Oh, no." He put his hands up in defense. "I don't know nothin' about that agency lady. Don't look at me. My time is all accounted for. I just meant, you know, our equipment, deciding which to pack, which to leave for the next day, just that kind of stuff. I had it all organized before lunch—this room to stay, this room to pack, this room to clear so I could clean it up—and then someone went and shoved it all in one room."

"Where were you working after lunch?"

"On your set. I did all your green-screen setup. The key grip can tell you. You were getting your hair touched up, so you probably didn't notice. I got a theory, though."

"You do?"

He looked left and right to make sure no one was listening to our conversation. "Yeah." He dropped his voice. "Check out Howerstein."

"The producer."

"He wasn't on your set. I didn't see him all afternoon. What I want to know is, where was he?"

"You're sure you aren't just angry with him because he said you can't work on Mindbenders' commercials anymore?"

"That's only one agency. There are hundreds of them, maybe thousands. I'm in the union. They're not going to blackball me."

I opened the door to the production office. "Is Daniel in here?" I asked Susan.

"He was here before, Mrs. Fletcher. But I think he's on Mrs. Bedford's set, or else Mr. Sevenson's by now."

"Are you alone?"

"Yep. Just me. Lily went on a Starbucks run. Jen went to talk with the location scout about next week's shoot."

"Anyone on your list?" I whispered, although no one else was in the office.

"Just one." She pulled a sheet of paper from beneath a folder and held it up for me.

"Put me down as the second visitor," I said, going to the cubicle and peering into Betsy's bag.

"I hear you've been looking for me, Mrs. Fletcher."

"Yes, Daniel. I wondered where you were yesterday afternoon. I didn't see you at my shoot."

"You didn't see me because I was looking for Betsy. We needed to clear an extra day for the location and I wanted her approval of the overage. Obviously, I never got to ask her."

"Did anyone see you while you were looking for her?"

"Lots of people. As I told the detective, I was in the production office part of the time. You can check with the girls. I got the cost approval from Kevin Prendergast—just ask him. Then I was out in the lot when they were packing the trucks."

"Ricky Pepper said he didn't see you all afternoon."

"Ricky can't see the broad side of a barn even with his glasses. If he wasn't in the union, he'd never get a job in production."

"Returning to the scene of the crime, Mrs. Fletcher?"

Kevin Prendergast stood in the doorway of the carpentry room. The burned-out fluorescent bulb in the ceiling fixture had not been replaced and the single tube remaining cast a harsh light on his angular face.

"I could say the same to you," I said.

I'd wanted to revisit the room where Betsy died to try to reconstruct what might have happened. Why had she come in here? Had someone lured her to this room? Was there an argument that culminated in an angry explosion and a vicious attack with the only weapon at hand? Or had the murder been premeditated, by someone with a grudge against her whose solution was to get rid of its source, and cover up the crime to delay discovery of the body until he—or she—could get away?

The carts had been moved out, most of the equipment in use or more readily accessed in areas closer to the sets. The room was empty except for a few stray light stands, and an outline in orange paint on the floor where Betsy's body had lain.

"Why don't you mind your own business and let the police do their job?" Kevin said.

"If I can help them uncover whoever killed Betsy, I intend to do it."

Kevin moved into the room, closing the door behind him. "Look, Mrs. Fletcher, Jessica. I'm interested in finding Betsy's murderer as much as you are, maybe more, but you've been poking your nose into my business. I don't like it."

"What don't you like, Kevin?"

"I don't like that you sneaked into my office when I wasn't there. You didn't think you could get away with that without me finding out, did you?" He moved close to one of the light stands, his fingers curling around the pole. "I'm warning you, stay out of my business."

"I wasn't sneaking around," I said. "I went to Mindbenders looking for you."

"How convenient that I wasn't there."

"I didn't know that in advance. When I didn't find you there, I went to your home."

"And neglected to mention that you'd been to the agency and questioned my staff. That particular art director will never talk to you again—or anyone else outside the office—if he wants to keep his job."

"Is there something you're trying to hide, Kevin? If so, it's too late."

"What's that supposed to mean?"

"I already know that Betsy was planning to open her own agency."

"So what? People do that every day. That's how most agencies get started. The creative directors leave and establish their own shops."

"How many of Mindbenders' clients was she planning to take with her?"

"She wouldn't have gotten any of them."

"Are you sure? Antonio was considering it."

"You're guessing," he said.

"You said at dinner that you wanted to send her to Italy. Wasn't that because Antonio was smitten with her? You used his infatuation to gain his business. How difficult would it have been for her to use that same attraction to draw him away from Mindbenders and into her own firm, Archibald Advertising?" I moved toward the door, uneasy at being closed in with him.

"Where do you think you're going?" Kevin said.

"Did you kill her, Kevin? You and Anne Tripper?"

"Leave Anne out of this," he growled, advancing toward me.

"Why should I leave her out of this?" I asked, backing up. "Her opal ring—the one she claims was lost or stolen—was found right here in this room."

Even in the dim light, I could see the surprise in Kevin's face. He grabbed my shoulders and shook me, knocking my head against the wall. "She was with me the whole afternoon, I tell you. She never left my side."

The door flew open and light from the hallway illuminated the darkened space.

"What are you doing in here, Kevin?" Anne Tripper said in a high voice. "They want me on the set. I've been looking everywhere for you."

I wrenched myself from Kevin's grasp and strode to the door. "Well, I'm pleased to say, you've found him." I pushed past her, drawing a deep breath as I walked swiftly down the corridor.

My cell phone vibrated in my pocket. I pushed the answer button and asked the caller to hold while I walked outside to get a better signal, and where I wouldn't be overheard.

"Hello, Detective Marshall," I said to the man with whom I'd worked on a case in British Columbia, when I'd taken a trip with a group of model-train enthusiasts. "Thank you so much for getting back to me."

"How are you, Mrs. Fletcher? It's nice to hear your voice again."

We chatted awhile, reminiscing about the Whistler Northwind, which, like so many of the old luxury passenger trains, was no longer in service. It was an elegant, leisurely way to travel, but people don't seem to have time for leisure travel these days. We're always rushing from one point to another.

"Interesting subject you brought up, by the way," Detective Marshall said.

"Were you able to find out anything about Lance Sevenson, or Laurence Stevenson, as he was known in his youth?"

"Canada is a big country," he said, "but the RCMP is a close family. I went through cadet training at Depot with some of the guys in the 'O' division, and they knew who worked the NES District in Ontario—that's 'North, East, Southwest' to you."

"You have something for me?"

"I do. Do you have a fax machine anywhere nearby?"

"I don't know," I said. "Let me find out and I'll call you back."

"You can reach me here for the next hour."

I headed for the production office, the brains of the production, as their intern, Lily, had dubbed it. The ladies there seemed to be the official problem solvers.

"Have him use this number," Susan said, writing it down for me on a slip of paper.

Minutes later, she handed over a sheaf of paper Detective Marshall had faxed me.

"I haven't seen you all day, Aunt Jess. Is everything okay?"

"Grady, can you do me a favor?"

"Of course. Anything for you."

"Is Frank home from school yet?"

Grady looked at his watch. "I think so."

"Would you please call and ask him a question for me?"

I found a quiet place and called my agent, Matt Miller, at his office.

"Hi, Jessica. You caught me on my way out the door, heading for the Hamptons."

"I won't hold you up, Matt, but I need to know something."

"What's that?"

"I need to know the subject of Anne Tripper's new book that's about to come out."

"Come on, Jess, you know I can't divulge that. There's

a strict embargo on it from the publisher. I just learned about it myself."

"I understand and respect that, Matt, but there's a murder at stake."

"Are you saying her book might have something to do with *that*?"

"What I'm saying, Matt, is that there's the possibility that it could. I don't need details, just the thrust of the book."

I waited out the silence on his end.

"Okay," he said, "but you didn't hear it from me."

"Fair enough."

"I have to tell you, I'm not exactly happy about it. It's going to cause me no end of headaches."

"Why's that, Matt?"

"It's another exposé, which I assumed it would be. But this time it's the advertising industry, how ad people, including the biggest names in the business, are cynically warping American values, especially when it comes to children. I don't know why I didn't see it before. She's been eavesdropping on the conversations of all my neighbors. They won't be happy with me—or Kevin."

"Interesting," I said. "Thank you, Matt."

"Only for you, Jessica, only for you. Got to run now."

I caught up with Detective Chesny and gave him the papers Detective Marshall had faxed to me.

"So Sevenson served time for fraud, huh?" he said. "A series of frauds. But why do we care?"

"If Betsy Archibald knew that he'd been convicted of

these crimes, and I'm confident that she did, she could have used that information to blackmail him," I said.

Chesny took a moment to think about the news, tapping the papers against the palm of his hand. "Maybe it's time to gather some of your friends together."

"I was hoping you'd see it that way," I said.

Chapter Twenty-one

Detective Chesny, a clipboard tucked under his arm, waited until Anne Tripper's green-screen filming was completed. As soon as the director called, "Cut," and then, "That's a wrap," Chesny passed the word that certain people were invited to join him in the library, the room that had been used as a set for my commercial. The grips had restored the furniture to its original arrangement; they'd removed the small desk that had been a stand-in for my home office, moved the large table back to the center of the room, and wheeled the chairs around it. I noticed that my novels had been taken from the shelf, replaced with several volumes on insurance law, an unabridged dictionary, and a thesaurus. There was still plenty of room for people to stand, and many of those filing in chose not to sit at the table. Instead, they clustered around a large plastic cooler filled with ice and cans of soda and bottled water, nervous laughter mixing with relief that the production was drawing to a close, and curiosity as to the purpose of the meeting, and what might be revealed.

I took a seat next to Grady and watched as people arrived, among them all but one of us who had attended the preproduction meeting at the agency, Betsy. The talent—myself, Cookie, Lance, and Anne—and those accompanying us—Grady, Jimbo, Lena, and, this time, Kevin—were joined by Antonio Tedeschi and Daniel Howerstein. Jason and Lucy, the production assistants, who had delivered the cooler, as well as a fishbowl of candy bars, took their leave before Chesny closed the door.

We were augmented by the director, Akmanian; the second AD, Dave Fitzpatrick; the grips, Ricky and Bob; and two of the three ladies from the production office, Jennifer and Susan.

Cookie plucked a candy bar from the bowl and dropped it into her purse. She took the chair next to Grady and motioned to her manager to join her by jerking her head at him and patting the seat of the empty chair beside her. Jimbo, who was talking with Akmanian, ignored her gestures. Frowning, she leaned across Grady and tapped my arm. "I did good today, Jessica. If Jimbo would just sit down, he would tell you. You would have been proud of me. I knew all my lines and everything went real smooth."

"I'm sure you were terrific," I replied.

"I was." She smiled up at Grady. "Too bad you didn't see me."

"I was there for part of the time," Grady said. "You were great."

"This spot is gonna help with my new restaurant, I bet. I hope this thing with Betsy won't keep it off the air. Do you think it will?"

I looked sharply at Cookie, but she had pulled out her candy bar and was delicately tearing off the wrapper.

"Well, this seems to be a convivial crowd," Lance said, nudging Lena, who slipped into a seat at the table and pulled out her steno pad and pen. Lance looped an arm around Antonio's shoulder. "Do you have any more gifts to distribute?" he asked.

Antonio's face reddened. He shook his head and glanced around, embarrassed.

"No little red packets to end the production the way it began, huh?" Lance teased.

"This is perhaps not a time to make fun," Antonio said. Then, feeling other eyes on him, he assumed he was expected to make a speech. He cleared his throat. "I thank you all for your wonderful work on behalf of Permezzo. I think . . . I hope . . . this campaign will make our company a big success in your great country. It is all due to your hard work, and to . . . and to . . ." He coughed and blinked several times, but a tear escaped and ran down his cheek. "And to our beautiful Betsy, who cannot be with us. I am so sorry for the death of my beautiful Betsy."

The room became very still.

"Is he sayin' he killed her?" Cookie asked in a stage whisper.

Antonio heard her. "No, no, please do not even suggest such a terrible thing. I would never harm Betsy. Never. I am just . . . I am just so sad." He pulled out a handkerchief and loudly blew his nose.

"Then who *did* kill her?" Lance asked, taking in all the faces around the table. "That's what we all want to know, isn't it? Isn't that why we're here, Detective?"

"We have some questions," Chesny said, ignoring him. "We think it makes it easier for us if all of you are here at the same time to answer them." He pulled a pair of reading glasses out of the breast pocket of his jacket and put them on.

"Oh, I get it," Lance said. "If we lie, there'll be someone who can point it out right away. Is that it?" Lance raised his reading glasses and peered at the detective through the lenses.

"Something like that," Chesny said, consulting his clipboard. "And as long as you're so eager to speak, Mr. Sevenson, would you like to tell us where you were on the afternoon Miss Archibald was killed?"

"I've already told you this," Sevenson snarled, "but I'll go over it again for the benefit of our colleagues. My assistant, Lena, and I were in 'video village,' as you call it. Well, maybe not as *you* call it, Detective, but as these production folks call it. Am I right, Prendergast? We were in video village with you."

Kevin had been leaning against the wall sipping diet soda from a can. "Not the entire time," he said, pushing himself upright and setting the can on a nearby table. He walked to where Anne Tripper sat and put his hands on her shoulders, lightly massaging them. "I seem to remember several times when you and Lena left the room, separately and together. Isn't that right, Anne?"

"That's right."

"Oh, for heaven's sake. People do need to use the facilities every now and then," Sevenson said. "We spent most of the afternoon with you two."

"Most of it, but not all," Kevin said.

Lance narrowed his eyes at him. "Of course, by your own calculation, that leaves some of *your* time unaccounted for as well."

"Anne can vouch for my presence," Kevin said.

"As Lena can vouch for mine."

Lena looked up from her pad. "Uh, yes, that's right."

"This posturing is ridiculous," Anne said, shrugging Kevin's hands off her shoulders. "If you have questions, Detective Chesny, please ask them so we can get out of here."

Chesny looked down at his clipboard. "All right," he said. "Did you kill Miss Archibald, Miss Tripper?"

Startled, Anne lifted a hand to her neck, her rings catching the light with the movement of her fingers. "I did not, as I have already told your assistants, or whatever you call them." She waved her hand toward the door, where two uniformed officers had taken up their posts. "And I was with Kevin all afternoon."

"I understand this is yours," Chesny said, holding up the opal ring.

"What? Where did you get that?"

"It was found on the floor near the body."

"Near the body?"

"That's correct. Would you care to explain?"

"I told you buying an opal for yourself was bad luck," Lance said, leering at her.

She gave him an icy stare. "It was stolen from my purse," she said, enunciating each word. "Just ask those two." She twirled around in her chair and pointed to Jennifer and Susan. "They should have been making sure that no one had access to where our personal items were stored. But they obviously fell down on their job. Or else they stole my ring themselves."

"We did not," Jennifer replied angrily. "We were there the whole time. We just make a handy excuse for you, don't we? You're always ready to blame someone else for your problems."

Chesny looked over at me. "Mrs. Fletcher, I believe you have a question for Miss Tripper."

I rose from my seat and walked to the other side of the table. "You went on an errand yesterday afternoon. I just wondered where you went."

Anne bristled. "As if it's any of your business."

Chesny raised his brows and peered at her over his half-glasses. "Answer the question, please."

"I . . . I keep a studio I use for writing," she said, smoothing a nonexistent wrinkle out of her skirt. "I went there yesterday afternoon to make some notes for my book."

"You told me you were going for a walk to get some exercise," Kevin said, frowning at her.

"I did go for a walk, but I also went to my studio."

"You went all the way up to the Upper West Side and back in an hour and a half?"

"I don't like the way you're questioning me, Kevin. I don't have to answer to you."

"No, but I'd like you to answer me," Chesny said. "Did anyone see you on your walk or at your studio?"

"I have no idea," Anne said hotly. "Why should I have to account for my private time? What does this have to do with Betsy's murder?"

"Someone ransacked Betsy's apartment yesterday," I put in.

"Well, it wasn't me."

"But you knew where she lived."

"Of course I knew where she lived. I made sure to know. She'd been Kevin's lover before he met me."

"You don't strike me as the jealous type," Lance said, grinning.

"Shut up, Sevenson. No one's interested in your opinion."

"People pay for my opinion all the time."

"So you deny being at Miss Archibald's apartment yesterday?" Chesny said.

"I do, and you can give me a lie detector test if you want."

"There's no need for that," he said quietly. "So, if it wasn't you, who was it?" He looked at me. "Mrs. Fletcher, any ideas?"

I scanned the room, looking at the women. Susan and Jennifer huddled close to each other, watching the exchange. Lena's eyes were focused on the pad in front of her, but she hadn't written anything down. Cookie had her bag in her lap and was pawing through it in search of something. She located a little velvet pouch, pulled it open, and slipped on her new diamond ring and bracelet, and sat back, admiring her jewelry.

"Mrs. Fletcher?" he repeated.

"Lena, can you tell us where you were yesterday afternoon?" I asked.

"Why do you need to know, Jessica? She was with me," Lance said, moving to stand near his assistant.

"No, she wasn't, Lance. But she was on an assignment for you. Isn't that right, Lena?"

"I . . . I don't know what you mean, Mrs. Fletcher." She tried to look me in the eye but immediately looked away.

"I understand you returned a wig to the Vanity Department this morning."

Her cheeks flooded with color. "I . . . I found it on one of the sets."

"Which set?" I asked.

"It was . . . let me see. . . . It must have been on Mr. Sevenson's set."

"I was setting up lights on his set this morning," Ricky said. "It's a bare room with a stool. I never saw any wig there."

"What's the big deal?" Lance said harshly. "She found a wig and returned it. She's an honest person. What are you beating up on her for?"

"Where did you find the wig, Lena?" I asked.

"Well, maybe it wasn't on your set," she said, gazing up at Lance with pleading eyes. "Maybe it was in one of the rooms I passed on my way downstairs." She took a breath and looked directly at me. "Anyway, I found it and I returned it to Maya," she added, ending strongly.

"Maybe it was in your shoulder bag all the time," I said, "and you returned it to Maya."

"Why would she borrow a wig?" Jennifer asked.

"Because the wig was the same color as Betsy's hair and she wanted to masquerade as her sister. That's what you told Betsy's neighbor when you were up there ransacking Betsy's apartment. Isn't that right, Lena? You told her neighbor that you were Betsy's sister. I must say that you did a good job going through her apartment. You left it in quite a mess."

She shook her head. "No, that's not true."

I reached into my pocket for the tissue I'd used to remove the bobby pins from the wig. "There were strands of hair left on the pins in the wig. If we analyze them, will we discover that they're yours? They're certainly the same color as your hair."

"That means nothing. She could've tried on the wig before she returned it," Lance said. "You need something better than that, Fletcher."

"Lena, if Betsy's neighbor is waiting outside," I said, pointing to the door, "she could identify you, couldn't she?"

Lena's eyes flew to the door and her faced drained of color. "No, I don't think so. She might say she saw me, but she doesn't see so well." She looked to Lance for confirmation, but he turned away from her, a disgusted look on his face.

"And how do you know that the neighbor doesn't see very well?" I asked.

Lena's mouth opened, but no sound came out.

"Perhaps," I continued, "you noticed that she wore thick glasses when she stopped you outside Betsy's door."

"I don't see that good either," Ricky said, pressing a finger against his glasses, "but I'd recognize you if I saw you again."

"How did you get into Miss Archibald's apartment?" Chesny asked.

Lena dropped her head.

"You took the keys from Betsy's bag, didn't you?" I said. "And you returned them this morning."

"She was the only one who came into the production office today, other than you, Mrs. Fletcher," Susan put in.

"I wasn't about to let them watch my bag anymore," Anne said, "not when things go missing in that office."

"Wait a minute," Kevin said. "I don't understand something here." He addressed Lena. "Why did you go through Betsy's apartment? What were you looking for?"

"Maybe Lance can tell you," I said.

"It's private," he barked. "Nothing to do with anyone here." Lance stood and paced the room. "Betsy had some of my papers, that's all. I wanted them back. I didn't want some stranger cleaning up her apartment and finding them. So I sent Lena to get them. But I didn't tell her to wreck the place. What the hell were you thinking?"

"The old woman was calling the police," Lena said. "I didn't have time to be neat. And you got them back, didn't you?"

"Is this what you got back, Mr. Sevenson?" Detective

Chesny said, holding up the papers that Detective Marshall had faxed me. He handed them to Sevenson, who quickly flipped through them.

"Where did you get those?" Lance said.

"What's in it?" Cookie said, her attention finally drawn away from her diamonds.

"That's private information, not for public consumption," Lance said, glaring at Chesny. "We can discuss this in private, can we not? I'd like a lawyer present."

"Betsy blackmailed you into doing the commercials, didn't she?" I said to Lance. "She knew of your past and held it over your head."

"If you don't mind, Jessica," he responded, "I'd prefer not to discuss this in public."

"Did she also demand money from you with the promise that she wouldn't tell the world your secrets?"

"Oh, no, my Betsy would never do such a thing," Antonio said, rushing to defend her.

"Wouldn't she?" Lance said acidly. "That witch would do anything to push her career. Yes, she pressured me to do the spots. And I agreed on one condition, that she kept what she knew about me to herself. My career depends on people believing in me. She threatened to sell a nasty story to the tabloids. I kept my part of the bargain, and I was going to make sure she kept hers."

"Blackmail is a good motive for murder," Kevin said triumphantly. "Isn't that so, Detective Chesny?"

"So is revenge," Lance shot back. "She was about to bolt from your agency and take your best clients with her. She bragged to me about that. If you didn't want her to

walk away with the prize pig"—he pointed to Antonio—
"you could've decided to take her out of the picture, for
good."

All eyes turned to Antonio. "Yes, yes," he said hesitantly.
"She did want me to go. I tell her I think about it."

"Tonio! How could you even consider it? We've known
each other for such a long time," Kevin said, obviously
wounded.

"Yes. Yes. Your father was my friend. But this was business, Kevin. She has the ideas, no? And so passionate, so
beautiful. But I think that maybe I would not go. I didn't
tell her that." He wiped his upper lip with his handkerchief. "Now, it doesn't matter."

"Maybe not to you," Kevin said.

Anne pulled her red quilted purse into her lap, opened
the flap, and checked its contents. Satisfied, she closed it
again. "I assume I'm free to go," she said, standing.

"Not just yet," I said.

Chesny looked at me and raised his eyebrows at what I
would say next.

"Does Kevin know the subject of your new book?"

Both Anne and Kevin looked quizzically at me.

I said to Kevin, "I assume that because you and Ms.
Tripper live together, you know the contents of the book
she's been writing."

"Of course I know," he said. "It's going to be a bestseller. Right, honey? It's a departure from her usual style.
It's about how advertising and marketing fuel the engine
of the economy, keep things humming."

"Care to disillusion him, Anne?" I asked.

"What's in my book is none of your business," she snapped.

"You're right," I said. "But it would be Kevin's business. It's about his industry after all, but it's not such a flattering picture as you've led him to believe, is it?"

"What are you talking about?" Kevin said, pulling at my elbow.

I shook him off and focused on Anne. "I wondered whether he knew your true intentions," I said, "because if Betsy had discovered them and threatened to tell Kevin—perhaps as a fitting revenge for your stealing him away from her—it might have been sufficient motive for you to kill her to ensure her silence."

"Wait a minute," Kevin said, addressing Anne. "Is what Mrs. Fletcher is saying true? Is this just another of your exposés? You swore to me it wasn't."

"It doesn't matter," she said, a cruel smile on her face.

"The hell it doesn't," he exploded. "It matters a lot to me. Is that why you moved in with me, to learn what I know about the ad business, tell you the inside secrets, introduce you to my friends, just so you could betray them? Betray me? You went off to that studio every day to write. To keep me from seeing your work. Oh, no, I was never to look at it before publication. Bad luck, you said. And I bought it. All the while you were tearing apart a business I love. You're despicable!"

She laughed. "Oh, Kevin, you are such a jerk. How I could put up with your ego for so many months is a tribute to my dedication to my project. Yes, the book uncovers the real motives behind advertising, and its truth twisters, including you."

"You've said enough, Anne," Kevin said, fists clenched, his mouth a slash across his face. "We'll discuss this at home later."

Anne blew a little puff of air through her lips. "You'll find I'm already gone from the apartment when you get home tonight. Ciao, baby. I'd like to say it's been good to know you, but that would be a lie." She plopped back down in her chair, long legs crossed, one foot moving up and down.

Kevin's eyes were wide with fury. For a moment, it appeared that he was about to physically attack her. But he backed away, mumbled curses under his breath, and stalked to a corner of the room.

Chesny looked at me. "Mrs. Fletcher, our next move?"

"I think you might have a few questions for Mr. Howerstein, our producer."

"Right," Chesney said. He consulted the notes on his clipboard. "Mr. Howerstein," he said, "you had quite an argument with the deceased. Care to enlighten us as to what it was about?"

Daniel moved forward from a shelf against which he'd been leaning. "Happened right down this hall," he said. "Did you tell him what you heard, Mrs. Fletcher?"

"I did, Daniel."

"Well, you were there, Mrs. Fletcher. So was Fitzpatrick. Betsy and I got into a fight. Big deal. Disagreements happen all the time. This is a pressure business. Tempers flare. You saw it yourself. I'm used to Betsy going off on my crew. She had a short fuse. I don't see where our argument could be a motive for murder. If you do, why don't you tell the detective about it?"

"You weren't fighting about Betsy's temper. You were fighting about money. You accused her of holding out on you. And she was. She said you'd get paid when the agency got paid."

"So? That's standard practice in the business."

"Perhaps it is, but I was there and so were you when Antonio said he'd already paid for the campaign and wasn't going to give any more money. You'd already paid Adam, and you had to put the money up for the crew salaries. You're desperate for money and Betsy lied to you, Daniel. The agency already had the money and they were sitting on it."

"Is that sufficient motive for murder?" Chesny asked.

"If it is, there would be a lot of dead agency creative directors," Howerstein answered bitterly. "They do that to us all the time." He looked up at me. "I didn't kill her, Mrs. Fletcher."

"I know."

"*You know?*" Anne exploded. "Then why are we wasting our time here?"

"Do you know who killed Betsy, Aunt Jess?" Grady asked. He'd sat silently, obviously fascinated as the confrontations took place.

"I believe I do," I said.

"Well, Ah sure would like to know. Wouldn't you, Jimbo?" Cookie said.

"Quiet, Cookie," Jimbo said.

Chesny sighed. "Let's get on with it," he said. "I'm eager to hear your conclusion, Mrs. Fletcher. I'm long on suspects and getting short on patience."

"Many people had a motive to kill Betsy. That's true, Detective," I said.

"Some people could say you had a motive, too, Mrs. Fletcher," Howerstein offered.

"Some people already have," I replied.

"Can it, Daniel," Kevin said. "I want to hear this."

"Betsy had a fiery temper," I said. "She was easily incensed and slow to cool. She lashed out, and unfortunately for her, someone lashed back. We needed to account for your whereabouts that afternoon, and we needed to examine your motives, because as Detective Chesny points out, many people could have had a reason to kill Betsy. But there were two important clues left at the scene, maybe three if we count Anne's ring."

Anne shot to her feet. "I'm telling you, I didn't kill her. I might have *wanted to*, but I didn't."

"Sit down, Miss Tripper," Chesny said. "What are these clues, Mrs. Fletcher?"

"First of all, someone had gone to a great deal of trouble to move the equipment into the room where Betsy was killed. They didn't want the body to be discovered too quickly."

"And the other clue."

"There were footprints in the sawdust around the body."

"That's right," Chesny said. "Unfortunately, there were a lot of them."

"You have my apologies about how those footprints were disturbed by my nephew and me, Detective Chesny. Grady and I didn't know that Betsy had been killed in that room until we found her body."

"I hope you're not referring to *my* footprints," Ricky said, looking down at his work boots. "I was in and out of that room all morning."

"I'm not, Ricky, unless you wore shoes with a poined toe that day," I said.

"Men don't wear shoes with pointy toes. That's for women," Ricky said.

"And that's why I concentrated on the women here. Anne, you wear pointy-toed shoes." I turned in a half circle. "And so do you, Lena." I looked behind me. "And you do, too, Cookie."

"And didn't Betsy?" Cookie replied. "She wore them fancy high heels at the agency meeting."

"Yes, she did," I said. "I'm not surprised you noticed. They were very expensive shoes with a pointed toe and very high heel. But Betsy wasn't wearing heels when she was killed; she was wearing sneakers."

"Well, I did wear my favorite shoes the other day," Cookie said, "but they don't have a real pointy toe, just a little, maybe. Anyway, when Betsy was killed, we were on your set watching your commercial. Weren't we, Jimbo?"

"I wish that was true, Cookie," I said, "but it isn't."

"What do you mean?"

"I didn't question it when you said you'd watched my commercial being made. I remember you saying that you didn't take your eyes off me."

"Because you were so very good. You looked like you'd been on TV your whole entire life."

"This morning, when Maya was doing your makeup, Cookie, you worried about it melting under the lights."

"You have to admit they're very hot. Maybe you don't perspire gallons under TV lights, but I surely do." Her eyes roamed the room. "Y'all pardon me for raising an indelicate subject."

"Cookie, you didn't know that Maya stays on the set, ready to fix your makeup and your hair between takes. If you had been on my set all afternoon as you claimed, you would have seen her powdering me and spraying my hair."

"Well, I could've missed something once or twice."

"True. But this was many more times, too many for it to have escaped your attention. No, I think it far more likely that you came to where my commercial was being shot just before the end of the day. And I don't think Jimbo was there at all."

"What are you sayin', Jessica?" Cookie asked, a hint of defiance in her voice.

I turned to her manager. "Jimbo," I said, "I don't believe the ladies here would have been strong enough to move all that equipment to block Betsy's body. But you are. Strong enough, that is. And you were very angry with Betsy. Cookie told me that you have a hard time reining in your temper once it's raised. Those footprints in the sawdust, the ones with pointed toes, were from your cowboy boots."

Jimbo pulled out his red kerchief and dabbed at his brow. "Now, Jessica," he began, "I think some explanation is in order." He slipped the cloth back into his pocket. "You see—"

"I'm going to ask you to give Detective Chesny that

kerchief, Jimbo," I said. "You had it out in the bathroom across the hall from the carpentry room. You used it to clean the sawdust off your boots. My grandnephew, Frank, saw you cleaning your boots with it. The police crime lab should be able to detect the sawdust residue still clinging to the fabric."

"It was a' accident," Cookie blurted. "He didn't mean it. Please, you have to believe me that Jimbo didn't mean to hurt her. He wouldn't hurt anybody on purpose."

Jimbo placed his hand on Cookie's. "It's all right, Cookie. I can speak for myself."

Chesny held out his hand and Jimbo laid the red kerchief in his palm. "That woman was just plain mean," he said, "takin' it out on Cookie, makin' fun of her accent, humiliating her in front of ever'body. It just wasn't right. I kept thinking about what she said to Cookie, and what she did. I got myself so burned up after lunch that I tracked her down, looked all over the building till I found her walking down that hall. I started in to yell, and she says if I want to yell, to take it in here, meaning that room. I'm giving her a piece of my mind and she picks up the nail gun, says I'm not to threaten her, and aims it at me. I wasn't threatening her. I'm a big guy, I know it. So maybe she was scared. But then she's accusing me and callin' me names, four-letter names, and I got so steamed, I wrestled her for it. And the damn thing goes off. Them things are supposed to have a safety latch on 'em. I know. I use one all the time around the house. It should never have gone off. I swear, I didn't mean to kill her. I swear it." Sweat poured down Jimbo's forehead and cheeks. He reached into his pocket, but came up empty and used the back of his hand to wipe his face.

"He didn't do it on purpose," Cookie said, her cheeks as wet as his, but from tears. "He wouldn't ever hurt anyone. He's just a big teddy bear. It was a' accident like he said."

"But then you tried to cover up what you did," I said to Jimbo.

"I just . . . I just went into a panic. I knew she was dead. She had no pulse. Just died instantly. All I wanted was not to see the body. I moved everything I could in there. Took it all out from the rooms next door and piled it up against her. I thought if I didn't see her dead, then maybe it didn't really happen." He collapsed into a chair and dropped his head into his arms on the table, sobbing.

"When did he tell you what had happened, Cookie?" I asked.

"He didn't tell me right away, but I went lookin' for him and found him moving all this equipment into one room. I made him stop and tell me what he was doing."

"And then you helped him."

"I did. I helped him move the light stands and a few other things that were not so heavy."

"I meant you helped him in another way. You took Anne's ring from her purse in the production office and threw it into the carpentry room."

Cookie hung her head. "I did do that, Jessica." She lifted her eyes to Anne. "And Ah am truly sorry."

"Why did you do that?" Anne demanded, her voice cold. "What did I ever do to you?"

Cookie sniffed. "You're just not a nice person," she said.

"And Jimbo is such a good man. I thought it would be easy for everyone to believe you killed Betsy. I would've believed it if I didn't know different."

"Well, that's just lovely," Anne said. She looked at Chesny. "I assume you're going to arrest them both."

"I know my business, Miss Tripper."

"I'd like my ring back," she said, holding her hand out to the detective.

"Sorry. It has to go in the evidence locker till the trial."

"Very well." Anne slipped the gold chain of her bag over her shoulder. "I assume I may leave now," she said over her shoulder as she walked to the door. She stopped in front of the two officers. At Chesny's nod, they opened the door and she disappeared through it.

Lance approached the detective. "About my papers," he said in a low voice. "You know, I paid my debt to society. I served my time. This doesn't have to be made public. I have a reputation to uphold. This gets out, my show could be canceled. Can we . . . ?"

Chesny gave him a hard look.

"I know," Lance said, "evidence, right?"

"We'll talk another time," Chesny said.

"Well, at least you know I'm not the guilty one. If the shoe doesn't fit, you must acquit." He laughed. "Lena, write that down."

One by one the others left the room until the only ones remaining were Detective Chesny and his two officers, myself, Grady, Cookie, and Jimbo.

Cookie went over to Jimbo and put her hand on his shoulder. "Come on, Jimbo. It's over now."

Jimbo raised his head. "Oh, Cookie. Ah made such a mess of things."

"Yes, you did. And so did I. But we still love you, and me and Homer will do ever'thing we can to help you. Ah can't forget that it was 'cause of me that you got into that fight with her." Cookie's eyes sought mine. "You're just too smart for me, Jessica. But you did right. We couldn't have held it much longer anyways." Her small smile was sad. "Ah hope we can still be friends. Ah'm still gonna hang your picture on my Wall of Fame."

Chapter Twenty-two

"How much time before your flight, Aunt Jess?" We were at La Guardia Airport again, this time for my flight to Boston, and then I'd have a short hop home to Cabot Cove in a small plane with my good friend and flying instructor Jed Richardson at the controls.

I looked at the long line for security. "I have an hour and a half," I said, "but I'd better start the process."

"That's a long time to wait," Grady said.

"I don't mind waiting as long as I have a book to read." I opened my arms and Grady leaned in for a hug. "Can I get a good-bye hug from you, too?" I asked Frank.

"Sure," he said, stepping into my embrace. "When are you coming back, Aunt Jessica? Michele and me, we're going to miss you."

"Me, too," I said. "But I hope you boys will come up to

Maine when school is out. I already spoke to your mothers. What do you think?"

"You mean just us, Michele and me?"

"Is it okay if your mother and father join us, too?" I said in a lowered voice. "I don't want them to feel left out."

Frank gave his father a sly smile. "Maybe," he said, drawing out his answer. "Okay. You can come, too."

"Nice of you to include us, sport."

"Oh, I almost forgot," I said, opening my shoulder bag. "This came for you this morning. Your mom gave it to me." I withdrew a package wrapped in brown paper.

"For me?" Frank said. "Is it a present?"

"I don't think so," I said. "Why don't you unwrap it?"

Frank tore at the paper. "It's my red earphones," he said, excited.

"Let's see what the note says." Grady retrieved the card that was taped to the earphones before it got lost. "It's from Detective Chesny," he said.

"Can I see?" Frank asked.

"Sure. Why don't you read it to us?" Grady handed Frank the card.

"It says, 'To Frank, who found the missing clue that solved the crime. Maybe you'll become a detective in the future.' I like that idea. I'd be a good detective, right, Dad?"

"You'll be good at whatever you do, as long as you work hard at it."

Frank looped the earphones around his neck, as he'd seen crew members do on the production. "Dad, do you think we could find another set of headphones for Michele?"

Grady winked at me. "We'll have to see," he said, "but I have a feeling there may be another set at home."

Several months later, I prepared for a visit from the boys and Donna. Grady would join us on the weekend. The financial machinations of the payroll company he worked for had finally caught up to the firm and the company closed its doors overnight, locking out not only the production companies whose payrolls they were supposed to distribute, but also their own employees, to whom they owed several weeks' salary. Before the closure, Grady and his boss, Carl, had confronted the management team with their findings, and had been assured that the company was turning things around. It wasn't true. Grady and Carl had to scramble to help their clients find a new payroll service, and in the end had decided to start their own company.

"We're calling it 'Zucker and Fletcher,' " Grady wrote me in an e-mail. "I held out for 'Fletcher and Zucker,' but we flipped a coin and Carl won."

I hoped Grady's employment woes were finally over, now that he had a company of his own. But of course, for many entrepreneurs, that's just the beginning of problems. Still, I had a good feeling about his new career move. Donna was thrilled that Grady would be working from home, at least until the company grew big enough to require office space. And they had purchased a second computer so she could help out.

The fall catalog for my publishing house had arrived with a large ad for Anne Tripper's new book, *Inside Advertising: The Scamming of America*. When we spoke shortly after I'd come back from New York, Matt had told me he was anticipating a rough few months after the book came out. He said, "I keep vacillating between being thrilled at its potential for bestseller status and cringing at how my Hamptons neighbors are going to respond."

I reminded him of the public relations theory that there's no such thing as bad publicity. Attributed variously to Mae West, Oscar Wilde, Mark Twain, and even President Harry Truman, the oft-cited quote goes, "I don't care what the newspapers say about me as long as they spell my name right."

"Sure, Jessica, I'll tell that to my wife when no one shows up at our Fourth of July picnic," he'd said.

Ads for Permezzo were appearing on television and on the Internet. So far, my spot and the one for Anne Tripper had aired. I'd received quite a number of e-mails from old friends who'd seen it. Lance's was going to break in the fall. He must have reached an agreement with Detective Chesny not to reveal his arrest record in Canada, because so far, at least, his sordid past has remained there—in the past. However, it wouldn't surprise me if the truth leaked out at some point. Very few people in the public eye are successful in keeping their earlier indiscretions a secret— as our politicians can surely attest to—and a criminal record is a pretty big indiscretion to hide.

Antonio had decided to shelve Cookie's commercial until the gossip died down about her involvement with the cover-up of Betsy's accidental death. Jimbo Barnes had been charged with involuntary manslaughter and his case was set to go to trial. Cookie's lawyer had managed to plea down the charges against her of accessory after the fact. She was given two years of community service and had chosen to cook meals for a homeless shelter in Dallas. I'd signed the photo Jimbo had taken of the two of us and sent it to her. It's now up on her Wall of Fame.